Unreasonable
Doubt

D1319329

Books by Vicki Delany

Constable Molly Smith Series
In the Shadow of the Glacier
Valley of the Lost
Winter of Secrets
Negative Image
Among the Departed
A Cold White Sun
Under Cold Stone

Other Novels
Scare the Light Away
Burden of Memory
More Than Sorrow

Unreasonable Doubt

A Constable Molly Smith Mystery

Vicki Delany

Poisoned Pen Press

Poisoned Pen Press
6962 E. First Ave., Ste. 103
Scottsdale, AZ 85251
www.poisonedpenpress.com
info@poisonedpenpress.com

Printed in the United States of America

To Mom

Acknowledgments

I'd like to extend my sincere thanks to Bonnie Taylor and Pat Bradley and their team HEAT from the Quinte Dragon Boat Training Centre for taking me out on the water and introducing me to the fun of dragon boating.

Thanks to Cheryl Freedman and Melodie Campbell for reviewing and advising on the manuscript of this book. Some advice I took; some I didn't. But all was carefully considered.

Thanks also to Barbara Peters for wanting another Smith and Winters, and for all her encouragement over the more than ten years I've been with Poisoned Pen Press, the world's best publisher.

And to Nelson artist Maya Heringa for letting me put one of her beautiful paintings in the window of the Mountain in Winter Gallery.

For Merrill Young, who lent me the use of her name. Hope you like what I did with you, Merrill.

"We know not whether laws be right
Or whether laws be wrong
All we know who lie in gaol
Is that the walls are strong
And each day is like a year
A year whose days are long."
—Oscar Wilde,
"The Ballad Of Reading Gaol"

Chapter One

Walter Desmond felt something move, something low in his belly that he might once have recognized as happiness. It had been many years since he'd known what happiness felt like. He gazed out the window of the bus, full of wonder. The mountains were so high, the slopes closing in on the highway, their ragged tops still white with snow even though it was July. In the valleys, lakes and rivers sparkled blue in the sunlight.

A shade of blue he had forgotten could exist.

He'd forgotten the smell also. The rich scent of pine trees, leaf mulch, fresh water moving fast over rocks and boulders. Clean air, most of all.

This bus, however, smelled of nothing other than too many people crowded too close together, a scent Walt knew only too well. When they'd had a rest stop in Hope, and his fellow passengers streamed into Tim Horton's, Walt had simply stood there, stunned, breathing it all in. Hope was the name of the town. Hope. He'd take it as an omen, because it had been a long time since hope had been more than a word with a meaning he'd forgotten. The mountains around Hope were almost vertical—a wall of dark green and brown. He might come back to Hope someday, but for now those mountains were altogether too close. He'd been hemmed in long enough. He closed his eyes and let his nose and ears explore the land around him until it was time to clamber back onto the bus.

As the bus travelled down the highway, and morning passed into afternoon, he could see that in all too many places the tall pines were a strange shade of brownish-purple, not the dark green he remembered. He'd read about the mountain pine beetle and the devastation the insects were bringing to this part of British Columbia as they killed every tree they encountered. He hadn't realized how widespread the damage was. He hadn't realized a lot of things. He'd read everything he could get his hands on and thought he'd be prepared when the day finally came.

He wasn't. Nowhere near prepared. Everything was so strange. Like that TV show "Life on Mars," in which the cop went back in time. Although in Walt's case, he'd gone forward in time. To life on another planet.

The bus had WiFi. He knew what WiFi was.

He'd read about it when he'd been allowed to use the library computers, where he'd tried to keep up with everything that was happening in the world without him. He'd heard about phones people carried in their pockets and were far more than just telephones, and about worldwide instant communication. He'd also heard about civilians using those phones to film cops smashing heads in. Or worse.

The woman in the seat beside him had a phone like that. It was white, but the case was brown with dirt. She spent a lot of time typing with her thumbs. He'd found typing difficult enough to get his head, not to mention his fingers, around. Back in the day, he'd had a secretary who did that typing stuff. But he'd worked hard at it; he'd been determined to learn. When he'd last been part of the working world, secretaries were being phased out. He understood that he'd have to type for himself. He had. And now was he was going to have to learn to do it with his thumbs or the tips of his fingers?

As a kid he'd loved those sci-fi TV shows and books where the astronaut, landing in some strange world that usually turned out to be Earth in the past or future, struggled to understand what was going on. It wasn't fun, Walter Desmond knew, not fun at all in real life.

The woman put away her phone. She pulled a dog-eared paperback out of her bag. She was wearing too much perfume. As well as a lot of things, he'd forgotten the scent of cheap perfume. There had been nothing cheap about Louise. Not her clothes, her makeup, or her hair. And certainly not the perfume she wore—subtle, enticing. He felt himself smiling. It was a strange sensation. He needed to get used to it.

He'd taken Louise's hand as the lineup to get on the bus edged forward. A few people openly gaped at her. Not because they recognized her, but because she looked so out of place in the grimy bus station in her designer suit, ironed blouse, patent-leather high-heeled pumps, and tasteful gold and diamond jewelry.

"You're sure this is what you want to do?" she said in her deep sexy voice.

"It's what I have to do."

"I might not approve, but I do understand." She'd advised him not to leave Vancouver. Not yet. Get accustomed to the modern world first. But he knew he had to do it. Now. While he still had the nerve. He could feel the softness of her skin, the warmth of the blood beneath the surface, the delicate bones, the pressure of her ring. He took a deep breath, and slowly, reluctantly, released her. It was like letting go of a lifeline in a storm-tossed sea. From this point forward, he was on his own. "Thank you. For everything."

Her eyes were warm. A smile touched the edges of her lips. "We won't meet again, Walt."

"I know."

She turned and walked away, her heels clicking on the sticky floor. She pulled her iPhone out of her Michael Kors handbag and began pushing buttons. She was talking as she walked through the doors, paying no attention to the people who'd stepped back to allow her to exit. He smiled at the memory: the moment she turned her back on him, she'd been thinking about her next case. Another poor schmuck waiting for her to save him.

"Hey, buddy. Haven't got all day here," a man behind him had called. And Walt clambered onto the bus.

The woman beside him, the one with the heavy hand on the perfume bottle, took his private smile as an invitation. "On vacation?"

"What?"

"Have you been in Vancouver on vacation?"

"Oh. Vacation. No."

"I'm going to Trafalgar to visit my daughter. And my grandchildren, of course. I have three now, two girls and a boy. There's another on the way, although early days yet. Would you like to see a picture?" Without waiting for an answer she began rummaging through her cavernous purse to once again pull out her phone.

"No," he said. He wished he could take back the word. He'd forgotten how to be polite. He shifted in his seat, stared out the window. The woman sniffed, but she took the hint and returned to her book.

What else had he forgotten? Pretty much everything that made life worth living. How to be polite, how to make money, how to drive a car, how to talk to women—other than Louise, and they'd certainly never engaged in small talk. He didn't know how to use one of those small, sleek phones that fit into a pocket or how to find a WiFi connection. He couldn't begin to understand the menu in the coffee shop, and when he asked for a coffee he didn't understand what the girl meant when she asked if he wanted Pike's Place.

His wife, Arlene, had passed away, shattered, defeated, brokenhearted, seventeen years ago. The day she died, he'd forgotten how to love.

But there was no forgetting how to hate.

Chapter Two

John Winters pulled up in front of a two-story heritage home close to the center of town. This was a nice street, the properties well maintained, the older houses either replaced by new ones of concrete, glass, and wood, or preserved in their historic glory.

The house he was interested in stood out from the others due to its state of considerable neglect. The front porch sagged at one end; the bottom step was broken. The fence and walkway were lined with what had once been lush perennial beds, but the hearty plants now struggled against an onslaught of weeds and invading grass. More weeds sprouted between the carefully laid bricks of the driveway.

"They're only in their seventies," Paul Keller said. "But not doing well at all. I believe the wife had a stroke a couple of years ago, and he has a bad heart."

"They have any other children?"

"A son. Name of Anthony. He lives in Toronto, I think. Several years younger than Sophia. They pretty much stay under the radar. We've not had any contact with them since…since then, not until these new developments hit the papers. As hard as this is going to be, we have to do it. Might as well get it over with."

The two men got out of the car.

A couple of kids came down the street on their bikes, enjoying the freedom of summer holidays. A sleek young woman in running gear passed, pushing a toddler in a jogging stroller. She nodded in greeting and went on her way, paying Winters and Keller no further attention. It was a hot day, and Winters felt the sun on his head and sweat under his arms.

A curtain twitched at a neighbor's front window and he knew they couldn't stand here all day. He let out a puff of air and walked up the cracked and weed-infested front walk beside the Chief Constable of Trafalgar. The porch steps creaked under their weight. An assortment of terra-cotta pots in various sizes lined the railing, overflowing with geraniums, begonias, and ivy. These plants, at least, were colorful and full of life.

Paul Keller knocked and the door opened.

The woman who stood there might have been in her nineties, but Winters knew she was only seventy-three. The years had been hard on her, indeed. She was very short at not much over five feet, wizened and frail. She leaned on a sturdy cane. Her face was heavily lined; her short, badly cut hair, steel gray; her brown eyes deep sockets in an olive face. "Chief Keller," she said, "you have come to tell me the bastard's dead. I'm glad of it."

A man appeared at her side. He was her age, but he didn't wear his grief and sorrow so prominently. "No, Rose," he said. "That is not why they're here."

"May we come in?" Keller asked.

"Of course," the man said. The woman, leaning heavily on her cane, turned without a word.

Winters and Keller followed them into the house. The carpets were threadbare in places, the paint on the walls in need of freshening, but otherwise things were neat and tidy. Winters recognized the symptoms: an old woman without the energy or dexterity to do a thorough cleaning anymore, but still house-proud; her husband losing interest in the minor handyman chores that had once kept him occupied.

He'd never been to this house before, had never met the D'Angelos. Yet he could sense the sorrow that hung over their house as if it were a dusty shroud draped over everything.

"I brought Sergeant Winters with me today,"

Keller said. "I thought you should meet. If you have any, uh, concerns, you can contact him. John, this is Gino and Rose D'Angelo."

The men shook hands. Mrs. D'Angelo went into the living room.

"What sort of concerns might we have, Chief Keller?" Gino D'Angelo asked.

"Why don't we have a seat," Keller said.

Gino led the way into the living room. Keller threw Winters a grimace.

The chief sat down, but Winters chose to stand. The living room was furnished in long-out-of-date shades of brown and orange. He recognized a collection of dark green glass ornaments as similar to ones he'd seen when Eliza dragged him to an antique fair in the spring.

Gino helped his wife into a stiff-backed wooden chair, and then dropped himself into a worn, cracked La-Z-Boy that had the best view of the TV. Alone in this room, the TV was modern. A thirty-inch flat screen. At the moment it was playing a game show, the sound turned up so loud they'd have to shout to be heard. The room was stifling hot, smelling of dust and mold. The air conditioning was not on, there were no fans; the windows were closed.

Winters' eyes were instantly drawn to the portrait dominating the room. It hung on the far wall, above the gas fireplace, showing a beautiful young woman on her graduation day. Her thick black hair, burnished to a high shine, fell in a waterfall past her shoulders, her olive skin was clear, her cheekbones prominent, her eyes a dark brown. Her smile was all-encompassing. One of her front teeth was slightly crooked, giving her a mischievous air. She wore a mortar board and gown, and held her diploma proudly. So young, so beautiful. Looking bravely, hopefully, toward a future that would never be. If he'd come into this house unprepared he would have thought her a granddaughter. Maybe even a great-granddaughter, if Rose and Gino had had their own child when very young.

He looked away. An abundance of smaller pictures sat on side tables. Most of them were of children, a boy and a girl, growing up, the years passing. Several of a boy, then a man, changed as time marched on. Of the young woman on the wall, none of the pictures were more recent than her graduation.

The sound from the TV ended abruptly. Silence filled the room.

"My daughter, Sophia," the woman said, her eyes fixed on Winters.

"She was...very lovely."

"Yes."

The police were not offered coffee or cold

drinks. Keller coughed. "You've heard that Walt Desmond's appeal was successful?

The man nodded. The woman's eyes blazed fire. "So," Gino said, "there will be another trial. Another ordeal for Rose. For me."

"No. The Crown has decided not to retry the case. They have withdrawn all charges."

"What does that mean?" Rose asked. "Gino, what is he saying?"

"It's over," Keller said, "There will not be a new trial."

"It will never be over. Not for us," she said.

"Mr. Desmond has been released from prison. I thought you should know."

Rose moaned. Her husband leapt to his feet. "You people, you did this."

"I…" Keller said.

"Your police didn't work hard enough. You didn't prepare a good enough case. You let this happen. What kind of a country do we live in where murderers…?"

"Please, Mr. D'Angelo," Winters said. "Mr. Desmond has served twenty-five years and is now out of prison. Recriminations won't help."

"Twenty-five years. What is twenty-five years to us, but twenty-five years that our Sophia did not get to live?"

"Nothing," Rose said, "can help us. Nothing ever has."

"Leave us now," Gino said. His fists were clenched, and a vein pulsed in the side of his neck.

Keller got to his feet. "There's one more thing you should know, sir. Mr. Desmond got on a bus in Vancouver this morning. He's coming to Trafalgar."

The couple stared at him, open-mouthed.

"He's free to come and go as he likes," Keller said. "You have to remember that. Leave him alone. If he attempts to contact you, call Sergeant Winters immediately. Stay away from him. Please."

Rose moaned again. Her husband made no move to comfort her. "Stay away from him? Leave him alone? No, Chief Keller. I will not leave him alone. If I see him, I will kill him."

Chapter Three

"What's up?" Molly Smith whispered to Dawn Solway.

"No idea. Maybe the chief's going to announce he's retiring. Your mom say anything about that?"

"Nope."

The conference room of the Trafalgar City Police station was filling with inquisitive officers and curious civilian staff. It was shift change, and a meeting had been called at this time so as to get the maximum number of people in the room. All the chairs were soon taken, and Smith and Solway had to stand against the wall. They waited.

When they'd been asked to report to the meeting room, Smith had initially assumed someone was being given a promotion or maybe a service medal of some sort.

That couldn't be it. Clearly, whatever was going on was not a good thing. Chief Constable Paul Keller and Detective Sergeant John Winters

stood at the front of the room. When everyone was
in place, Keller stepped forward. He was not smiling, and Smith figured he wasn't about to announce
his retirement. His face was too grim, his back too
straight for that. John Winters didn't look all too
pleased either.

Worst-case scenarios galloped through her
head. All around her people mumbled darkly.

Geeze, Smith thought, *don't tell me the city's
decided it can't afford to have its own police service
anymore and we're being handed over to the Mounties.*

"I'll get straight to it," Keller said. Every whis-
pering voice died. "I trust some of you have been
following the Walter Desmond case."

Nods all around. Desmond had served twenty-
five years for the murder of a young Trafalgar
woman. For more than twenty-five years he'd
protested his innocence. Last year, an organization
dedicated to overturning wrongful convictions had
taken up his case and launched an appeal. The
original evidence against him turned out to be
shoddy at best. Out and out police incompetence,
or corruption at worst.

The appeal court of British Columbia had
ordered a new trial. The Crown prosecutors,
faced with the total collapse of their original case,
dropped all charges. Desmond had been incarcer-
ated at the Kent Institution in Agassiz, B.C., near

Vancouver, where he'd been transferred a few years before on the closing of the penitentiary in Kingston, Ontario. He'd been released only last week. As he was fully cleared of the crimes for which he'd gone to prison, he was not on parole and no restrictions or limitations had been placed on his movements; he'd simply walked out of the prison and been allowed to go his own way. A free man. But a man who'd done a lot of years, and who had no support to help him integrate back into the community.

"He's on his way here," Keller said.

Groans filled the room.

"Doesn't he have to go to a halfway house or something first?" one of the clerks asked.

"He's not guilty, or so say the laws of Canada, Marjorie. He can do anything any citizen can. No restrictions."

"Does he still have family here?" Solway asked.

"No. His wife followed when he was sent to Kingston Pen. They didn't have any kids."

"Why do you suppose he's coming back then?" Dave Evans asked.

"I've no idea," Keller said. "But it can't be good."

No, Smith thought, it couldn't. The murder of Sophia D'Angelo and the arrest and conviction of Walter Desmond had happened a long time ago. The case had been forgotten by the members of the Trafalgar City Police and most of the towns-people. Then the appeal had filled the local and national papers, and got everyone talking about it again. Walt Desmond and his wife had lived in Trafalgar. He'd been a real estate agent; his wife owned a woman's wear shop. He belonged to Rotary, coached soccer, had even served on the city council for a few years. A respectable member of the community. He'd been sent away for the sexual assault and murder of a woman who'd been viewing a house for sale. He'd always maintained his innocence, even when to confess would have given him a shot at parole. Officers of the Trafalgar City Police had arrested him, prepared the case against him, testified against him in court. Celebrated when the verdict came down.

And, twenty-five years later, those officers had been found to have been complicit in concealing evidence in Desmond's favor.

Thank God, they all thought, although they didn't say, no one who'd been on the force back then was still working here.

"He's arriving on the five o'clock bus," Keller said.

"Want someone to meet him?" Sergeant Jeff Glendenning asked.

"Emphatically not. I want no contact between our members and Desmond whatsoever. Other than in circumstances that would happen with any citizen."

"I'll do it," Glendenning said, as though he hadn't even heard the chief. "Someone needs to tell him he's not wanted here."

"I said, no. Stay away from Desmond. All of you. I know you're friends with Jack McMillan, Jeff, so I'll advise you strongly not to discuss the case with him."

Smith was standing behind Glendenning, seated in the back row. She heard him mutter under his breath. Dave Evans threw him a glance.

"John or I will find out where Mr. Desmond's staying, and pay a courtesy call tomorrow. That's all."

"Do the D'Angelos know about this?" Solway asked.

"They do. John?"

Winters stepped forward. "Chief Keller and I called on them a few hours ago, soon as we got word that Desmond had bought a bus ticket to Trafalgar. They were not, shall I say, pleased at the news. For those of you who don't know, Sophia D'Angelo was a local girl. She'd been in Victoria for university and came home the previous summer. Her parents wanted her to stay in Trafalgar, and they gave her the money for a down payment on a house to encourage her to settle down."

"So the family had money?"

"They were comfortable, but no more. Remember, twenty-five years ago property in the Kootenays didn't go for anything like it does now. Even taking inflation into account. The family has never had the slightest doubt that Desmond killed their daughter. They were extremely upset to hear the case was being reopened."

Upset was an understatement. Molly Smith had been in the constable's office a few months ago when Mr. and Mrs. D'Angelo had arrived, demanding to see the chief. Mr. D'Angelo's bellows and Mrs. D'Angelo's weeping could be heard throughout the station.

"We had to tell them Desmond's coming back. Can't allow them to run into him unexpectedly on the street or in the grocery store." Winters pressed his lips into a tight line. The meeting had obviously not gone well.

"You think they're going to do something?" Dave Evans asked.

"Wouldn't blame them if they did," Glendenning mumbled, although he made sure it wasn't loud enough for the men at the front to hear.

Winters and Keller exchanged glances. "God help us, I hope not," Winters said. "Mr. D'Angelo made threats against Mr. Desmond, but he's seventy-four, his wife seventy-three. Both of them are in poor health. I advised them to stay out of Desmond's way, but I don't have to remind you people that this is a small town, the chances of them running into him in a public place are considerable. If that happens, all we can do is try to de-escalate the situation. I remind you that Walt Desmond, in the eyes of the law and thus in the eyes of the Trafalgar City Police, has not committed any crime. He was, apparently, a model prisoner...."

"What about the rest of the town?" Solway asked. "How do they feel about this?"

"Divided," Keller said. "Those who were here back then anyway. To newcomers it's nothing but an interesting news item. At the time, the town was convinced Desmond was guilty. When the appeal began and news of the police... uh..."

"Incompetence is the word you're looking for," Detective Ray Lopez said.

"That's not fair." Barb Kowalski spoke for the first time. The chief's administrative assistant, she'd been with the TCP for almost thirty years. She was the only person in the room who'd been working here back then. "Jack and Doug and the rest of the guys did a thorough investigation. What the paper said about them was a lie."

"Enough," Winters said.

Smith suppressed a sigh. Not only the town was divided.

"Some people," Keller said, not looking at Barb, "are still convinced Desmond is guilty. Some believe he was treated unfairly. We can only hope people will keep their opinions to themselves and go about their business."

"In Trafalgar!" Solway said. "That would be a first."

People laughed, but the laughter wasn't comfortable. This was a passionate town, full of passionate people. Passion, Smith sometimes thought, was a requirement for living here. Whether for the environment, justice, peace, or politics, the people of Trafalgar could be expected to have strong opinions on any issue.

"The bus from Vancouver," Keller said, "will be pulling in soon. I want everyone to be aware that this is an extremely delicate situation. We are to stay strictly neutral if conflict does break out."

"Do you have any idea what Desmond's long-term plans are, Chief?"

"Not a clue. We can only hope he decides he doesn't like it here after all and moves on. Dismissed."

"Tough one," Solway said to Smith as they began to file out of the meeting room.

"I can't imagine spending twenty-five years in prison for something you didn't do."

"That's a heck of an assumption, Smith,"

Glendenning snapped at her. "Didn't you hear the chief? We have no opinion."

"I'm allowed to have an *opinion*, Sarge. I am not allowed to act on it, and I have no intention of doing so." Glendenning was new, came in from Edmonton several months ago. He was an older guy, probably looking for what he thought would be an easier small-town job to fill in the time until he could retire. He'd rubbed her the wrong way right from the start. She could guess why he didn't like her: he didn't get on too well with Dawn Solway, either. Solway was the only other woman on the force, and not only that but she was an out-lesbian as well. Glendenning might not like them, but he did nothing, said nothing, that would cause either of the women to lay a complaint. As long as it stayed that way, she was fine with it.

"Dave," Glendenning said, "give me a moment, will you?"

Chapter Four

The town hadn't changed all that much, Desmond thought as the bus pulled next to the small building that served as the Greyhound station. The surrounding mountains, not tall enough to be snowcapped in summer; Koola glacier in the distance; the wide, fast-moving Upper Kootenay River. The big black bridge crossing the river. More traffic, maybe, or perhaps that was just because this was summer and he'd last seen the town in the early fall.

Last seen, out of the small window in the sheriff's van taking him, shackled, shamed, defeated, to prison.

All that was over now. Over, thanks to Louise and her team.

There were more houses than he remembered, a new condo development down by the water, homes marching further up the mountain on the far side of the river. Most of the shops were different. The town looked good—prosperous, doing well. He'd followed the news from Trafalgar over the years. Ecotourism had been a boon for this area. The streets, he noticed from the bus, were full of young people, and many cars had kayaks or bike racks mounted on the roof.

The bus stopped and the doors opened. The building hadn't changed much, except to get a bit older, a bit shabbier. The woman in the seat next to Walt lumbered to her feet with a groan. "Thank God, that's over," the man behind muttered.

Walt waited until everyone was off before standing up and taking his backpack down from the overhead rack. A line of cars waited in the lot. People greeted friends and hugged and cried. Walt's seatmate was surrounded by a pack of squealing kids and a smiling woman. The bus driver unloaded luggage. Passengers waited impatiently for their own bags, and then snatched them up and hurried away.

Walt had no luggage. He owned nothing in the world other than the few toiletries and clothes Louise's secretary had taken him shopping for with the credit card Louise's organization had given him. They would, she'd told him, be asking the government for substantial compensation for his lost years.

He hefted his bag, unzipped it, and got out

his hat, making sure to keep concealed the single thing Louise's secretary had not helped him buy. In just one way prison had been good for him: He was a heck of a lot fitter than he'd been twenty-five years ago. He hadn't had a lot to do in prison other than work out and study law books.

He glanced around, getting his bearings. His house, their house, his and Arlene's house, was over there—to the east, about halfway up that hill. He squinted. He thought he spotted it, but the trees had grown over the years so it was hard to tell. He wondered who lived there now. He hoped they were happy. As happy as he and Arlene had been.

Once upon a time.

He'd looked up B&Bs on the Internet and booked the first one he recognized. It wasn't far from the bus station, and he'd enjoy the walk.

A cop stood in the entrance to the convenience store attached to the bus depot. A young man who would have been nothing but a toddler when Walter and Arlene lived here. He was tall and well-muscled in his short-sleeved uniform shirt. Walt recognized the red stripe down the pant leg, the patch on the sleeve. Trafalgar City Police. A deep shudder ran though Walt's entire body. The cop stared openly at him, his thumbs hitched through his laden utility belt. Walt began to turn away, to lower his eyes. Then he remembered. He was a free man. He had nothing to fear, not from this cop, not from any of them. He stared openly at the cop, until the man turned away and went into the store.

"What do you remember about the Walter Desmond case, Mom?" Molly Smith asked.

"Too much," Lucky replied. "Far too much. It was a terrible thing, Moonlight. There hadn't been a murder in this town in a hundred years or more. We thought we were so safe here in peaceful Trafalgar. It was an enormous blow to the town. And then to find out the killer was a local man, one of us, not a drifter passing through." She shook her head and her masses of curls, far more gray than red now, moved. Molly Smith's straight blond hair and blue eyes were her inheritance from her late father, Andy.

"The police arrested a suspect almost right away, didn't they?"

"Yes. And we all breathed a sigh of relief. Safe in our beds once again." Lucky's face tightened. "But it looks like they got the wrong guy."

Smith didn't know what to think about that. She'd read the newspaper reports. That the investigating officers had screwed up mightily was beyond doubt. Didn't mean the guy wasn't guilty. Just meant they hadn't been able to prove their case.

"I won't go into a rant about police corruption, dear," Lucky said with a smile. "That was before Paul moved here, and all the others involved are gone now, aren't they?"

"A couple of the old guys still live around here, but they're retired, so they don't have to talk about it if they don't want to."

They were in the tiny, cramped office of Lucky's store, Mid-Kootenay Adventure Vacations. Flower and the summer employee, Tyler, were out front. The bell over the door tinkled as customers came and went, and voices inquired about sizes and prices.

"Did you know him, Mom? Walter Desmond, I mean?"

"Not well. I knew his wife, Arlene, better. She was in my yoga class. We didn't socialize, other than an annual summer potluck and the occasional coffee after class. She owned a dress shop on Front Street. Where Eliza's art gallery is now. I never shopped there myself. I thought the clothes were better suited to older women. You know, pastel colors and polyester." Today, Lucky was dressed in a sleeveless, knee-length cotton dress in a swirling print of blues and greens worn over black leggings. Feathered earrings danged at her ears. She lifted her arms and her bangles clattered.

Smith smiled at her mom. Since Lucky was

now the official "partner" of the Chief Constable of Trafalgar, she'd invested in more sedate clothes than she normally wore for police and town functions. But still, pastels and polyester were not her thing.

"The yoga group was very supportive of Arlene when Walt was arrested," Lucky said. "I remember that. The poor woman. She was simply devastated, as you can imagine. She put up a strong front, and insisted that Walt was innocent. She must have aged ten years over the course of the trial."

"No one thought she might have been involved? Like a Karla Homolka sort of thing?"

Lucky shook her head firmly. "That was never even considered. Back then who would have believed that a wife would help her husband kidnap, rape, and murder young women? It was a winter afternoon, as I recall. Arlene was at her store the entire time in question. She couldn't provide her husband with an alibi."

"What happened to her?"

"Nothing good. She sold their house to pay his legal bills. After he was convicted and sent to prison, she moved away. She went to Ontario, to be closer so she could visit him regularly, we were told. I seem to recall that she died a few years later. Cancer, I think they said. So sad. And now, it looks like he was innocent all along. Why are you asking about that anyway?"

The office door burst open and a woman swept in. "Lucky, you will never believe who I just saw! Walt Desmond. Walking down Front Street as bold as brass. I almost crashed my car in shock. I swear the guy hasn't aged a bit. Oh, hello, Moonlight. I'm glad you're here." Lucky and many of her friends still called Molly by her birth name, Moonlight. That, Smith knew, was no name for a police officer. The visitor's face was flushed beneath her wide-brimmed hat, and not from the sun, Smith suspected. "What are they saying at the police station about Walt? Do they know he's here? Back in town?"

"We're not saying anything," Smith said.

"You'd better let them know."

"Mr. Desmond is free to come and go as he likes," she parroted the chief's line.

"I know, but..."

"Now I know why all the questions," Lucky said. "I think the best we can do is to leave the poor man alone, don't you agree, Judy? Let him get on with his life. What's left of it."

"Well, of course," Judy said. "I wonder how long he's planning to stay. Good heavens, do you think Gino and Rose know?"

"They know," Smith said.

"Mustn't keep you." Judy gripped the brim of

her hat and dashed out, presumably to spread the news far and wide.

"This," Lucky said, "is not going to end well."

Chapter Five

Ellie Carmine lugged the bucket of cleaning supplies down the stairs. Her back ached. She was
getting too old for this nonsense.

The B&B was almost full with women from
one of the dragon boat teams, and she'd decided
to give herself a small break and not rent the last
room. Then, scarcely knowing what she was doing,
she'd gone and done just that. Accepted another
reservation for five nights. Still, she needed the
money and empty rooms didn't pay the bills.

She put the bucket in the closet and shut the
door. The new arrival was due at five p.m. She
might have time for a quick cup of tea before he
got here. Despite her sore legs and aching feet, she
smiled to herself. She hoped the single man would
enjoy staying in a house full of fun-loving, highly
athletic women, all of them taking a break from
husbands, children, and jobs.

She plugged in the kettle.

The doorbell rang.

Oh, well. Get him settled in and then she could have her tea. She tidied her hair and went to answer the door.

Something was vaguely familiar about the man standing there, but she couldn't say what. He smiled at her, but the smile didn't touch his eyes and his look was wary. He'd booked online, using a credit card. Ellie never read the papers or watched the news on TV. She worked too hard, she told anyone who would listen. Although she always tried to find time in her day for her favorite soaps. And she did enjoy watching *Ellen* and *The View*.

"I'm Walt," the man said. "I have a reservation?"

"Certainly, come on in."

Ellie's place, the Glacier Chalet B&B, was one of the largest, nicest old houses in Trafalgar. A Victorian gem, bought by Ellie and her late husband many years ago. They'd been able to afford it only because it was falling apart. Most of the other houses of that era had been torn down, replaced with characterless modern boxes.

They'd worked hard to restore the house to its original glory, right down to the elaborate gingerbread trim. The front porch, graced with dove gray pillars, wide enough for lounge chairs and tables where guests could enjoy a drink on a summer evening, ran across the front and down each side wall. Inside, the guest rooms were large and comfortable, decorated to match the period of the house. A ground-floor common room was fitted with couches and chairs, an old computer, a small TV, a full bookshelf, and board games and puzzles were stacked in wicker baskets. The house was large enough that Ellie and her daughter, Kathy, had their own apartment. Kathy, much to Ellie's displeasure, used her valuable business diploma not to help run (with the intention of eventually taking over) the B&B, but to get a job in town at a dental office.

Soon it would be, Ellie thought, not for the first time—not even for the first time that day— time to sell. The place was worth a small fortune and would see her into a very comfortable retirement. The problem would be in finding a buyer. Not much call for six-bedroom houses with seven bathrooms, plus a separate apartment, two kitchens, and a half-acre of garden. Maintaining the garden alone was a full-time job. She'd had to finally give in and hire a landscape company when Kathy began ignoring her pleas to get the lawn cut.

"You can park your car around back," she said to the new guest.

"I don't have a car. I came in on the bus." He stepped inside and politely removed his hat, a wide-brimmed beige Tilley.

"Oh. All right then." That was odd. The Glacier Chalet was the most expensive B&B in Trafalgar. She didn't get a lot of customers who arrived on the Greyhound. She studied the man. He was tall, lean, seemed to be in good physical shape although he was exceedingly pale. His clothes looked new: khaki summer-weight pants, a golf shirt, black loafers. He carried only one piece of luggage—a bulging backpack, also looking quite new.

A table in the front hall served as the registration desk. Ellie handed Walt a sign-in sheet and a pen. He wrote his name. Then he stopped and thought. "I'm sorry," he said at last, "but I've just come back after an extended time away, so I don't have an address at the moment."

"That's okay," she said, "I have your credit card number on file." Better remind him of that. "The house is full. I hope it doesn't get too noisy for you." Also a good idea to remind a single man that she wasn't alone in the house. Although, at the moment, she was. "Breakfast is served in the dining room, from six-thirty to nine on weekdays. Seven to ten on weekends. Coffee's on all day, and I put some light snacks out in the early evening, around five-thirty or six. You're welcome to make use of the TV or the computer in the common room at any time. If you want suggestions as to places to eat or things to do, I'd be happy to help." She smiled at him.

"I've… I've been here before. But it's been a long time. Thank you, Ma'am."

Ellie liked politeness in a man.

Now, if only she could remember where she'd seen him before.

Walt Desmond lowered himself gingerly onto the bed. For a moment he felt as though he were going to fall right through, all the way to the floor. The mattress was soft, yielding and yet firm at the same time. The duvet was thick, the cover almost blindingly white. He hadn't slept in a bed like this since…No, he was here now. He had to enjoy every moment without remembering all he had lost. The only room left in the B&B, so the Internet had told him, was a single. He was glad of it. He didn't want to sleep in a big bed, where memories of Arlene curled up next to him would haunt his dreams.

The room was beautiful, although startlingly feminine to his prison-accustomed eyes. Arlene would have loved it. The duvet cover on the bed was as white as fresh snow in the prison yard before the men started trampling down the drifts. The pillow-cases were a deep blue. The walls were painted pale blue and the prints hanging there featured scenes of the lake in winter. A child's stuffed polar bear, with a blue ribbon around its snow-white neck, sat on the dresser beside tea things. A coffee pot, a small kettle, two blue-and-white china teacups, a silver tray containing packets of hot chocolate mix, sugar, packaged whitener, and several packages of cookies. The blue-and-white striped curtains were open, giving him a view of rows of houses and winding roads marching up the side of the mountain.

Louise's assistant had checked him into a motel when he'd been released. The room had been plain and functional, yet he'd thought it magnificent. He couldn't really afford this place, should have stayed at a cheap motel, tried to save some of what little money he had. But, he'd learned the hard way, there was no sense planning for tomorrow. Tomorrow might well turn out to be just another nightmare. Blue, he'd read somewhere, was a calming color. Not that he needed anything to calm him down. He thought that he could lie here, on this bed, forever, looking up at the white, unmarked celling. Breakfast, Ellie Carmine had said, was from six-thirty to nine. Tomorrow morning he'd have two and a half hours in which he could decide if he wanted to get out of bed or not. Imagine, no ringing bells, no lines of sullen, shuffling men. Probably a heck of a lot better breakfast than the slop they'd served at the prison too.

He lay back on the bed. Ellie Carmine. He remembered her. She and her husband had bought this old house and fixed it up. They opened the B&B the summer before....Her husband's name was Daniel. Danny, she called him. Walt wondered if Danny was still around. He'd been about to introduce himself, tell Ellie they were acquainted. But he'd closed his mouth, the greeting, the reminder unsaid. Time enough to find out if people here remembered him.

He heard the front door open and a burst of female laughter. Footsteps on the stairs. Several pairs by the sound of it. More laughter.

Of all the things he'd missed, perhaps what he'd missed the most had been the sound of women laughing.

He almost leapt out of his skin at a rap on the door. "Yes?"

"Hi, I'm Darlene, your neighbor."

He lifted himself, reluctantly, off the bed and opened the door. The woman was in her early sixties, extremely well-preserved sixties, with gray-blond hair pulled back into a high bouncy ponytail. She wore a pair of tight black shorts and a red shirt made of a stretchy material with Kelowna Pepper printed across the front, and her feet were wrapped in sturdy sandals that looked like they'd been fashioned from old tires. Her skin was bronzed from the sun and her teeth almost shone. She held a bottle of wine in her hand. "Welcome. We've had a great day and are in the mood to celebrate. We're going to have a drink or two in the common room before heading out for dinner."

"I…" he found himself at a total loss for words. He'd thought Louise beautiful, with her expensive suits, her perfume, her high heels, and sleek black briefcase. But this…this tall creature, with the tanned face, swinging hair, muscular arms and legs—long bare legs—firm breasts under the tight shirt, that smile, was beyond beautiful. "I'm Walt."

"Pleased to meet you, Walt. We tend to get a mite loud sometimes, so you're welcome to join us if you'd like. No pressure." She waved the bottle in the air. "And the drinks are on us."

Further down the hall a door opened. Another beautiful woman, much the same age, dressed in identical black shorts and red shirt as Darlene, stuck her head out. "Oh, goodie. Just what we've been missing. A man." She barked out a laugh. "I'll be down soon as I've hit the shower."

"That degenerate is Nancy," Darlene said. "You need to watch out for her, Walt."

Nancy slammed her door with another peal of laughter.

"Come on down when you're ready," Darlene said. "If you want to."

She took the stairs at a gallop.

Walt stood in the doorway to his room, stunned.

Carolanne sank onto her bed with a grateful sigh. She ached. Her whole body ached. Easier to catalogue what didn't ache rather than what did. She was definitely getting too old for this. All she wanted to do right now was to sleep. Take a nice long nap, then order in a pizza—an extra large would be nice—and stay in bed with the pizza, a bag of chips, and a stack of mindless gossip magazines.

But, as was becoming usual these days, what got her to her feet, running the bath and laying out clothes to wear to dinner, was the thought that the other women were older than her. Stronger, fitter, better-looking. But still *older*.

She climbed into the bath with a grateful sigh. The water was piping hot, the towels big and fluffy, the soap and bath products lightly scented. She was pleased she'd thought to get a smaller, single room. She didn't mind paying a bit extra, as long as she could have *some* desperately needed moments of peace and privacy. These women were tireless. A morning jog, a day on the water, drinks and snacks in the common room, and then out to dinner. At least they didn't want to go clubbing after. Carolanne sank further into the water.

What had she gotten herself into?

Carla had dragged her to the dragon boat club, telling Carolanne what she knew well enough but couldn't convince herself to do anything about: she needed an interest in life. She needed a reason to get up in the morning and get out of the house, to go somewhere other than just her excruciatingly boring job as a bank teller. She needed to meet new and fascinating people. She needed, Carla said, to meet men. Carolanne had put her foot down at that. She was not, she insisted to her sister, interested in dating or in doing anything that would make anyone think she, a recent widow, was looking for a new husband.

Carla had smiled and said, "Have I got the perfect thing for you."

Carolanne had never been one for exercise. She'd gone to the gym when she was younger, more because everyone she knew was a member of a gym than because she enjoyed it. Frank played hockey in the winter and fished in the summer. Carolanne had absolutely no interest in participating in those things with him. He didn't mind. He did his thing, she did hers, and when they got together at the end of the day all was right with their world.

She felt tears behind her eyes and blinked them away. No regrets. Her marriage wouldn't have been any stronger, Frank's all-too-short life any longer, if she'd learned to skate or pretended interest in sitting in a leaky rowboat or over a hole in the ice waiting for some hapless fish to swim past.

She'd joined the women's dragon boat team expecting a few pleasant summer hours out on the lake. Instead she'd fallen into a group of *determined* women. These women lived and breathed their boat. They had jobs and families, but otherwise they seemed to exist only for their time on the water. The water, and the team. It was the camaraderie, the teamship, which drew Carolanne in. Even when she discovered that the women worked out to get in shape for boating, rather than paddling to get in shape. In the winter, when they couldn't put the boat in, they just worked out.

To her considerable surprise, she turned out to be good at it. She had long legs and long arms, perfect, the team's coach had told her, for paddling. Carla soon dropped out. She said she didn't have the time, with the job and her kids, but Carolanne knew her sister wasn't getting the pure joy out of it that she was. Perhaps that was another thing that drove Carolanne on. Carla was the older sister, always more accomplished, more successful with her lawyer-husband, two perfect kids, and her position as an executive in an insurance company.

The team went to California for a week in February. Not to swim and relax in the sun, but to practice on the water. And, of course, to work out. It had been the best week Carolanne had in a long time.

Although, when they got home she had to take two extra vacation days, just to recover.

She started at a knock on her door. "Drinkies downstairs in five minutes," Darlene shouted. "If you're late we won't save any for you."

Carolanne blinked. She must have fallen asleep. The bath water was cool, the bubbles nothing but soapy scum. She climbed out of the tub and reached for a towel.

These women—this team—had given her life meaning again. But sometimes she wished they hadn't given it quite so much activity.

Chapter Six

Ellie Carmine put down the phone. She could scarcely credit what she'd been told.

Walt Desmond. Back in town. Now she knew why she thought her newest guest seemed familiar. He looked good, she thought. Better than she might have expected. He'd been a somewhat overweight man, round and flabby, on the verge of going to seed like so many men his age. Now he was lean, muscular. His face had slimmed into handsome lines, the short gray hair suited him, and he even seemed taller than she remembered.

One of her friends had called, bursting with the news. Walt Desmond had been seen getting off the bus from Vancouver. He was back. Ellie had heard something over the spring about an appeal of his case. Some reason to believe he hadn't actually killed poor Sophia D'Angelo. Of course he'd killed her. Everyone knew that. The police case was rock solid. Criminals were getting away with anything these days. She was only glad her Danny wasn't around to see Walt strutting around the streets as if he had a right to move among law-abiding folks.

A peal of laughter came from the common room. Those women, part of a dragon boat team from Kelowna, sure knew how to have a good time. But it wasn't all drinking and laughing, Ellie knew. Teams had come here from all over British Columbia for a week of training and competition. On Saturday, they were having an open house down at the river. The women headed out first thing every morning and spent a good part of the day in their boat, preparing, they'd told her, for a big race in September in Italy. The rest of their team and women from the other teams were spread out in B&Bs and hotels all across Trafalgar. Ellie liked having them here. They were a fun bunch, and she hoped they'd inspire Kathy to get up from the computer and head out for some exercise. No luck there yet.

She just wished they hadn't invited Walt Desmond to join them in the common room.

She picked up the phone.

"Trafalgar City Police," said the polite voice.

"Uh, hello. I'm uh…"

"Do you have an emergency, Ma'am?"

"No. Nothing like that." She dropped her

voice. "This is Ellie Carmine from the Glacier Chalet B&B."

"Hi, Ellie. What can we do for you?"

"Ingrid, I thought you people would want to know…that's all."

"Know what, Ellie?"

"Walter Desmond is back in town."

"We're aware of that."

"He's staying here. With me. I mean in my B&B."

"Is that a problem for you, Ellie?"

"No. I thought you should know. In case, well, in case anything happens."

"Thanks for calling. It's the position of the Trafalgar City Police that Mr. Desmond has been cleared of all charges and is free to come and go as he likes."

"Okay. Uh, thanks, Ingrid. Bye." Ellie put down the phone. She didn't know what she'd thought the police could do. She didn't know what she wanted them to do. Tell Walt to leave, probably. She'd rather he wasn't here, but she didn't think she could out-and-out demand that he leave. He was a paying guest, after all.

She'd have to warn Kathy to have no contact with him. She lifted the tray. As she did every night when the house was occupied, she'd arranged a few bowls of nuts and olives, a platter of crackers and inexpensive cheese, some supermarket pâté, and a sliced baguette from Alphonse's French Bakery, which she bought at the end of the day when he was discounting the leftovers. It wasn't expensive, but it made the guests feel spoiled.

Ellie entered the common room as the last drops of a bottle of white wine were being poured into Walt's glass. The women held full glasses, and their faces glowed with drink and health and good humor. They were an attractive bunch, Ellie had to admit. Sleek, well groomed, fit and lean. They all appeared to have some money behind them, and had arrived in a convoy of high-end SUVs and luxury sedans.

Walt looked up with a smile for Ellie. She studied his face. Looking for something, anything, that would tell her what he had done. His smile faded. He put down his glass. She turned quickly away and put the tray on the coffee table.

"Everything okay, Ellie?" Darlene, who seemed to be the group's leader, asked.

"Of course. I mean, why wouldn't everything be? You ladies have a nice evening now. Don't worry about the dishes, I'll clean up before I go to bed." With another quick glance at Walt, she fled.

"Did anyone think that was odd?" Nancy said, as

the kitchen door slammed behind Ellie. "She was so friendly a few minutes ago, and then out of the blue she looked like she'd swallowed a goldfish."

"I heard the phone." Carolanne scooped up a handful of nuts. "Maybe she got some bad news."

Walt got to his feet. The wine tasted sour in his mouth. He hadn't had a sip of wine in twenty-five years and had been really looking forward to it. As well as to spending time in the company of these women, listening to them laugh and chatter about inconsequential things. To drink wine and eat cheese and nuts and pretend, for a little while, that he was a normal guy, leading a normal life.

That phone call had been about him. Ellie Carmine, kind gentle Ellie, came back into the room after answering the phone, and looked at him as if expecting him to whip a knife out from under his shirt and run amuck through the house.

"Hey," Darlene said. "You're not leaving us already are you, Walt?"

"Sorry," he said. "I've had a long day, and I'm all in. I'm going for a walk. Clear my head. Thank you for your kindness."

As he turned to leave, the woman named Carolanne gave him a shy smile. He felt himself smiling back. She was slightly younger than the others, younger and quieter. She wasn't beautiful, like Darlene, or all muscle like some of her friends. But she was lovely in a gentle, quiet way, with her chin-length brown hair, huge dark eyes, small breasts, slim hips, and long limbs. "Enjoy your walk," she said.

The setting sun had outlined the mountains to the west in shades of purple. The sky was clear, the air warm, and a light wind ruffled the hairs on his face and arms. He stood on the porch for a few moments, breathing deeply. He was looking forward to seeing stars, a blanket of stars, maybe even the Milky Way if he was lucky.

He hadn't seen anything but the brightest of stars in so long. He and Arlene had owned a telescope. They weren't exactly astronomers, but they enjoyed sitting out on a clear winter's night, wrapped warmly, sipping hot chocolate, and watching the movement of the night sky.

In prison the lights, inside and out, had burned all through the night, and when he was released and staying in Vancouver, the glow of the city hid all but the strongest of the stars.

He walked through the quiet streets as dusk lengthened. He needed to think about joining a gym. Too much rich food and no workouts and, before he knew it, he'd be slow and fat again. He didn't much care if he was fat or not, but he'd never again be slow. He'd learned, fast, that the only way to survive in prison was to look as tough and as mean as any one of them. To *be* as tough and as mean as any one of them.

The streets of comfortable homes with well-groomed gardens and cars parked in driveways were quiet. Lights glowed inside houses and curtains were drawn.

Louise had not been happy when he told her he was coming home, to Trafalgar. People have long memories, she'd said; they won't have forgotten. But I'm innocent, he protested, you proved that. She'd merely shaken her head.

The short hairs at the back of his neck twitched. In prison he'd quickly learned never to ignore his warning senses. A car fell in behind him, moving at the same slow pace as his walking. He stopped abruptly and whipped around, fists clenched, prepared for a brawl. He did not relax when he recognized it as a cop car, white with the logo of the Trafalgar City Police. The same car that had taken him away, so long ago. The car he'd been stuffed into after they marched him out of his house with his hands cuffed behind his back, while curious neighbors gathered on their front steps and he shouted for Arlene to call a lawyer. Any lawyer.

She couldn't have found anyone more incompetent and useless if she'd tried.

This wasn't the same car, of course, but similar

enough. Same cops, too: two guys bristling with aggression and attitude.

The car pulled to a stop beside him.

The one driving was the man he'd seen earlier at the bus stop, a young one. The other was older, edging close to retirement. They got out of the car. They shifted their equipment belts and approached him.

"Help you, gentlemen?" Walt said. He did not relax one bit.

"Let's see some ID," the older one said. He was shorter than Walt, starting to run to fat, but not quite there yet. His jowls jiggled when he spoke. This guy was old enough to have been around when he lived here. Walt studied him, looking for something familiar. Nothing.

"No," Walt said.

"What?"

"I said no. I have no ID on me, as I'm out for a simple walk on a summer's evening, and you have no authority to ask for it, in any case." Walt's wallet was, in fact, in his pocket. But he knew the law.

"I…" the older one said.

"Doesn't matter," the young one interrupted. "You've got quite an attitude, Walt."

"If you know my name, you know I've committed no crime and you can't stop me from peacefully going about my business." He kept his head up, his chin forward, his back straight, arms at his sides. But his heart was beating so hard he feared those two goons would hear it, and a cold sweat ran down his spine.

Show no fear. Never show a trace of fear.

"Word of warning, Walt," the young one said, "you might have fooled the judges on high, but we've got your number. Hope you're not planning on staying in town too long."

"I'll stay until I feel like moving on."

"See, it's like this." The older one spat out the words. "Some of us know that Jack McMillan and Doug Kibbens were good solid cops. Old-fashioned cops, the kind who recognize a scumball when they see one and have the guts to do their jobs without the approval of some fancy-ass judge-lady. Doug's gone now, died in his boots like a good officer should, but Jack's still around. His friends don't like to hear his good name slandered."

Doug Kibbens was dead, Walt knew that well enough. Rather than dying while doing his job, he'd been killed in a single-vehicle accident. Gone over the side of a mountain to crash and burn at the bottom. Walt had shed no tears when he heard the news.

"It's over," Walt said. "Leave me alone and I won't be slandering anyone."

"Is that a threat?" The cop rested his hand on the butt of his gun.

"No. It's a comment."

A woman turned the corner and walked toward them, almost running to keep up with the frisky golden Labrador straining at its leash. The dog headed straight for the group of men, tail wagging, long pink tongue flapping. The woman gripped the leash tighter and hurried on, dragging the dog behind her, throwing curious glances at the men as she passed.

"I checked the bus schedule for you," the older cop said. "The next bus out leaves tomorrow at eight. Be on it. Come on, Dave. We're done here." He walked around the car and climbed into the passenger seat without giving Walt another look. The young one, Dave, didn't move for a long time. Then he said, "A word to the wise."

He got into the car and they drove away.

Walt had been planning to walk to the out-skirts of town to get the best view of the stars. He decided against that, better not to be alone in the dark. He still wanted to see stars. They wouldn't be as bright on Front Street, not with all the people and the shops and traffic.

He wondered if those two cops had been acting with the approval of their superiors. He let out a long sigh: he'd find out soon enough.

Chapter Seven

Eliza Winters' smile collapsed the moment the customer's back was turned. She flipped the sign on the door to CLOSED and gave the lock a satisfying twist. It had been a long day and she was dead tired.

Long, tiring, but profitable, she reminded herself. The gallery had been busy all day and a good number of customers had bought. Her assistant, Margo Franklin, was fighting off a bad cold and this was the third day she'd missed work. Eliza kicked off her Jimmy Choos and slipped her aching feet into a pair of comfortable flip-flops. Much better. She'd spent most of her working life in heels, but even now when her feet ached from standing all day, she couldn't bring herself to wear pumps or flats with the sort of stylish suit she insisted on wearing to work. She was the boss; she could dictate that the staff (meaning Margo) could wear shorts and tee-shirts if they wanted. But training dies hard, and from the age of sixteen when she'd first become a model, Eliza Winters had been taught that appearances were everything.

She glanced around the gallery. For the summer months they were featuring paintings of the Kootenays. Most of the work was by local artists, but they had some pieces by people who'd visited the area and been inspired to try to re-create the beauty. The variety was what appealed to her most about this collection. Everything from one enormous brilliantly colored canvas that took its inspiration from street graffiti to her favorite piece, a tiny pencil sketch of blue flowers in a mountain meadow with the barest hint of the outline of the glacier beyond. She was tempted to buy the sketch for herself, but she resisted. If she bought all the art she loved, their house would be full and the gallery empty.

She stepped mechanically through her end-of-the-day chores, wondering if she'd be able to get away for a few days later in the week as she'd planned. Other than Margo, there was no one Eliza could rely on to open and close and watch the store for an entire day. She owned another gallery in Vancouver, in the trendy, high-end Kitsilano neighborhood. At that gallery she employed a proper manager and stocked recognized art with prices to match. So far, after rent and wages, the Kitsilano store hadn't made a dime, whereas the little shop in Trafalgar, intended to be more of a hobby than a business, was doing great.

She glanced out the wide front window. Night was arriving. Street lights illuminated people window-shopping or heading to bars and restaurants and a steady parade of cars driving down Front Street. It was the middle of summer, and the tourists were here in force. She switched off the light behind the sales counter, turned on the night lights, and headed toward her car and home, thinking of a quick shower, comfortable clothes, a glass of cold white wine, and supper on the deck. Her husband had called earlier to say he was finishing work and would have dinner ready. She sighed happily at the thought and let herself out.

The Mountain in Winter Gallery was in the center of a row of shops, all of which backed onto an alley. The bright lights of Front Street weren't visible here, and the alley was lit by lamps perched at the tops of utility poles so their light shone in circles amidst puddles of shadowy gloom. A single red light flashed from the top of the nearest mountain, warning airplanes to keep their distance. Something rustled near the bags of garbage piled at the rear of Crazies Coffee next door, but Eliza paid it no mind. A cat probably, or a mouse. She pressed the button on the key, the headlights of the BMW flashed a greeting, and the car's interior lit up.

She fell forward, hard, crashing into the hood of the car. A heavy weight landed against her, pinning her down. For a moment she had absolutely no idea what was happening. All she knew was she couldn't move and the car was cold and hard against her chest. She opened her mouth, but could make no sound. Something was covering it. She heard a mumble and pure fear washed over her. A man had shoved her up against her car, his bulk had trapped her in place, and his hand was over her mouth. She kicked back, hard, and made impact. He merely let out a quiet grunt, and she spared a thought for the three-inch stiletto heels she'd kicked off so gratefully. She felt hot wet breath on the back of her neck, and a hand scrambling at her legs. Her skirt was lifted, and rough nails scratched her thigh. Against every instinct she had—to fight, to resist— she let her body go limp. A voice whispered, "That's better. Don't fight and I won't hurt you." The hand over her mouth relaxed as the other squeezed and prodded her flesh. He sighed. She gathered all the strength she could and jerked her head to one side. Her mouth came free and she screamed. She continued screaming as she turned, wrenching herself out of his grip. She kicked out and made contact. She could see him, black hair, white face, red eyes full of lust and surprise. He snarled and pain exploded in her face. She screamed again.

White light washed the alley, and for a moment Eliza thought she was passing out. Or perhaps he'd killed her and she was approaching the gates of...whatever lay beyond. A car engine revved and the headlights were stronger, brighter. "I'm calling 911!" a woman shouted into the night. The man stepped backward. He held his hands in front of his face, trying to block the light. He looked at Eliza. She reached for his face, fighting to ignore the pain in her own face. She'd scratch his eyes out if she had to. She'd kill him, if she could. Pain exploded in her belly, then he turned and ran. He jumped over the garbage bags and dashed down a side alley. Her legs collapsed and she was falling.

Chapter Eight

Molly Smith wiped barbeque sauce off her chin. Her napkin was so saturated it was useless. She reached for another.

"Enjoying those?" Adam Tocek asked.

"Yum, yum, good." A chicken graveyard lay on the plate in front of her. She scooped up the last wing and ripped at the tender meat with her teeth.

He sipped his beer. He was having nachos. Wednesday night wings and nachos, when schedules permitted, had become one of their routines. Now that they were engaged and living together, Smith thought it important to keep the romance alive. Not easy for anyone these days, particularly not when both partners were police officers, and Adam, the RCMP dog-handler for the district, could be called out just about any time. And often was. More than once Smith had had to find her own way home. Tocek's schedule had its advantages, though: she was rarely asked to be the couple's designated driver, as he always held himself to one beer.

"This a private party or can anyone join?" Dawn Solway stood behind Tocek's chair. She was in uniform and carried a glass of ice water.

"Take a seat," Smith said. "Doing the rounds?"

"Yeah." Solway snagged an empty chair and pulled it up to their table. "Dave and Jeff are on the road. Lucky buggers." She subtly shifted her Kevlar vest. "I think I might melt if it doesn't cool down soon." She gulped water. Tonight it would be Solway's job to walk the streets and alleys and pop in and out of the bars. On a night like tonight, heat and humidity lingering after a scorching day, the air-conditioned patrol cars were popular spots.

Summer in Trafalgar was a busy time. This was a tourist town, but far off the well-travelled route between Vancouver and the Rocky Mountains used by bus companies. Most of the tourists who came here were young people, looking for mountain air and views, backcountry hiking and kayaking in summer, some of the world's best skiing in winter. The sort that liked to burn off excess energy when they emerged from a week in the wilderness.

At the table next to them, six women stood up all at once. They headed for the door, calling out goodnights. Solway grinned. "Thank heavens for athletic middle-aged women." She made a great display of checking her watch. "Almost nine o'clock. Time for them to be heading to bed."

Tocek laughed and dug through his pile of nachos, searching for more salsa.

Solway leaned over. Smith did likewise. "Ellie Carmine called the station. Walt Desmond's staying there."

"Any trouble?" Tocek asked.

"No. She just wanted us to know."

"Bad business," Smith said.

"I can't imagine why the hell he's come back," Tocek said. "Does he really think people are ready to forgive him?"

"Whyever not?" Smith asked. "He didn't do it."

Tocek snorted. "Some big-city lawyers on a mission found that the investigating officers had stretched the truth a bit. Things were more…shall we say…flexible, back then. They knew they had their man. They simply helped the proof along."

"You can't be serious," Smith said. "They lied in court. They hid a witness from the defense. They denied the guy a fair trial."

"Shouldn't have even come to trial," Solway said, "from what I've read."

"Come on, you two. None of us were around then. They wouldn't have exaggerated the evidence if they weren't positive he'd done it." Tocek shook his head. "They knew."

"Travesties of justice happen all the time," Smith said. "Look at Truscott, look at Moran, at..."

"I don't know the details of those cases. And neither do you, Molly. But I know that Jack McMillan and Doug Kibbens had decent records. They never fudged..."

"You're defending Jack McMillan?" If Smith hadn't been trained in how to behave in a public place (by parents as well as at police college), she would have screamed. "The same Jack McMillan who called me a drag queen?"

"He didn't actually call you that, Molly," Solway said, trying to lighten the mood. "He was simply making an observation. As I recall, Adam put a stop to his observation."

McMillan was an old-time cop who hung around the station when retirement got too much for him, trying to interest the current officers in how things had been done in his day. He was sexist, racist, and homophobic and most of the staff, police, and civilian, ignored him. About the only ones who had much time for the old guy were Jeff Glendenning and Dave Evans—probably because they approved of, but could never say, the things McMillan said. Glendenning was an old guy, and he'd be gone soon. But Dave Evans was the same age as Smith herself, and she'd have to work with him for a long time. Until he got the new job on a big-city force which they all knew he was desperate for, and not having much luck finding. A couple of years ago when Smith and Tocek had first started dating, Tocek overheard McMillan goading Evans into making a comment about the sexual habits of female officers in general, and Smith in particular. That incident had ended in a hideously embarrassing brawl in no less a place than the police station in front of all her coworkers.

Smith had told Tocek never to defend her honor again.

He'd been pretty good about it. As far as she knew.

"That's all irrelevant," he said now. "Walt Desmond was a straight white man, so no one can accuse McMillan of railroading him because of prejudices."

"I didn't say that was what happened."

"If they'd deliberately created evidence against an innocent guy, then they had to know they were letting the guilty one off. They wouldn't have done that."

"I didn't say that either. I said that in some cases, we know—because it's been proved—that innocent people are convicted of crimes they did not commit, and sometimes it's because the police were either shoddy and careless or deliberately vindictive. If you want to give McMillan some credit, I'd put my money on shoddy."

"You're saying the entire TCP covered up a crime?" Tocek asked.

"No! I'm not saying that at all, Adam. Plant some false evidence, hide some exonerating stuff, then step back and watch everyone around you believe it. Easy enough."

"As fun as this is," Solway said, getting to her feet, "I have to get back out there. It's my job tonight to stop any potential fights from breaking out. I won't be getting a call here, I hope."

Tocek laughed but Smith glared at her friend. "Soon as Adam admits he's wrong, this is over."

"Not gonna happen, Mol."

"As Adam pointed out," Solway said, "neither of you were around then. I'm sure the case files are easily available. They would have had to have been brought out of storage for the appeal, right? Read up on it. Then you can argue with some idea of what you're talking about." Her radio crackled. She lifted a hand, asking her friends to be quiet, and bent her head to listen. "Two-two here. Do you need backup? I'm in the Bishop, can be there in a sec. Okay." She pushed herself to her feet. "911 call. Dave's got it, but I'd better go and see what's up. A woman's been attacked in the alley just down the way. Sounds like the attack was interrupted by

a passerby and the perp took off. Catch you later."
She weaved her way through the crowded room,
heading for the back door at a rapid clip. She threw
a wave to Mike behind the bar as she passed.

Smith glared at the man she loved. He finished
his beer and returned her look with the sexy grin
that always made her heart melt.

Right now, it didn't exactly melt, but perhaps
it softened, if only a little.

"We can argue about this 'til the cows come
home," he said. "But I'd rather not. Let's get Norman
and have a walk. I'm in the mood for ice cream."

"Okay," she said.

He waved at the waitress to bring the bill.
Smith glanced around the room. People were eating
and drinking, laughing and talking. If she and
Adam were divided about the Walt Desmond case,
what must the mood be like in the rest of town?

Adam's phone rang. He rolled his eyes as he
answered. "I'm in town now. On my way." He hung
up and threw Smith a grimace. "They want me at
Dawn's call. The guy got away on foot. It happened
only minutes ago so they're hoping Norman can
find the trail."

"I'll go with you. No need to call someone out
to watch your back."

Chapter Nine

"I've called for help," the woman said. "Oh, my God, I can't believe it. Are you okay? Eliza, help's coming."

Eliza looked up. She was sitting on the pavement, her back against the front tire of the BMW. A woman crouched over her. She'd gotten out of her car but left the engine running, and the headlights on. Brilliant white light flooded the alley. The car radio was playing classical music. Mozart, Eliza thought. Suitable music to walk into heaven by. "Merrill?"

"Yes. It's me."

"What are you doing here?" Eliza said.

"I was baking granola bars for tomorrow." Merrill Young worked at Rosemary's Campfire Kitchen, a shop further down Front Street. "While Rosemary's away, I've been running the place, and I got it into my head that I forgot to turn the oven off. I've been known to have a touch of OCD on occasion."

"I'm glad to hear that," Eliza said. She laughed. Merrill laughed.

By the time they heard sirens, and red and blue lights were sweeping the alley, both women were laughing so hard tears ran down their faces.

"Is everyone okay? What's happened here?" A male voice said. "Mrs. Winters, is that you?"

Constable Dave Evans stood over her, his handsome face full of concern. She stopped laughing, and began to cry.

"Let's get her inside," Merrill said.

Eliza flinched when Evans touched her arm.

"It's okay," Merrill said, her voice as calm and soothing as though she were speaking to a frightened toddler. "Let us help."

Eliza's legs felt like they were made of rubber. She pushed Evans away and leaned against Merrill.

"Do you need to go to the hospital, Mrs. Winters?" Evans asked.

"No. I'm okay." She breathed. It hurt.

"You look like you took a couple of punches," Evans said. "You're going to be darn sore tomorrow. Let the medics check you out."

"No," Eliza said. "I want to go home."

"She needs to sit down," Merrill said. "Let's get her inside."

"I'm going to call the Sarge," Evans said.

Eliza shook her head. That hurt too. "I will. Where's my bag?"

"I see it," Merrill said. She scooped up Eliza's purse as well as the key ring she'd dropped.

"Everything okay here?" a woman called. Constable Dawn Solway stepped out of the darkness into the circle of light.

"Eliza's been attacked, but I chased him off," Merrill said. "Help me, please. Dave, you get the door." She passed him the ring of keys. He opened the door to the gallery and switched on lights, as Solway and Merrill half-carried Eliza inside. Two brown leather chairs were arranged around a chrome and glass table displaying a collection of art and architecture magazines. Eliza had envisaged the comfortable space as somewhere for the spouse to rest while the art lover browsed, and thus was able to make an unhurried decision.

Eliza dropped into the soft, warm, buttery leather. Merrill placed her phone in her hand. Eliza's hands shook as she struggled to find the right buttons. Merrill took the phone back. "What's your password? Is John in your contact list?"

Eliza nodded and recited the numbers. Merrill made the call and handed the phone back to Eliza.

Evans gave Merrill a jerk of his head, telling her to come with him. "While Mrs. Winters is on the phone, why don't you tell me what happened?"

John Winters liked to cook, but he wasn't very good at it. His wife, on the other hand, neither liked to cook nor was she any good at it. She'd spent too many years as a model, when her meals consisted of a handful of lettuce leaves without dressing and an ounce or two of broiled fish, to take any pleasure in the preparation of food. He'd been raised in the sort of home where cooking was considered women's work. His father hadn't known how to so much as make himself a piece of toast and a boiled egg.

Winters' work schedule didn't leave a lot of time for meal planning or complicated prep, but over the years he'd learned how to make a few nice dishes, and he had some tricks for getting a good meal on the table quickly. Tonight, he was making pizza. Homemade crust was far beyond his skillset, so he'd bought the dough ready-made from the supermarket. He'd sliced mushrooms, onions, and green peppers, laid out pepperoni, grated a mountain of cheese, and opened a can of pizza sauce. While Eliza was getting out of her work clothes and hopping into the shower, he'd assemble the ingredients and put the pizza in the oven. He smiled at the thought of Eliza eating pizza. She continued to get modeling work into her middle age and had to pay even more attention to what she ate as she got older. But, eventually, she decided it was all getting too difficult and announced her intention to retire. He'd been delighted, secretly imagining the little wife at home instead of traveling the world, ironing his shirts and having a hot, hearty meal on the table when he came through the door at the end of the day.

He should have known better. Before she'd so much as finished her last modeling gig, Eliza had bought two art galleries, one of which she planned to manage and staff herself.

Now that she wasn't modeling, she'd relaxed fractionally and started eating slightly better. He hated to think what her bone density must be after a lifetime of Melba toast and carrot sticks. In her early days, before they'd met and married, she'd supplemented her lack of food with substantial quantities of cigarettes and illegal drugs. Most models had to, she'd told him, to keep the hunger pangs at bay, particularly when they were young and still growing. She'd been able to give up that part of the life, and although her diet had always, to his eyes, been sparse, she'd eaten with an eye for adequate nutrition.

She'd enjoy a small piece of pizza tonight, although he made one quarter of it without pepperoni and only half the amount of cheese. He glanced at the clock on the wall. She was running late.

His phone rang. He checked the display. Eliza. Delayed by a last-minute customer perhaps, or a friend wanting to talk. "Winters' Pizza Parlor. Head chef speaking."

All he heard was sobs.

"Eliza? What's the matter? I can't hear you. Where are you?" A car accident, he thought. That she was well enough to make the call had to mean she wasn't trapped or injured.

"Sarge?"

"What the…? Dawn is that you?"

"Yeah. I'm at your wife's art gallery. Got a 911 call. She's okay, but really shook up. You'd better come down."

He was out the door before he'd even hung up the phone.

Chapter Ten

It was too hot tonight to leave the dog in the truck and Tocek didn't like to keep the engine running and the air conditioning going for hours, so he'd asked the manager of the Bishop and Nun if Norman could stay in the office while he and Smith were in the place. It was never a problem; Norman was a very well-behaved dog.

Smith ran for the truck to get Norman's police vest as well as Adam's RCMP jacket and a police-issue vest for herself, while Tocek got the dog. They slipped out the back of the Bishop and Nun into the alley. Norman could usually be counted on to attract a crowd when he was working, but the alley had been sealed off. Cruisers were stationed at the intersections, breaking the gloom with rotating red and blue lights.

Smith would follow while Tocek gave the dog his head and Norman cast about for a scent. She'd done this before. The dog-handler's total concentration had to be focused on his animal: someone had to watch their backs.

No problem spotting the scene. A civilian car was parked askew across the alley, engine running and lights on. No bodies that she could see, and that was a good thing.

"What you got?" Tocek said.

Detective Ray Lopez said, "Woman attacked. A passerby arrived and the perp ran off."

"Here?" Smith said, "That's Eliza Winters' art gallery."

Lopez nodded. "She's inside. Dawn's with her. John's on his way."

"Is Mrs. Winters okay?" Tocek asked.

"Well enough to refuse to go to the hospital."

While they talked, Norman sniffed about, nose to the ground, searching for a scent. The only thing he had to go on would be a trail recently laid down.

Lopez pointed down the alley, away from the Bishop and Nun. "The woman who intervened said he went that way. I've tried to keep people from walking around too much, knowing you were coming, Adam."

"Thanks. Looks like it's show time." Norman had found something. His ears stood up, his nose swept the pavement, and he set off at a rapid clip down the alley. Tocek kept a light hand on the leash and Smith followed. Officers stopped what they were doing to watch them pass.

Norman kept to a straight line close to the wall of shops on his left. They reached Elm Street, where a patrol car was keeping people out of the alley. Norman didn't hesitate and turned left. The heavy traffic and bright lights of Front Street were only a few yards ahead. He walked up the hill. People spotted him and pointed. Phones came out of pockets or bags and snapped pictures. Norman and Tocek paid not the slightest bit of attention. They were used to attracting a crowd. "Stand back, please. The dog is working," Smith told the over-friendly and over-curious.

They reached Front Street. Norman hesitated, and then he walked in slow, searching circles. He found something of interest and went left, but he stopped after a few yards and cast around again. He sniffed at the ground under a late-model Explorer parked at the curb. Smith put her hand on the hood. Warm.

Norman continued sniffing. He glanced back at Tocek and seemed to say, "Sorry, partner."

Tocek gave him a pat on the head. "You tried, buddy."

A couple dashed across the street at a break in the traffic. They were in their mid-thirties, dressed as though going out for dinner. "Everything okay, Officer?" the man asked.

"Is this your car, sir?" Smith said.

"Yes. Yes it is."

"May I ask how long you've been parked here?"

The couple exchanged glances. "No more than two or three minutes. We're early for our dinner reservation so we were window shopping at the jewelry store across the way and saw your dog checking out our car. What happened?"

"Did you see the vehicle parked here before you?"

"No. The spot was empty, wasn't it hon?"

The woman nodded in agreement. "I said we were lucky to find a place so close to the restaurant."

"Thanks," Smith said.

"Come on, buddy." Tocek pulled at the leash and Norman gave up the search.

"It was a long shot," Smith said, as they walked back to the alley. "Worth trying, though. If only he'd stayed in the alley and hid behind a garbage bin, we'd have had him."

"Just like in the movies," Tocek said. "It's not too late and Norman needs a win. Do you mind?"

"Go for it," she said.

"You distract his attention, and I'll set it up," Tocek said.

Smith led Norman behind a parked car. She

crouched down and gave him a scratch behind the ears, so he wouldn't try to find out what his partner was up to.

A few minutes later Tocek was back. He took the leash and said, "One more job for you, buddy." He led the dog to the scene of the earlier attack. This time he gently edged Norman to the wall on the far side of the alley from the Mountain in Winter. Norman cast about and instantly found something. He set off at a determined pace, Tocek and Smith following. When they reached the hardware store, he didn't hesitate before cutting into the narrow driveway running beside the building. A collection of garbage cans was set by the back door. Norman leapt forward and came to a halt. He barked, once only.

"Hey! You got me. I give up." The woman concealed there popped up, a huge smile on her face.

"You're under arrest," Smith said, in her toughest voice. She grabbed the woman's arm and led her away while Tocek praised the dog to the skies.

"Thanks," Smith said to Constable Liz Farrens of the RCMP. Farrens was new and had not met Norman yet.

"Nice dog," Farrens said. "Nice guy, too. Yours?"

"Yes," Smith said.

Farrens pretended to pout. "That was fun.

Anytime. Ron's calling me. Gotta go." She went to help Ron Gavin, the forensic investigator.

Tocek and Norman joined Smith. The man was grinning and the dog had a satisfied swagger to his step. They hadn't had a successful conclusion for the last several outings. Norman didn't work for money, and he considered being sheltered and fed nothing but his due. He worked only because he wanted to; it was important he get regular doses of praise. Tocek couldn't congratulate him on a failure so when it had been a while since a successful search, he set Norman up for a win.

Smith sometimes wondered who thought he was fooling whom.

John Winters had joined the group by the back door of the art gallery and was talking to Ray Lopez, his detective constable. As Smith and Tocek approached, Winters went back inside.

"Need me for anything more?" Tocek asked. Ron Gavin crouched on the ground, dabbing at a few spots of what looked like blood. Fortunately, there was very little of it.

"No," Gavin said.

"Look, you gotta at least pick him up," Evans said to Lopez.

"No."

"Pick who up?" Smith said. "Do you know who did this?"

"No, we do not," Lopez said.

"A known sex offender arrives in town and no more than a couple of hours later a woman's attacked and you think that's a coincidence?" Evans said. "When's the last time we heard of a stranger attack around here, eh? It's been months."

"A sex offender?" Smith said. "You don't mean Walt Desmond? The court says he didn't do it."

"Get real, Smith," Evans snapped. "Do you believe everything the lawyers say?"

"I don't..."

"I said leave it," Lopez said. "We have no reason whatsoever to bring Walter Desmond in for this. Besides, our witness says it was a young man."

"Witnesses say a lot of things," Evans said. "Not always true, even if they think it is. Desmond was seen heading toward town not more than an hour or so ago."

"We were told to stay away from him," Smith said. "Didn't you hear?"

"I don't need the likes of you to tell me what the chief's orders were." Evans glanced over Smith's shoulder. She sensed Adam behind her. He said nothing. "I saw the guy walking down the street earlier, okay?" Evans said.

"We have no more reason to question Desmond than anyone else you saw out walking tonight," Lopez said. "Leave it, Dave."

For a moment Evans looked as though he were going to keep arguing. Then he abruptly deflated and walked away. He glared at Smith as he passed.

"What was that about?" she said.

Lopez shook his head. "Dave's got a heck of a bee in his bonnet, but I don't entirely blame him. To be honest, I wouldn't mind asking Desmond what he was up to earlier myself, but John reminded me of the chief's orders. That guy just being here is a can of worms."

"Let's let these people get back to work," Tocek said. "I feel like ice cream."

Chapter Eleven

"You ever done any paddling, Molly?" Dawn Solway asked.

Smith glanced up from the computer in the constable's office. She was beginning her shift, checking in, reading over last night's reports. The biggest incident of the night, by far, had been the attack on Eliza Winters.

"Sure. I've kayaked all my life."

"I mean competitively. On a team. Like these dragon boats." Solway had changed into shorts and tee-shirt before heading home after her shift.

Smith shook her head. "Looks like fun, though."

"It does. I've been thinking I might like to give it a try. How about you?"

"You mean join a team?"

"You're off Saturday, right?"

"Yeah, but I've pulled a double shift today. Then I'm on afternoons tomorrow. I'll be beat."

"Fresh air and exercise'll perk you right up. The dragon boat people are having an open house at the river on Saturday. Anyone's welcome to come by and give it a try. Game?"

Smith had gone down to the park to see the women practice yesterday. She'd sat on a bench for a long time, just watching. The sleek, brightly colored boats moving low and fast across the water, powered only by the strength of the women's muscles working in unison, appealed to her. "You're on!"

Solway grinned. "Good. See you Saturday. Everything, uh, okay with you and Adam after I left last night?"

"Yeah," she said with a grin. "All good. Norman got the call out and I helped, but we came up with nothing." Before heading home, they'd gone for ice cream—triple chocolate fudge for Adam and a single maple walnut for her—and walked with Norman down to the park by the river. They'd held hands and exchanged nibbly little kisses while Norman sniffed at benches and lampposts, the chase forgotten, checking out the news from the dog neighborhood. Adam had tasted of chocolate and beer. And love. He always tasted of love.

"Word's spreading of the attack on Eliza," Solway said. "I must have been stopped a dozen times last night."

"By the sounds of it, Merrill was the hero of

the hour. It's probably natural she's going to be telling the story far and wide. How's Mrs. Winters?"

"Shook up, but she should be fine. She took a couple of punches, but she refused to go to the hospital." Solway lowered her voice. "As you can imagine, John's on the warpath. I swear, Molly, I've never seen anyone so silently angry in all my life."

"Could Eliza or Merrill identify the perp?"

"The usual. White guy, average height, average weight, average age. Merrill said he was wearing a denim jacket; Eliza said he had on a gray sweatshirt."

"Typical."

"Catch you later."

It was seven in the morning. The sun was up, and outside the office windows traffic moved slowly, most of it heading into town bringing people to work. A quiet time. Time to catch up on paperwork. Tough about what happened to Mrs. Winters, but by the sounds of it she got off easy. Smith didn't know Eliza Winters well and found her cool and distant the few times they'd met. She wasn't the typical cop's wife, that was for sure.

Smith could only hope that when she and Adam had been together as long as Winters and his wife had, Adam would still love her that much. If the perp knew what was good for him, he'd be halfway across the country by now. Which was probably the case. There hadn't been reports of any stranger assaults around town lately, so this was likely someone passing through. He'd be afraid the women could identify him if they saw him again, and be long gone.

She turned to her computer and opened up Google. She searched for information about the Sophia D'Angelo/Walter Desmond case. Like pretty much everyone in town, she knew the bare bones of it. The murder itself had been largely forgotten over the years by anyone who didn't know the people involved, but the arrival of lawyers from Waterston and Gravelle and the subsequent national publicity of the appeal brought it crashing back to the town's radar.

In the summer of 1990 when she was twenty-two years old, Sophia D'Angelo moved back to her hometown of Trafalgar from Victoria where she'd earned a BA in history. She found a job in a bank as a teller. Apparently she'd been unhappy working at the bank and living in the small town, and wanted to go back to Victoria. Her parents tried to encourage her to stay by offering to pay the down payment on a house for her.

On the afternoon of Tuesday, January 15, 1991, Sophia D'Angelo asked permission to leave the bank early to view a property for sale. She left work at three-fifty and was observed by one of her coworkers getting into her car, which was parked in the staff lot behind the bank, and driving away.

At four thirty-nine p.m., the Trafalgar City Police received a call from 176 Pine Street. Walter Desmond, Trafalgar resident and employee of Town and Country Realty, had arrived to show the house to a potential buyer. Sophia's car was parked in the alley at the rear of the house. Desmond found the back door unlocked and upon entering had immediately discovered the body of Sophia in the kitchen. She had been tied up, sexually assaulted, and her throat had been slashed.

Desmond claimed he'd been late to the meeting, having had a flat tire on the highway as he returned—alone—from showing a mountain property. At the time of the initial investigation, no one reported seeing him fixing his tire at the side of the road where he said the incident occurred, although police found a tire in his trunk which had been punctured by a nail and the temporary replacement tire on the car.

The homeowners had been in Ontario visiting relatives at the time of the murder. The house had been for sale for a long time, as it needed a substantial amount of work. Fingerprints lifted off the front and back doors and kitchen surfaces were all identified: the homeowners, Walt Desmond and two other realtors, both female, and the few people who had viewed the house, most of whom were women.

Desmond had been arrested at his home two days later.

On a quick superficial read, Smith thought the case looked weak. Yes, Sophia had an appointment to meet Desmond at the place she was killed. When police arrived Desmond had blood on him, but he claimed he'd touched the body to check if she was still alive. The back door had been unlocked, Desmond said, and that had surprised him. A key to the house was kept in a coded lockbox for access by real estate agents. The homeowners told police they had given a spare key to a neighbor to keep an eye on the house. The neighbor was a seventy-six-year-old woman who emphatically claimed she'd never lent the key to anyone. Smith read quickly. She'd need to search court documents, but it didn't look as though the defense lawyer had bothered to point out that keys were easy to duplicate, or that the code to the lockbox was available to anyone who worked in a real estate office. The neighbor said that when Desmond visited the house, he always parked outside by the front sidewalk, where the car would be visible to anyone passing by. But that day he parked in the back alley, so no one could say what time he'd arrived. Desmond claimed he parked in the front or back alternately, depending on the direction he'd come from at any given time. But the defense had not raised that point in court.

Innocent or guilty, Walt Desmond's lawyer had put up a mighty shoddy defense.

She checked another page. The lawyer had died of bowel cancer about a year later. She wondered if he were already ill at the time of the trial.

According to one of her coworkers, Sophia had been wearing a new bracelet the day in question which she, the coworker, particularly admired. A tennis bracelet, thin and sleek made of gold with a single inset row of diamonds. The stones were glass, not real diamonds, and the gold was cheap, but it had still been very pretty. It had been a gift, Sophia boasted to her friend, from her boyfriend.

The bracelet was not on her body when she was found. The police had searched the house, Walter Desmond's home, yard and garbage, Desmond's clothes and his wife's clothes. The thin bracelet made of glass stones and impure gold had never been seen again.

Smith pulled up the archives of the *Trafalgar Daily Gazette*. Some of their old stories had been converted to digital, anything to do with the D'Angelo killing among them. Tensions in town had been running strong, and not many people were on Walt Desmond's side. She wondered about that. The man had no prior record of any sort, evidence wasn't conclusive, he protested his innocence, yet people were quick to condemn him. She made a mental note to talk to her mother.

One of Sophia's coworkers at the bank testified that Sophia said she found Desmond "creepy." The witness couldn't say why, in that case, Sophia had continued to deal with him. The realtor's office had other agents. A friend from high school testified that Sophia never liked to "make a fuss." The defense lawyer had not objected to testimony that amounted to little more than hearsay and implications, and jurors were left free to conclude she hadn't asked for another agent for that reason.

Other than the fingerprints, no forensic evidence had been submitted.

Walt Desmond was found guilty of first-degree murder, largely on the basis of the timing of the killing. Sophia left the bank at three-fifty saying she had an appointment to view the house at four o'clock, and was seen getting into her car at that time. The house was a five-minute drive from the bank. Desmond had left his other clients, at the property a good half-hour outside of town, at quarter after three. He phoned the police from the house phone at four-thirty-nine. He was known for his punctuality, witnesses said, and although he did have a flat tire in the trunk of his car, no one could say when the flat had happened. The police had not examined his car at the scene, leaving the prosecution to claim the man had deliberately run his car over a nail and changed the tire in his own garage after the killing, in order to set up an alibi.

Sophia, by all accounts, was a timid young woman. A stickler for the rules, they said. Her parents and boss insisted that she would never have gone into the house without the realtor letting her in. Even if the door had been unlocked when she arrived, she would have waited outside in the cold.

It was a weak case, built on timing and impressions of what the dead woman had supposedly been like. Timid. Shy. A stickler for the rules. No forensic evidence tied Desmond to the sexual assault or the killing. The victim did not have any defensive injuries, thus it was easy to conclude that she'd inflicted no wounds on her assailant. She had probably been taken by surprise and subdued immediately.

Smith then accessed the police files, starting with the autopsy report, wondering why, if there had been a sexual assault, there hadn't been any useable forensic evidence. She read quickly.

She leaned back in her chair and closed her eyes. Oh, God.

Poor Sophia had been raped with a knife.

Blood would have been everywhere. No wonder Desmond had the woman's blood on him.

Anyone walking unknowingly into that room would have been covered in it. The knife was a kitchen one, a good sharp chef's knife, taken from the wooden block on the kitchen counter. No prints, other than those of the homeowners, were found on the knife.

But, the Crown claimed, Walt Desmond had been wearing gloves when the police arrived. The gloves had been soaked in blood.

Sure he was, Smith thought. It was January. The gloves were light leather, not big bulky warm ones, the sort one would wear driving and might not remove before entering a house.

Reading these reports, all these years later, and only a quick overview at that, led Smith to conclude the case had been so flimsy it never should have gone to court. Walter Desmond had a right to be in that house, where Sophia was killed, at the time he was. His excuse for being late was believable. He had no record of any sort, certainly not of violent attacks on women. A witness had testified that Sophia thought Desmond was creepy. The jury was left to conclude that meant he'd been making unwelcome advances on her. It was nothing but hearsay, and Smith was surprised it had even been allowed in court.

Walt Desmond was found guilty of the murder of Sophia D'Angelo and sentenced to life in prison.

Over all the years he'd steadfastly maintained his innocence, even knowing that confessing and expressing remorse would have helped him get parole.

Then, a couple of years ago an organization dedicated to helping the wrongfully convicted took up his case. An appeal can only be launched if new evidence is found. Simple reinterpreting of previously given evidence or testimony isn't enough. The lawyers, headed by Louise Gravelle, dug up that new evidence.

And it looked mighty bad for the TCP.

She'd begun to read the report of the appeal when her radio cracked to life. "Five-one?"

"Five-one. Go ahead."

"Altercation at 1894 Victoria Street."

"I'm on it." She abandoned the computer and headed out back for a car. She slapped the console. Brought up lights and sirens. "Isn't that the Glacier Chalet?" she asked the dispatcher.

"Yes. Ellie Carmine called it in. A man has attacked one of her guests."

Chapter Twelve

Smith pulled her cruiser to a halt half on the sidewalk outside the gorgeous Victorian mansion. She ran down the path and bounded up the steps. The door opened before she reached it. A woman, not Mrs. Carmine, someone Smith didn't know.

"Thank heavens you're here, Officer. He's gone berserk."

Smith told dispatch she needed backup and stepped cautiously into the front hall. "Follow me," the woman said. She led the way into the dining room. The room was large enough for four tables of varying sizes, set with white tablecloths and pink-and-white china, and a long buffet with coffee and tea things, boxes of dry cereal, a crystal bowl full of sliced fruit, and containers of yogurt. The walls were papered in a dusty rose pattern; a chandelier dripping crystal tears hung in the center of the room; the windows were set into deep recesses overlooking the garden. Portraits in gilded frames, of stern-faced Victorian ladies and rigid mustachioed gentlemen, graced the walls.

Smith glanced around the room quickly, checking everyone out. They were all on their feet, the remains of breakfast abandoned on the tables. Aside from the two men who'd apparently been fighting, the other occupants of the room were women of a similar age, dressed in identical outfits of black spandex shorts and red tee-shirts with the name of their team, Kelowna Pepper, across the front of them.

The two combatants had been separated, placed in their own corners like boxers. The younger man seemed to have gotten the worst of it. He sat in a spindle-legged chair, more ornamental than designed to hold a person, with a box of tissues on his lap. A woman stood over him, holding his head back, pressing tissues to his nose. A pile of discarded tissues, red with blood, lay on the floor around him.

He pulled his head away from the woman's gentle hold as Smith came into the room. She recognized Walt Desmond immediately from the picture Winters had shown them.

The other man was older, much older. He was pressed up against a corner, Ellie Carmine planted firmly in front of him, while a dragon boat woman, short but powerfully built with close-cropped gray hair, held his arm.

Gino D'Angelo. Sophia's father.

Not good.

"What's going on here?" Smith feared she didn't need to ask. Ellie Carmine had phoned the police station yesterday evening to say Walt Desmond was staying at her B&B. It was entirely possible she'd told half of Trafalgar as well. And so Sophia D'Angelo's father had come looking for him. Outside, sirens announced the arrival of her backup.

"I've no idea," the woman helping Walt said. She was close to six feet tall with a cheerful blond ponytail that swung as she talked. "That man barged in here, yelling his fool head off, and without a word he slugged Walt. I'm a nurse. I don't think his nose is broken."

"We were having breakfast," another woman said. "The doorbell rang, Ellie went to open it. We heard yelling. I went to see if Ellie needed help, but that man pushed right past me. "He kept yelling that he was here to see Walt."

"Walt got up, went to the door," the nurse said, "to see what was going on. And—wham—he got a punch in the face. That guy's a lunatic."

Brad Noseworthy came into the room. Smith gave him a nod. *Everything okay here.*

"Mrs. Carmine, you can let Mr. D'Angelo go now," Smith said. "He won't be causing any more trouble. Will you, sir?"

Ellie stepped back; the short-haired woman released D'Angelo's arm.

The old man lifted his head, and looked at Smith for the first time. His eyes were sunken pools in a dark face. He spat on the beautiful cream and rose carpet. Ellie gasped.

"You'd better leave, sir," Smith said. "Constable Noseworthy will drive you home."

D'Angelo did not move.

"Mr. Desmond is entirely within his rights to ask us to lay charges. Do you want that?"

"You would charge me? And let the man who murdered my daughter go free? Where is the justice?"

The watching women threw questioning glances at each other and at Walt.

"Mr. D'Angelo, you are aware that the appeal court ruled in Mr. Desmond's favor and the Crown withdrew all charges. In other words, not guilty."

"Oh, my God." The short-haired woman gasped.

This was a situation they hadn't gone over in police college. Smith had no idea what she would do if Gino D'Angelo refused to leave. Wrestle a seventy years plus man to the ground, haul a murder victim's father off to jail in handcuffs? Her mother had always maintained a healthy mistrust of police and the justice system. Lucky, and people of like mind, were easily persuaded that a miscarriage of justice had happened. But not everyone would agree. Longtime residents were talking of little else, and newcomers were eager to find out what all the fuss was about.

Walt got slowly to his feet. The bleeding had stopped but his nostrils were crusted with drying blood. "It's all right. I understand how difficult this must be for you and your wife." He stepped forward. He held out his hand. Smith could almost feel Noseworthy brace himself.

Gino D'Angelo looked at the offered hand for a long time. He growled and spat again. Walt didn't move his hand out of the way. The phlegm formed a puddle in the center of his palm. "I'm sorry you feel that way, sir. I'm going to finish my breakfast now." Walt turned and crossed the room. The nurse handed him a tissue. He accepted it and wiped his hand. Then he sat down. Poached eggs were congealing on his plate. He reached for his fork with a hand that shook ever so slightly.

"Breakfast," the short-haired woman said. "What an excellent idea. I'll be no good on the water without a full belly."

"With five kids I'd have thought you'd have had enough of that, Nancy," the nurse said.

The women laughed. It was tight laughter,

with no mirth in it, but sufficient to break the tension.

"Come on, sir," Smith said, "let's leave these ladies to finish their breakfast in peace."

D'Angelo walked out of the dining room. Smith and Noseworthy followed. Ellie bustled after them, wiping her hands on her apron.

"Did you come in your own car, sir?" Smith asked.

"Yes."

"Then Constable Noseworthy will follow you home. To make sure you're safe."

"That man. You will let him sit there, eat his food. With women."

"Mr. D'Angelo," Noseworthy said, "we have no choice. Nor do you. Leave Desmond alone."

"If you...if the police, will do nothing, then I will." D'Angelo walked out of the house. He did not close the door behind him.

Noseworthy and Smith exchanged a glance before he hurried after the old man.

"Do you think he'll do something, Moonlight?" A longtime friend of Lucky's, Ellie still used Molly's proper name. "Perhaps I should ask Mr. Desmond to leave."

"That's up to you, Mrs. Carmine, but it doesn't seem to me as if Mr. Desmond did anything wrong here."

"I know they say he's innocent, that he didn't kill that poor girl. But I can't believe the Trafalgar police could have made such a mistake."

"I'm going to have a word with Mr. Desmond before I go." Smith headed back to the dining room. The women were seated, chattering like birds, birds trying to ignore the tornado gathering on the horizon. Someone had picked up the bloody tissues and tossed them into a wastebasket. Walt Desmond hunched over his plate, fork in hand, but he was only stirring his food into mush. He'd put a lot of ketchup on his sausages and the sight made Smith's stomach roll over.

"Everything okay, Officer?" the nurse said.

"Mr. D'Angelo has gone home," Smith said.

"Good. Isn't that good, Walt? It's all a silly misunderstanding. Obviously the poor gentleman is well known to the police. I'm Darlene, by the way, Darlene Michaels. We're here for the dragon boat training."

"I guessed that," Smith said.

"You should give it a try, Constable," another woman said. "It's loads of fun and an unbeatable workout."

"Maybe I will. Mr. Desmond, do you mind if I have a word?"

He stirred his food. "Might as well."

"In private, perhaps?"

"I have no secrets. These women, I hope, are my friends." He seemed to take in the entire room as he said it, but out of the corner of his eyes he glanced at one woman, slightly younger than the rest, tall and slim with brown hair cut in a neat bob and wide dark eyes.

They chorused yes. The younger woman flushed ever so slightly.

"Please, sir," Smith said.

He got to his feet in a quick, sharp move that had Smith almost taking a step backward.

"Why don't we step outside, sir? Won't be long."

Walt followed her into the hall. Behind them the room fell silent.

The porch had a big swing and a cluster of white wicker chairs around a black iron table. Thankfully, it was in the shade. She took a seat and Walt Desmond dropped into a chair beside her. It was going to be another hot day. She could feel the heat building under her Kevlar vest. They desperately needed a heavy, soaking rain. The forests surrounding the town were tinder-dry, waiting for a dropped match or lightning strike to burst into an inferno. "I'm Constable Smith. I know who you are, Mr. Desmond."

"As does everyone in town, it would seem." While Smith had been seeing Noseworthy and

D'Angelo off, Walt had wiped the last of the blood off his face. He was, she thought, not a bad-looking guy for his age. Short-haired, well-muscled, with full lips and chiseled cheekbones. Good looking, except for the pasty-white skin and the dark, empty eyes. She suppressed a shudder.

"I'm sorry about what happened there, sir. Chief Constable Keller paid a visit to the D'Angelos, to tell them to leave you alone. I guess Mr. D'Angelo decided to ignore that advice."

"I guess he did." Walt sat perfectly still. His large, rough, and scarred hands were folded in his lap, his feet flat on the floor. He stared out over the street. "Ellie called you Moonlight. Moonlight Smith. Are you Andy Smith's daughter?"

"Yes."

"How's he doing?"

"He died a couple of years ago."

"Sorry to hear that. A lot of things change when you've been away for a long time. I'll have to get used to that."

"Mom's good, though. She still has the store. Mid-Kootenay…"

"I remember it. Your dad ordered a telescope for me. It was a Christmas gift to Arlene. My wife." He turned his head suddenly and studied her face. "You'd be too young to remember us."

"Yes." Uncomfortable under his stare, she got

to her feet. "If there's any more trouble, give us a call, eh?"

"I can count on the single-minded dedication of the members of the Trafalgar City Police to protect me?"

She couldn't blame him for being bitter. She had no idea what he must have been through all these years. "Yes, you can. Chief's orders."

"Your chief. How long's he been here?"

"He wasn't around when...your case happened, if that's what you're asking."

"Glad to hear it."

She walked down the stairs and went to her car, feeling his eyes on her back every step of the way.

Chapter Thirteen

Chief Constable Paul Keller stormed into the police station. He did not look happy. Staff scattered, everyone suddenly searching for something to be doing, preferably someplace else. He smelled of fresh tobacco and that was never a good sign. The chief was trying to quit smoking. He wasn't having much success as every time he was under any stress at all he could be seen dashing into a nearby convenience store. He marched into his assistant's office. "Is John in?"

"As far as I know." Barb was never intimidated by the chief or his moods. Over the years she'd dealt with some *really* hard-assed chief constables.

"I need to see him," Keller said. He went into his own office, slamming the door behind him, and Barb reached for her phone. "You're needed, John, ASAP."

Winters was at her door in less than a minute. "What's up?"

She shrugged and whispered, "Meeting with the mayor. At a guess, I'd say it didn't go well."

Winters knocked lightly on the door that joined the chief's office to Barb's and then opened it. "You wanted to see me, Paul?"

"Take a seat. Barb, you better join us. You won't need the laptop. No minutes."

Barb and Winters exchanged glances. She shut the door behind her.

Now he was sitting down and had some time to compose himself, the high color was fading from Keller's face and his breathing was settling into a normal pattern. He'd already grabbed a can of Coke out of the bar fridge he kept behind his desk and had popped the tab. He took a long swig. Barb hid a grin. The habitual Coke had turned to the diet version. The poor man was trying to lose weight and give up smoking at the same time.

Barb's eyes moved to the pictures on his desk. There was a new one, of the chief's son, Matt, and Matt's girlfriend, Tracey, taken on a recent holiday in Banff, with the famous hotel looming majestically in the background. Another recent photo showed the reason for the diet and attempt to give up smoking: Lucky Smith smiling at the chief as they posed together on the lakefront at Chateau Lake Louise.

"Bad meeting with the mayor?" Winters

asked, and all thoughts of love and diets flew out the window.

"No, thank heavens. I'd left him when I got the call. The mayor wanted to talk about the Walt Desmond situation. He's worried some people are going to react badly to news that the guy's back in town. He asked me what we could do about it. I said we can do nothing, nothing at all. The man's as free to conduct his life as anyone of us is. I had to remind the mayor that Desmond is not under bounds of parole. He does not have to report to a police station nor account for his affairs in any way."

Barb and Winters exchanged curious glances once again. "We know that," Barb said. "So what's the problem?"

"I've told the dispatchers to let me know if there are any calls related to Desmond. I'd left the mayor's office and was walking back, when I got a call. Gino D'Angelo showed up at the Glacier Chalet, where Desmond is staying."

"That was a foolish thing to do," Winters said.

"He attacked him."

"Walt Desmond attacked that old man!" Barb gasped. "I knew he…"

"No, Barb. Gino assaulted Desmond. In front of a dining room full of guests, I might add."

"Oh. Sorry." Barb sank into her seat. What

was she supposed to think: a convicted murderer, an old man. Who's more likely to be the aggressor?

"What happened then?" Winters asked.

"The fight had been broken up when Molly and Brad arrived. I called Molly a few minutes ago. She said one punch only had been thrown. Desmond made no attempt to defend himself, and the B&B guests stepped in and separated the men. Brad saw Gino home, and Desmond did not want to take the matter any further. Very wise of him, in my opinion."

"Are you going to pay another call on the D'Angelos?" Winters asked.

"I think not. What on earth can I say that hasn't already been said a hundred times? I wanted you to be aware of the situation. Feelings will be running high. I had planned on paying a friendly visit to Desmond this morning, just to say hi. I've changed my mind. Molly and Brad have been there already. Another one of us going around so soon is going to look like harassment. I want you to keep your distance, too, until and unless you have some specific questions for him about the murder case itself."

Winters nodded.

"So far Desmond's kept to himself and maintained a low profile. Let's hope it stays that way. The incident last night didn't help." Keller cleared his throat. "Sorry, John, that sounded harsh. All I meant was I've heard whispers saying Desmond was behind the attack on Eliza."

"I don't think so," Winters said. "Eliza says the perp had longish dark hair and Merrill agrees. The picture you showed us of Desmond was of a guy with short gray hair. Innocent or guilty, rumor can be a dangerous thing."

"Why did he come here, anyway?" Barb said. "To cause trouble that's why. More misery to that poor family."

"I asked you to come in, Barb," the chief said, "because you're the only one of us who was here back then. Did you know Desmond and his wife?"

"I knew them as in saw them around. I knew who they were. Arlene Desmond owned a dress shop on Front Street. I shopped there now and again. I felt dreadfully sorry for her. Married to that man."

"You felt sorry," Winters said, "before or after the killing?"

"Well, after, of course. When we found out what happened. Some people thought she must have known all along what he was like, but I figured he'd fooled her as well as everyone else." Even now all these years later, Barb's blood began to boil. She'd been a junior clerk back then. In the days when, without the widespread use of the Internet and only the most rudimentary of police databases, they had more civilian staff. The chief hadn't even had a computer on his desk. His secretary took dictation and typed his letters. She also fetched his dry cleaning, and bought flowers for his wife when he forgot her birthday. If Paul Keller ever tried to ask Barb Kowalski to run personal errands, she'd give him what for. Not that she wasn't happy to bring him back a coffee when she took a run to Big Eddies, or sneak a little of her home baking into his office. She was rather fond of the old coot. Still, couldn't allow them to start taking liberties. Then, before you knew it, it would be dry cleaning and birthday gifts.

"I've read the files, Barb," Winters said. "The entire case against Desmond was flimsy to begin with, and the appeal evidence was overwhelming. The TCP, to put it mildly, screwed up. Big-time."

"I don't believe it," Barb said. "Doug and Jack, they worked like dogs on that case. They were determined that Walter did it, and they proved it! Doug's gone now, and that's probably a good thing. I can't imagine what Jack must be thinking, to have his judgment questioned after all these years."

"That's just it, Barb," Winters said, his voice soft and low. "They focused on Desmond like a laser beam, didn't seem to even bother looking at anyone else."

"That," she said firmly, "is because he did it. And we all knew it. Heavens, Sophia told one of her friends Walt was making unwelcome advances."

"Hearsay," Winters said. "Reading between the lines, I wonder if the witness was encouraged to expand on that idea."

Barb jumped to her feet. "Never! Never. I read those reports, I saw those pictures. What he did to her was unforgiveable." Unbidden images flashed behind her eyes. In all her years with the police, Barb had never seen anything so dreadful. She wasn't supposed to, she was just a civilian clerk. But she'd opened the wrong file, and there they were. Photographs of that beautiful girl. Desecrated. Barb had nightmares for a long time, and her husband had taken to walking her to and from work for a while.

Then came the trial and the just verdict. Walter Desmond was sent away, to where he could do no more harm, and they were all safe again. The nightmares ended; she mocked her fears.

And now he's out, walking our streets, laughing at us. To her horror, she began to cry.

The chief started to stand.

"I'm going to take an early lunch." She ran from the room and out of the police station, while startled officers and staff watched her go, not even stopping to get her purse.

Keller dropped into his chair. Winters let out a breath he hadn't realized he was holding.

"What was that about?"

"I asked Barb to join us because I wanted her take on what the old-timers are saying about this all being stirred up again. Looks like I found out."

"I wouldn't convict a cat on the evidence presented at that trial," Winters said. "Never mind what the appeal uncovered."

"I understand where Barb's coming from. The murder was shocking, truly dreadful. The sort of thing that had never happened here before. People were terrified. Monsters were living in their midst. A quick arrest and subsequent conviction went a long way toward reassuring them."

"Right. Except that, when I read the evidence, Paul, I have to conclude that they might have gotten the wrong guy. I'm not saying they did, even though the appeal court thinks so. It might be that Desmond was as guilty as sin, although the case wasn't solid. But, if Desmond was railroaded to keep the town happy, then someone else, the guilty person, walked away. And that's what really bothers me about this. The TCP didn't even look at anyone else. Drifters, known sexual criminals, small-time troublemakers, current or ex-boyfriends of the dead woman. No one. They found their man, and built a case around him."

"Has anyone heard from Jack McMillan since this started?" the chief asked.

"Not as far as I know."

"I'd like you to pay a call on him. A nice friendly chat. Cop to cop. Tell him to stay the hell out of town for the time being. Maybe he can take a long tropical vacation. Now that the court's decreed Desmond didn't do it, it's an open case. You'll have to spend some time looking into it, but after all these years I don't expect much of a result. Still, has to be done."

"What about Desmond himself?" Winters asked.

"I want him gone, but our hands are tied. Hard to believe the man's so stupid as to come back here, but there you have it."

"I'll ask Molly if he said anything to her about his intentions."

"Do that. I'd like to know, too. She does have a way of making men talk to her." A ghost of a smile crossed his face. "Sorta like her mother."

Chapter Fourteen

Winters decided not to call ahead. He'd never had much time for Jack McMillan, and the feeling was mutual. He was pretty sure the old cop would tell him not to come if he suggested a meeting. He found McMillan's address in the files, took the department van, and drove out of town. When he left the highway, the road curved up the side of the mountain. Neat homes, well-tended gardens, and sidewalks fell away as he climbed. The paved road ended and became gravel and then dirt, getting progressively rougher as trees gathered closer. But even up here the wilderness was being pushed back. A new house, a huge modern palace of glass and concrete, grew out of a shelf of rock off to the right. The view, Winters thought, must be magnificent. He drove on. The road ended at McMillan's place, the entrance marked by a No Trespassing sign. He turned in. The driveway was as welcoming as the sign: a rough track that would be pretty much impassable in heavy rains. His back teeth rattled along with the van's chassis on the washboard surface.

The trees opened and the driveway ended in a circle of bare dirt in front of a substantial garage. The house itself was made of wood, a good size, with large windows overlooking the forest, a welcoming front porch, and a spacious deck off to one side. But one of those windows was covered in plywood, paint was peeling in long strips from the porch pillars, and a section of the deck railing had broken away. The yard, which might have once been a lawn, was a mess of struggling saplings and triumphant weeds. A garden shed sat beside the house, not touching but titling toward it as though it needed the support. A dog, a big male German shepherd, came around the side of the house. His muzzle was heavily gray, and he moved with an awkward gait as if something was wrong with his right hip. Nothing wrong with the teeth, though, and he displayed them in a hostile snarl.

Winters switched off the engine, and felt heat seep into the van as soon as the air conditioning died. He waited. A truck was parked close to the garage; someone was home.

He didn't have to wait long. Jack McMillan came out of the house, a second dog with him, younger but no less aggressive. McMillan was dressed in an oil-and-food-stained tee-shirt with the Toronto Maple Leaf logo across the front, and jeans that had seen a lot of wear. He didn't look good, Winters thought. McMillan's eyes were watery, his face blotchy, and he needed a shave and a haircut. The skin on the back of his right hand was raw and red. He shuffled across the yard toward the van. McMillan snapped at the old dog, who closed his mouth and went to stand with his partner at the man's side.

Winters opened the van door. The sun beat down on the unshaded yard.

"John," McMillan said, "what brings you out here?" He scratched at his right hand with dirty, torn nails.

"I'd like a word," Winters said.

"Seein' as to how you've never been to my home before, I have to wonder what brings you here. Walter Desmond, I'd guess."

"You heard he won his appeal. The Crown withdrew all charges."

"Yeah, I heard. Fuckers."

McMillan made no move to invite Winters inside, to sit down and crack open a beer and talk about the good old days. Winters had not expected him to. Winters had checked the man's service record before coming out. McMillan started his career in Vancouver, like John Winters himself had. He'd come to Trafalgar with his wife and three children in the late seventies. His wife left him a few years before the D'Angelo killing, taking the children with her. Winters glanced around. This would have been a nice home, a good place to raise kids. Now, it was a dump falling into ruin through neglect and disinterest.

"What you lookin' at?" McMillan snarled. He looked a great deal like his dog had moments earlier.

McMillan had not had a distinguished career. There were a couple of complaints from the public about overly aggressive arrests, searches without reason or warrant, harassment. No charges had ever been laid, no disciplinary action taken.

One complaint, from a woman who stated McMillan pushed his way into her house at night on the pretext of searching for an armed suspect and then asked her for a beer, had caught Winters' attention. The woman left town shortly after. Her complaint left with her. No further action taken. On paper, McMillan came across as somewhat of a bully, a bit too quick to push people around. That came as no surprise to Winters, who'd met the man previously. But otherwise, there were no stains on his record. No highlights or commendations, either.

McMillan had retired several years earlier and retreated to his cabin in the woods. He came into town now and again, to hang around the station lunchroom looking for someone to tell old war stories to, and got together once a month or so at a bar with some of the other retired guys (and they were all guys) or nearly retired ones like Jeff Glendenning.

"Just looking around," Winters said. "Nice piece of property you have here. That's quite the house next door."

"Fuckers," McMillan said. "From Calgary. Oil guy. They spend a couple of weeks a year here, if that. Keep their dammed security lights on all night, though, whether they're here or not."

"Still," Winters said, trying to sound friendly, "having that place next door will increase your property value."

"Increase the taxes, anyway. What do you want?"

So much for being friendly. "To tell you Walter Desmond has arrived in town."

"Has he now?" McMillan didn't sound at all surprised. Winters suspected the phone lines had been buzzing up here. Some of the calls would have come directly from the police station itself.

"It would be best if you kept your distance for the time being, Jack."

"Why would I want to do that? Maybe Walt and I can get together, knock back a couple of beers. Talk about the old days."

"Don't give me that attitude, Jack. I'm asking you to do us all a favor and keep away from trouble." The old dog sniffed at Winters' pant legs. He shifted a few steps, lifted his leg, and peed against the tires of the van. McMillan laughed.

"Old service guy," he said. "Put out to pasture when he was shot in the leg."

For a moment Winters wondered who McMillan was talking about. His record said nothing about being shot. But McMillan was watching the dog. "Nice of you to take him in."

"Someone has to look after us old guys. Work hard his whole life, give everything to the police. Guard the taxpayers of this town, some of whom deserve it, plenty who don't. And what's your reward? For him?" McMillan nodded at the dog. "The long walk, if I hadn't said I'd take him. For me? Told to stay out of the town you spent the best years of your life protecting."

A bit of an exaggeration, but Winters let it go. He knew plenty of cops who'd retired. A lot of them loved it. They'd taken consulting jobs, gone into the carpentry business, travelled to all the places they'd dreamed of. Winters knew one former RCMP sergeant who'd become a best-selling romance novelist. But for too many, being a cop was all they'd ever had. It was all they were, and when they weren't any longer, they found themselves with nothing left.

Winters wondered what side he'd fall on when the time came. Unlikely Eliza would let him sit around feeling sorry for himself. She was already trying to get him interested in the business of her art galleries. He suppressed a shudder.

McMillan could start by fixing up this place, rather than letting it fall to rack and ruin around his ears. It wasn't much past noon and the scent of beer was strong on the man's breath.

"A friendly warning, Jack. Just stay away, eh? Desmond's out of prison and there's nothing you can do about it except cause trouble."

"I was the first officer on the scene. Did you know that, John? I saw that girl. I saw what he did to her. I saw him standing there, drenched in her still-warm blood, holding the knife, smiling at me like he was inviting me to share in the joke. Butcher."

"As far as the Crown and the law are concerned..."

"The Crown can go fuck itself and take the law with it. Time for you to be leaving. I'm sure you have reports to fill out, good cops to harass. Maybe even pretty little ones to screw. How's Moonlight Smith working out by the way? Imagine, a cop named Moonlight."

"Talk like that won't help…"

"See, *Sergeant* Winters, the way I see it is, I'm not trying to *help*." More scratching of his hand.

"Stay away from Walt Desmond, Jack."

"Or what? You'll arrest me? That'll go down well with the citizens of this town. The decent ones, anyway. The honest ones. Killer runs free while the cop who caught him is locked up."

Coming here had been a mistake. About all Winters had achieved was to get McMillan riled up. He turned and headed back to his car.

He had to swing the van in a circle to go back the way he'd come. Jack McMillan made no move to get out of the way.

Winters glanced in the rearview mirror before the clearing disappeared from sight. The young dog had lain down in the sun. The old one watched him through one rheumy eye. His expression was identical to that of the old cop.

Chapter Fifteen

It was going to be a very long day. Smith had offered to take a shift for one of the guys so he could get to his daughter's soccer tournament. Seemed like a good idea at the time, as he'd return the favor when she needed one. But right now—approaching six o'clock, and with another twelve hours to put in—not so much.

She stuck her head in the door of Mid-Kootenay Adventure Vacations. "Hi, Flower. Mom still here?"

Dinner time and the store was quiet. Flower glanced up from her magazine. "In the back. I heard about what happened last night, Molly. Everyone's talking about it. The art gallery's just across the street from us. Scary. Did you catch him yet?"

"No," Smith said. "He's probably long gone by now."

"I told your mom I'm bringing my bike into the shop from now on," Flower said. "And I'm going in and out by the front door. I'm not leaving it tied up out back anymore."

"He's long gone," Smith repeated, "but to be on the safe side, we're stepping up patrols in the alleys and walkways. I'll be checking them regularly tonight."

"I suppose that's good," Flower said. "But I'm still not going out there alone. Particularly not after dark."

"Is that you, Moonlight?" Lucky called.

"Yes, it's me."

"Come on through. I'm off the phone."

Smith had to suck in her stomach and swivel sideways to squeeze past Flower's bike, parked in the hallway, to get to her mother's office.

Like Flower and everyone else Smith met today, Lucky had heard about what happened last night. Eliza's art gallery hadn't opened this morning, fueling rumors. Smith had spent most of the day trying to calm people down and reassure them that Mrs. Winters had not been harmed. Lucky greeted her daughter with, "Have you caught him?"

Smith closed the door behind her. "No. He's probably long gone, but we'll be patrolling the alley regularly for a while."

"Poor Eliza. I thought I might pop around to her house after work, bring her flowers or something."

"Better not, Mom. She's an exceptionally private person. She might think you're only wanting the inside scoop."

Lucky sighed. "I suppose you're right. John called Paul last night. Paul was furious."

"Fair enough," Smith said. She still wasn't entirely comfortable with the thought that the Chief Constable—her boss—was regularly spending the night at her mother's place. When she visited the house in which she'd grown up, she tried not to notice signs that Paul Keller wasn't sleeping in the guest room.

"Between you and me," Lucky said, "Paul wonders if this was a random attack or something more...personal."

"You mean aimed at Sergeant Winters? That's possible, but not likely." Still, it did happen, and Winters was checking to see if anyone he'd been responsible for convicting, who might still be carrying a grudge, had recently been released from jail. If it were Doug Kibbens or Jack McMillan's wife who'd been attacked, they'd be asking questions of Walter Desmond. But Winters hadn't been anywhere near Trafalgar at the time of that case.

"Some of the shop owners have asked the town to allow them to park on Front Street all day, for no charge," Lucky said. "People, women, are worried about parking in the alley."

"I bet that wasn't well received."

Lucky shook her head. "Parking's hard enough to come by at this time of year without us blocking the street. I've told everyone I speak to that they'll be okay if they stay alert. Carry their keys in their hand, check the shadows. I'm still parking in the alley."

Smith had seen her mom's car earlier. Today, it was the only one parked behind the shops in the entire block. "Good advice, Mom. Anyway, I'm not here to talk about that. I was thinking about Walt Desmond earlier."

"Why? I should tell you that more than one person is pointing out the coincidence of the attack on Eliza coming the very day Walter got to town."

"They can point as much as they like, Mom, but that doesn't mean anything. Plenty of people arrived yesterday. It is summertime. If it will help squelch rumors, I can tell you Eliza and Merrill both said the attacker was young with long hair."

"Why are you asking then, dear?"

"I'm curious. The case is interesting. Whether Desmond did it or not. I've been reading some of the old reports. Once he was charged, everyone and their dog rushed to tell the police they'd always figured he was a strange one. But before Sophia was killed, Desmond had no record. So I'd like to hear your take on him."

Lucky leaned back in her chair. She closed her eyes. Smith let her mom think. Lucky could be impulsive, passionate, sometimes overbearing. But she was unfailingly honest and always thought the best of people. She never failed to be surprised when people let her down.

"It's hard to pick apart what my impressions were before and after the arrest, dear. I knew his wife better than him."

"Tell me about her."

Lucky was silent for a long time. "She didn't seem to be a happy woman. Again, I might be mixing up before and after, but I don't think so. They didn't have any children. Now you know I don't believe a woman needs children to lead a fulfilled life." Lucky tried not to glance at her childless daughter. "But I did suspect Arlene might be lonely. She didn't have many friends. She kept largely to herself."

"Lonely sometimes means a lot of things in a marriage," Smith said. "Was Walt rumored to have affairs?"

Lucky shook her head. "Not that I ever heard."

Smith hid a smile. If Lucky and her friends hadn't heard rumors, then Walter Desmond had either been one careful guy or totally on the straight and narrow.

"I remember…" Lucky said.

"Remember what?"

"It's starting to come back to me now. I remember being surprised after he was arrested, at how vehement Arlene was in her defense of him. I hadn't thought they had a very good marriage. Nothing I can put my finger on, you understand, dear, but sometimes you can tell. Couples who bicker over nothing, never smile at each other or casually touch. No, I'm wrong. It wasn't *them*, it was her. She'd make jokes at his expense, jokes that weren't at all funny, complain about the small inconsequential things he did or his irritating habits. But when he was arrested, Arlene supported him completely. She sold everything they had to raise funds for his defense. She was...*destroyed* isn't too harsh a word, when he was convicted. I heard she died of cancer, but some people whispered she'd killed herself. Just goes to show, you never know what goes on in someone else's marriage. Or how deep people can truly be."

And that, Smith knew, was the problem with legal cases. Secrets, always secrets.

"Did you know the dead girl, Mom?"

"I can't say that I ever met Sophia. I didn't know her parents at all. You were just starting primary school when she died. Although..." Lucky's voice trailed off and Smith's ears perked up.

"Although...?"

"I had never met Sophia, no. But I was aware of her. The youth center was just getting going in those days, and with you and Samwise still young and the store to manage, I didn't spend as much time there as I do now. We got a grant to buy computers for kids to use after school. Twenty-five years ago, most people didn't have a computer in their home, and certainly not one in every room as well as in their pocket. It was after the killing, during the trial, I believe, when I overheard some of the girls talking about Sophia." Lucky's voice trailed off.

"What did they say, Mom?"

"The papers were full of what a lovely young woman she was. It seemed as though everyone had fond memories of her."

"But…" Smith nudged. This was like interrogating a hostile witness.

"One of the girls at the youth center said her sister, who'd been in Sophia's classes in high school, said it was good riddance to bad rubbish. Everyone has enemies, of course, and no one more than high school girls."

"And, boy, do I remember that." Smith suppressed a mental shudder.

"The thing is, dear, the other girls said they knew what she meant. It seems her peers didn't have quite the fond memories of her that other people did."

"Did you tell anyone?"

"Heavens, no. What difference did it make? It was a horrible, brutal murder. That was all that mattered."

Smith wasn't so sure. The problem with secrets is that no one knows which secrets are important and which aren't. When the rush is on to sanitize the memory of the dearly departed, the truth can get buried as deeply as the dirty laundry. "I've gotta go. Thanks, Mom. Catch you later."

"Are you off work next Saturday, dear?"

"As it happens, I am. Why?"

"Paul and I are planning a barbeque in the afternoon. Nothing big, just a few friends coming over. I'd like you and Adam to come."

"Okay. What time?"

"Three. Bring Norman. Sylvester misses him." Sylvester was Lucky's aging golden retriever. Sylvester adored the police dog, and in moments of whimsy Smith wondered if dogs could experience hero worship.

She went back to the street. And the heat. As she walked, watching faces, peering into shops, checking out the traffic, she thought about her mother. So, Lucky and the chief were going to start entertaining family and friends as a couple.

It wasn't that she wanted, or expected, her mom to spend the rest of her life in widow's weeds.

Lucky and Andy Smith had had a good marriage; they'd loved each other until the day he died. All the more reason for her mom to want, and deserve, to find happiness with a new man. The chief was divorced, so no problems there. But he was the chief; he was her boss. Oh, well, she'd have to get used to it.

Now there's an accident looking for a place to happen. A giant black Escalade, all clean and shiny, swung into the oncoming lane to pass a Toyota Yaris waiting patiently for the car in front of it to maneuver into a parking place. The driver of the Escalade leaned on his horn, whether at the Yaris or at the Escape heading toward it in its proper lane, Smith didn't know. She made a mental note of the license plate, suspecting she'd be seeing the Escalade again.

Chapter Sixteen

When he returned to the office after his useless visit to Jack McMillan, Winters' day didn't get any better. His desk phone rang and he picked it up.

"Guess who," the cheerful voice on the other end said.

Winters didn't bother to hide his groan. "Meredith Morgenstern."

"Got it in one. Your favorite girl reporter. Miss me?"

"No."

And wasn't that the truth. Meredith was a Trafalgar native. She'd been born here, lived most of her life here until a couple of years ago when she moved to Montreal. She was a journalist. The sort of damn-the-torpedoes reporter Winters hated. A few bodies strewn in her wake was the price she was prepared to pay to achieve her ambitions. Her blind stupidity had almost gotten Molly Smith killed a few years ago. When Meredith had landed a job with a muckraking Montreal tabloid, Winters hoped he'd seen the last of her. The paper she worked for featured giant scare quotes on their front pages, photos of politicians and celebrities looking their absolute worst, and as-naked-as-the-law-would-allow women on page three.

But Meredith had strong ties to Trafalgar: her parents still lived here, and he always knew he'd be hearing from her some day.

"How's *Montréal*?" he said, in his hideous high-school French accent.

"Lovely. But I'm not there right now. Guess where I am?"

"What do you want, Meredith?"

She sighed. "Very well, I'm in Vancouver. At the airport. Heading home for a visit with the folks. And, as long as I'm going to be in Trafalgar anyway, my editors are interested in what's happening with the Walter Desmond situation. I'd love an official statement from the TCP."

"Then you should be talking to Chief Constable Keller."

"I figured I'd start with you, John. Come on, what can you tell me? Desmond's back in town, I hear."

"Walter Desmond is as welcome to enjoy the amenities of Trafalgar as any other law-abiding citizen."

"It doesn't look good for the TCP, though, does it? I've only starting reading the appeal judge's decision. Turgid stuff, although at a quick skim I noticed the words 'failure to' and 'neglect' and 'ungrounded.' Do you have anything to say about that, John?"

"Long before my time, Meredith." Mentally, he added, "Thank God."

"I know that, but I'd like your personal opinion. Did the TCP knowingly arrest and charge an innocent man, or was it pure incompetence?"

"Will you look at that," he said, "where has the day gone? Time for my donut run." He hung up.

His personal opinion—one he would never share with anyone, Meredith Morgenstern least of all—was that Desmond had been deliberately railroaded. Set up for a murder the police knew he didn't commit.

The question was, why. Was it a couple of bad cops, or was the whole department in on it? With the detective sergeant dead, and the arresting officer not talking, they'd probably never know.

Walter Desmond had been seen that day, on the highway outside of Trafalgar, fixing a flat tire where and when he said he was. A man, one Ryan Smethwick, had been travelling from Salt Lake City, where his parents lived, to Anchorage, Alaska, where he lived. He'd seen Desmond at the side of the road, looking helpless, Smethwick said. Smethwick pulled to a stop and helped replace the flat with the temporary tire. The men had shaken hands and he'd carried on his way.

A few days later, he'd been in a motel room in Fort Nelson, B.C. watching the news. A man by the name of Walter Desmond, resident of Trafalgar, had been arrested for the "brutal murder" of Sophia D'Angelo. Smethwick recognized the man he'd stopped to help being hustled out of his house in handcuffs between two grim-faced police officers.

Smethwick's first reaction, so he told the investigators from Waterston and Gravelle twenty-five years later, had been gratitude that he himself hadn't ended up dead on the side of the road. But when the news article mentioned the date and time of the murder, he'd turned off the TV and phoned the police station in Trafalgar. He told the officer on the phone about the emergency tire repair. He was positive of the time because he'd stopped at a gas station not more than fifteen minutes earlier, to call his wife from a pay phone and tell her he'd crossed the border. He checked the time before making the call, knowing she got home at three-thirty from the lunch shift at the restaurant where she worked. He'd made the call at three forty-five and they talked for no more than a minute or two.

He'd been with Walter Desmond from four o'clock until at least four twenty or twenty-five.

The officer had taken down his details. Name, phone number, address in Alaska. Smethwick said it would be inconvenient—he was due to start a new job when he got home—but if necessary he'd go into the nearest police station to make an official statement.

He'd been told that wasn't necessary, at this time, and someone would be in touch later.

He'd never heard anything more about it. The next afternoon when he again called home to check in, the answering machine message told him to phone his mother-in-law immediately. His wife had been seriously injured in a car accident and was in the hospital, fighting for her life. Smethwick had driven all though the dark winter night to get to her bedside.

Over the next weeks he spared no thought at all for Trafalgar and the man stranded at the side of the road. When Smethwick's wife was home again, facing months of physical therapy, he did wonder if he should go down to the police station and make a statement.

Not to bother, he decided. The cops would contact him if they needed him.

He hadn't thought about the case again until Waterston and Gravelle found him.

Winters leaned back in his chair and idly rubbed his thumb over the face of his watch. Impossible to believe that whomever Smethwick had spoken to at the Trafalgar police station would have forgotten the call. Particularly considering Desmond claimed the flat tire as his alibi. He flipped through pages. Desmond had stated that someone stopped and helped him. He hadn't gotten the man's name or noticed his license plates. The prosecution said that was obviously a lie, a desperate attempt to provide himself with an alibi. As this Good Samaritan could not be produced, the jury agreed with the prosecutor. Unfortunately Smethwick hadn't made a note of the name of the person he spoke to. A male, was all he remembered, Officer Someone. Officer was not a rank, and there were no women on the force at that time. It could have been just about anyone.

Chapter Seventeen

Walt Desmond stirred his chicken and noodles. The meal was good, but he wasn't used to spice and heat, so he took only a few bites. Prison food had been nothing but repetitive, bland, and heavy on the carbs. Arlene had been a good cook. An adventurous one, too; she would have loved the new locovore movement: locally grown foods, organic vegetables, delivered straight from the farmer's field or barn. Most of all, Arlene been a great baker. He'd missed, among all the other things he missed, her fruit pies and delicate cakes. Sure, they had cake and pie at the prison. The pastry was the taste and consistency of cardboard and the cakes could have been used to patch drywall.

He thought about Arlene. How over the last years of her life her face had turned pale and doughy, and the color drained out of her eyes, like a watercolor painting left out in the rain. She'd put on weight, a lot of weight, and her muscles softened and turned to jelly. Her expensive, fashionable clothes no longer fit and, not caring, she bought replacements at Walmart or Zellers. The few good pieces of jewelry he'd bought her over the years had been sold for legal fees, along with her diamond engagement ring. Only the plain gold band that was her wedding ring remained for her to be buried in.

He hadn't been granted a pass to go to her funeral. Just as well. Her parents and siblings had turned against him, and tried to turn Arlene also. He didn't need to stand at her graveside, while everyone openly stared at him and nudged and whispered to each other, in order to mourn her. He wasn't even all that sure how she'd died. The chaplain had broken the news to him with weasel words like disturbed state of mind, depression, given up hope. In other words she'd killed herself.

Although, ultimately, it had been those bastards who'd framed him, who'd killed her. All these years later, he still had not the slightest idea *why* they'd framed *him*. Louise had advised him not to return to Trafalgar, not to attempt to go back in time, to instead put it behind him and move forward. "No," he said, "I have to know *why*."

"Sometimes," Louise said, "there *is* no why."

Trafalgar Thai was full on a Thursday night, and a line snaked out the door. He thought he'd heard a collective gasp when he came in, but that might have been his imagination. A few people, some of whom he vaguely recognized, had stared as he crossed the room following the young, menu-carrying waitress to his table, and then quickly went back to their food and companions as if embarrassed to be caught gaping. Once he was seated, sipping at the green tea he'd been served without asking for it, no one paid him any outright attention, although he did catch a few peeking at him out of the corners of their eyes.

"I'll have the bill now, thanks," he said to the passing waitress.

She glanced at his nearly full plate. "Was the food okay?"

"It was fine. Very good. But I don't have much of an appetite tonight."

The dragon boat women had invited him to come to dinner with them. He'd been tempted, but in the end declined. He was trouble in this town, and they didn't need to be saddled with Walt Desmond. After the altercation at breakfast with Sophia's father, and his chat with Constable Smith, Walt had gone back into the B&B. He'd almost expected the women to run in horror at the sight of him, to insist he be evicted from the Glacier Chalet. Instead, they'd been sitting in the dining room, breakfasts finished, sipping coffee.

They stopped talking when he came in. They'd been waiting for him.

"If you don't want to tell us what that was about, Walt," Darlene said, "that's okay."

"But if you do want to talk, we're here," Carolanne said. She gave him a soft smile, before dipping her head.

He'd almost cried. Instead, he gave them the barest of bones of his story: "That poor man's daughter was murdered. I didn't have anything to do with it, but I went to prison for it. The appeals court found that there had been a miscarriage of justice. I have been completely vindicated. And now, here I am, having a little holiday. You can read all about it on the Internet."

He'd started to leave, to return to his room. He hesitated, and then turned back to the watching women. "Thank you for your kindness."

He paid cash for his unfinished Thai dinner and left a twenty-five percent tip.

It had been too cool in the restaurant, the air conditioning turned up high, but outside the last of the day's heat hung in the air. The streets were busy, young people mostly, tourists, checking out the restaurants and bars.

He stuffed his hands into the pockets of his jeans and walked down the street. He kept his head up and his eyes moving. He wasn't in prison any more, but he'd never again allow himself to let his guard down. A woman approached from the opposite direction. She was about his age; there was a trace of something familiar about her. He could tell the moment she recognized him. Her eyes opened wide and her jaw dropped. She turned and darted across the street as horns honked and cars squealed to a stop.

Oh, well. He hadn't expected to be welcomed with open arms.

Mid-Kootenay Adventure Vacations was still open. Andy Smith's store. Walt was sorry to hear he'd died. He hadn't known Andy well, but from what he did know, Andy had seemed to be a good guy. Like a lot of old-time Trafalgar residents, he'd been a Vietnam War draft-dodger who'd never gone home again. What was Andy's wife's name? Some hippie thing? The interior of the store was brightly lit, and he could see her through the window, talking to a young woman with blond dreadlocks standing behind the counter. Mrs. Smith was older, rounder, and her shock of curly hair had turned gray, but she was still dressed in the sort of clothes that would have been popular at Woodstock. Lucky, that was what they called her.

On impulse, he opened the door. The bell tinkled.

"Let me know if you need anything," the clerk called.

He studied the equipment. Everything looked so new, so modern. Even the bright colors of the athletic clothes were strange to his eyes.

"See you tomorrow, Flower," Lucky Smith said. She turned to leave. She smiled at him, not really seeing him. Then she stopped and took a second look. "Walt. How are you?"

"I'm good. Lucky, right?"

"Yes. Uh…welcome home."

"Thank you. Do you know, you're the first person who's said that to me? It's nice to hear."

"I…uh…"

"I was sorry to hear about Andy."

"Thank you."

He decided not to tell her he'd been talking to her daughter earlier. Everyone in town probably knew about that dustup with Gino D'Angelo, but if they didn't, he wasn't going to be the one to tell them.

"I'm off home now," Lucky said. She swallowed, and then she visibly relaxed and gave him a smile. It was a nice smile. "It is good to see you, Walt. Are you back here to stay?"

"I haven't made any plans yet. I'm still getting the lay of the land, so to speak."

"If you need anything, let me know. I was

sorry to hear about Arlene. I'm…sorry about everything."

"It's all over now," he said. But that was a lie.

"Good night." Lucky bustled out of the shop.

The clerk was watching the exchange with much interest. Walt said thank you and left the store.

The place next door was new, to him at least. Rosemary's Campfire Kitchen. Some sort of catering business. The display in the window showed tin plates and cups, foldable cutlery, and battered cooking equipment arranged around birch logs and a paper fire. Inside, he could see shelves of nuts and chocolate bars. He pushed open the door. It took him a long time to make up his mind, but he eventually decided on a bag of honey-roasted almonds. The young clerk barely glanced up from her phone long enough to take his money.

The night was a warm, soft blanket on his shoulders, and the town an oasis of light and civilization, surrounded by the dark, looming bulk of the mountains. He munched on almonds as he walked through the busy streets, enjoying the bright lights and the happy chatter of people around him.

A police car drove past on the other side of the street. It made a U-turn at a break in traffic and came back. It moved at walking speed, slowly, keeping pace with him. The driver was not Lucky's daughter, but one of the cops he'd had a run-in with last night.

Walt's heart accelerated. He told himself to keep walking. He was in a public place, minding his own business, eating nuts he'd paid for. He even had the receipt in his pocket.

He dared a glance at the cop. The man stared back at him, his young, handsome face set into tight lines. Then the car accelerated, lights and sirens came on, and roared away.

Walt kept walking. Time to return to the B&B. Maybe the women would be back from their dinner, enjoying a nightcap in the common room. He realized, with a small degree of surprise, that he hoped they were. He'd like to spend some time with them. With all of them, but particularly with the quiet one named Carolanne.

He left the busy shops and restaurants and the crowded streets behind him. This part of Front Street was mostly offices. Accountants, lawyers, an addictions help center. The real estate company he'd worked for was still there. He hadn't bothered to drop in and say hi. The cop car slid up beside him, its lights and sirens off. He kept walking. The car pulled ahead, the front tire climbing onto the sidewalk, and the officer got out.

He was alone this time. He walked around the car and planted himself on the sidewalk, blocking

Walt's way. Walt tried to go around him. The cop spread his legs and rested his hand on the butt of his gun. "Going somewhere?"

"To bed."

"Tomorrow?"

"I haven't made my plans yet. You'll be the first to know when I do."

Walt realized he was standing at the entrance to an alley, a dark spot equal distance between two streetlights. A couple walked by on the other side of the street, but no one else was nearby.

"I brought an old friend of yours," the cop said. "Wants to have a chat."

Walt glanced to his right. The alley was a dark tunnel. Cables and wires stretched overhead forming an urban jungle. The cop moved. He didn't so much grab Walt as bump him. Walt was fitter and stronger than he'd ever been, but the cop had thirty or more years on him, never mind being armed. Walt stumbled. He felt a hand on his arm and he was jerked into the alley. The cop placed his bulk firmly behind him, blocking any exit. For a moment Walt cursed himself for not bringing his backpack. Then he thought *no*. He couldn't chance getting caught with its contents on him.

As Walt's eyes became accustomed to the dim light, he saw two figures standing against a building, draped in the deeper shadows. "What the hell's going on?" To his relief his voice stayed strong.

The men stepped away from the wall. One was the older cop he'd seen yesterday, not in uniform tonight. At first he thought he didn't know the third guy. He was older than the others, overweight, with wet red eyes and a nose like a billiard ball. He sported a scraggy goatee and badly cut, greasy hair.

"Well, well, if it isn't my old pal, Walter."

Despite the heat of the night, a line of ice ran down Walt's spine. He knew that voice. He still heard it, in his nightmares. "Jack McMillan. I wouldn't have thought you could get any older or uglier. Guess I was wrong."

"I heard Arlene died of shame. Sorry about that."

"You keep your problems with me between us. Leave my wife out of it."

McMillan took a step forward. He poked Walt in the chest. The two cops stood back, watching. Ready to move. "You don't like me talking about your wife. Well, you said bad things about me in the press. Things I didn't want my ex-wife and kids to hear."

"I'm not going to engage in a pissing contest with you. Not now, not ever. You and your idiot sergeant set me up, you drove my wife into her grave, you ruined my life, and you let a killer go

free. I don't know why, and these days I don't care."
Walt cared very much, but this wasn't the time,
nor the place to try to find out what Kibbens and
McMillan had been up to. "I want to get on with
my life. What little of it you bastards left me with."

"You killed that girl. You raped her with a god-
damn knife and then you slit her throat. She was
a nice girl, never did any harm to anyone. Want
to talk about ruined lives? How about her life, her
parents'? You did it, and I know you did."

McMillan's face was up against Walt's now,
almost touching. He could feel the spittle landing
on him like a light rain. He kept his arms to his
side, slightly bent. Ready. He'd had his share of
beatings in prison. He could take it, if it came to
that. Which it probably would: three against one.
One of the three a young cop with heavy boots and
a baton. He sensed the older cop shifting from one
foot to another. Getting ready to move in.

Chapter Eighteen

It was going to be a long, boring night. The bouncer at the Potato Famine had called to say a fight had broken out, but by the time Molly Smith jogged over, the miscreants had taken off. Dave Evans was in the car tonight, but she hadn't seen him in hours. She shifted the weight of her utility belt. She accepted a glass of water from the bartender and sipped it, watching the crowd, letting everyone know she was there. The Potato Famine wasn't one of Trafalgar's tourist highlights. Except among those tourists who arrived in a convoy of motorcycles, with leather jackets bristling with colors and badges, and the occasional vacationing university jerks who wanted to try their hand at slumming it.

A band was playing heavy metal. Smith enjoyed listening to a good, live heavy metal band in a bar as much as the next person, but this bunch wasn't good, and they were scarcely even live. Not that anyone was paying attention anyway.

She put her empty glass on the counter. "I'll be around," she said.

"Catch you later."

"God, I hope not," she muttered. He didn't hear her over the racket.

She went through the main room, down a dark passageway past the kitchen, all noise and steam and hot grease, and out the back door that opened into the alley. More than once she'd caught a couple out here too impatient to find themselves a hotel room. Or even the backseat of a car. Tonight, the alley was quiet. An orange cat slipped between garbage bags at the back of the shop next door.

It was early, barely past eight o'clock, the sun dipping toward the mountains. Give it time, and the action at the PF would be heating up, inside and out.

She walked to the corner and turned into Front Street. Busy tonight, a nice evening and the height of the summer tourist season. She and Adam had vacation time scheduled in a couple of weeks. They were going to Ontario to spend a few days with his parents (gulp!) in Toronto and then taking his nephew and two nieces for a week's canoe trip in Killarney Park. She was looking forward to it very much. The camping and canoeing part, that is, not the staying with the parents part. She hadn't met them yet, although they seemed okay the couple of times they'd Skyped. She'd never been to Ontario, and figured it couldn't hold a candle to B.C. when it came to the wilderness, but the pictures she'd seen of Killarney on the Internet when Adam made the bookings did look nice. Unspoiled and remote, exactly the way she and Adam liked it.

She strolled down Front Street, showing the flag so to speak. Most people she passed nodded and smiled, a few turned their heads away, and one guy, well-known to the police, bolted down a side street. She checked her watch. Time for a rest stop and something to eat. She touched her radio. "Four-two, this is Five-one."

"Go ahead." Evans said.

"I'm popping into the office for half an hour. The PF is quiet now, but looking like a big crowd tonight."

"I'm on a call. Stay on the street until I'm clear."

"Ten-Four." She hadn't heard any call come over the radio recently, other than the one sending her to the Potato Famine. No matter. She could wait. She debated what to get for supper. Shanghai noodles from Trafalgar Thai would hit the spot. She pulled out her phone and called to place the order. She kept her favorite restaurant on speed dial.

"Can you wait about an hour, Molly?" the hostess said. "I'm really sorry, but we're short in the kitchen tonight with one cook off sick and the lineup's out the door."

"I can see the line from here. Sure, an hour's fine."

She breathed in deeply as she passed the restaurant. Fragrant spices and the scent of warm cooking oil drifted out. She waved to her friend Christa, standing in the line with a man Smith vaguely recognized. He had his arm around her shoulders. Smith and Christa had been close once. As close as sisters. But they'd drifted so far apart Smith hadn't even known Christa was dating someone.

At Fleures des Menthe, tables and chairs were set out on the patio. The eating area protruded across the sidewalk into the street, marked off by a neat, white wooden fence, adorned with pots overflowing with purple and yellow petunias. The patio was full; people laughed and glasses clinked. Smith ran her eyes over the crowd, not that there was ever much trouble at this upscale restaurant. Her heart sunk into her stomach. The last person she wanted to see was here, having dinner with an older couple.

"Hey, Molly!" Meredith Morgenstern spotted Smith. She jumped to her feet and carried her wineglass over to the fence. "Nice to see you."

"What brings you to town?"

"Vacation. A duty visit to the old folks."

Meredith nodded to her dinner companions. They smiled back. Vacation was okay, Smith thought, as long as Meredith wasn't moving back to Trafalgar. She had to reluctantly admit the other woman was looking darned good. Her hair was brushed to a brilliant shine, cascading in black waves down her back. Her makeup was light and perfectly applied, and her eyebrows formed a flawless arch. She wore a navy-blue linen jacket over a blindingly white tee-shirt and blue capris. She was taller than Smith remembered. She glanced down to see blue and gold sandals with three-inch heels on Meredith's feet.

Smith felt like an ungainly lump in her black boots, heavy uniform, Kevlar vest, and fully laden equipment belt. She was melting under all that, while Meredith looked as light as a breeze and sipped white wine with beautifully manicured hands.

Something about Meredith Morgenstern still made Molly Smith feel as though she were back in high school, desperate for the approval of Meredith and her gaggle of in-girls.

"I heard you and Adam got engaged. Congratulations."

"Thanks."

"When's the big day?" Meredith checked Smith's left hand for a ring.

"We haven't decided yet." She never wore the gorgeous square-cut diamond when in uniform.

"I was going to give you a call," Meredith said. "How about lunch? If you're working tonight, you'll be free tomorrow, right?"

"Lunch?" Smith said.

"My treat. Come on, say yes, we can talk over old times and laugh about all the fun we've had over the years."

Smith couldn't remember having ever had any fun in Meredith's company. "Sorry. I've pulled a double shift today, and I have to be back at three tomorrow. Another time, maybe."

"Saturday, then?"

Smith heard herself saying, "I was planning on going to the dragon boat thing down at the river. I suppose I can do lunch after."

"Perfect. One o'clock? Right here?"

"Okay. See you then." Smith walked on. Why on earth had she agreed to that? Shouldn't be a problem. After all, Meredith was here to visit her parents. Not in search of a story.

She heard low voices coming from the next alley, and ducked into it. A group of teenagers stood in the shadows. She checked for cans of beer or the scent of pot. Nothing. They eyed her warily, as teenagers do. She recognized most of them. Middle-class kids from good homes who went to school and had part-time jobs. Not the sort to be looking for trouble, just bored and restless.

Smith remembered what that felt like. "Everything okay, guys?"

"Yeah."

She carried on down the alley, then turned right and headed west. She had no particular route to walk, just went where the mood took her. Downtown Trafalgar was only a couple of blocks. She'd spend the night popping into bars, checking dark corners, peering into the windows of closed stores. Her stomach rumbled and she checked her watch. Only fifteen minutes had passed since she'd ordered her supper. She was starving.

As she approached the intersection of two alleys, she heard a soft grunt, and a man saying, "You don't seem to able to take a hint. So maybe it's time to do more than hint."

She rounded the corner, her hand on the radio at her shoulder. Four men were wrapped in shadow. One had his back against the wall, while another stood in his space, too close to mean anything good. Two other men held back, watching, but braced as though they were ready to move. She recognized Dave Evans first, as the weak light from the street reflected off the word "Police" printed on the back of his Kevlar vest. Then Sergeant Jeff Glendenning, not in uniform.

She dropped her hand. "What's up, guys?"

The men jumped. The entire body of the man against the wall sagged in relief. The fellow threatening him stepped back and turned to face her.

Walt Desmond and Jack McMillan.

Definitely not good.

"Get lost, little girl," McMillan said.

"I don't think so." She looked at Evans. "What's going on here, Dave?"

He shifted from one foot to another, eyes on the ground.

"He's protecting the peace," MacMillan said. "Keeping our streets safe for law-abiding folks, right, Sergeant?"

"Let's go," Glendenning said.

"What are you doing here, Jeff?" Smith said. "You're not working tonight."

"Good cops are always working," McMillan said.

"Stay out of what doesn't concern you, Molly," Evans said.

Her head spun. Clearly Evans and Glendenning were helping McMillan to harass Desmond. Glendenning wasn't a direct boss of hers, but he was a superior. And Evans, she had to work with Evans. She had to be able to rely on him to protect her life if need be.

"Mr. Desmond," she said, "how about I walk you back to the B&B?"

"I'm sure that won't be necessary," he said. "We've finished our little talk. Right boys?"

"Nevertheless," she said, "I happen to be going that way."

Walter Desmond stared at Jack McMillan for a long time. Then the edges of his mouth turned up. "Glad we all understand each other. Gentlemen." He made a crook out of his arm and held it out to Smith. She ignored it.

"This is a private matter, Molly," Evans said. "Don't be reporting it."

"Let's go," she said to Desmond.

He preceded her into the street. She followed, the hairs on the back of her neck prickling, conscious of the three men watching her. She didn't think for a minute that they'd jump her. No, even McMillan would be more subtle than that.

They passed under a streetlamp, the yellow light bright and welcoming. Desmond let out all the tension he was holding in one long sigh. His shoulders slumped and his hands uncurled. "Thanks."

"If," she said, "you want to report them for harassment, I'll back you up. I'll say what I saw." Behind them, she heard the police car start. It sped past. Only Evans was in it, and he didn't turn his head as he drove away.

"Let it go," Desmond said.

"It's unlikely McMillan will. Let it go, I mean. Suppose I'm not around next time?"

He laughed. It was a good laugh, deep and heartfelt. He turned to look at her, and once again she thought he was a good-looking man, despite the deathly pale skin and the eyes that had seen too much. "I mean absolutely no offense and I appreciate your intervention, but I can imagine telling the guys on my cell block that a pretty little thing, young enough to be my daughter, was worried about not being around to protect me."

She felt herself smiling back. Any other time, she would have taken great offense at being called a pretty little thing. Desmond, she felt, deserved a break. She patted the patch on her uniform shoulder. "Goes a long way."

His face fell, and the laughter died in his eyes. "Yeah. So it does. I'm not worried about McMillan. He was never anything but a bully, and he's sure as hell gone to seed. I could take him blindfolded with both hands tied behind my back. Probably even with the old cop on his side. The young guy, the one you called Dave? He'd be a threat, if he wanted to be, but I think you've smartened him up a bit. He'll be worried you're going to report him. Are you?"

She didn't answer. She didn't know what she was going to do. "Look, Mr. Desmond. Why are you here? Why have you come back? You must know feelings are running high. Not everyone agrees with the appeal court."

"Have you read up on my case?"

"Some of it."

"What do you think?"

She hesitated. *That he was framed, railroaded, and a guilty man allowed to walk free.* "I'm not going to comment, sir."

"I saw your mother today."

"You did?"

"She's looking good. I noticed signs in the store window. Political action posters. Against the Grizzly Resort, whatever that is. For marijuana decriminalization. I guess your mom hasn't changed much."

"She hasn't changed one little bit." *Despite being the partner of the chief of police.*

The welcoming lights of the Glacier Chalet sparkled in the distance. It looked, Smith thought, like a picture on a post-card or the box of a jigsaw puzzle. They walked on in silence.

"Why have I come back?" he said as they reached the B&B's front gate. "I don't truly know.

Maybe because this place, this town, surrounded by these mountains, was the last place on Earth where I was happy."

Chapter Nineteen

John Winters eyed the mountain of paper on his desk. Walter Desmond had been determined, by a court of law, not to have murdered Sophia D'Angelo. As her death was, beyond a doubt, not an accident or a suicide, that meant that someone else—person or persons unknown—had murdered her.

And that meant the case was now active and on his desk.

Twenty-five years had passed. Witnesses had died or moved away. The investigating detective was dead, his closest colleague uncooperative. Chances were good that the perp had left town a long time ago—probably thanking his lucky stars that some other poor guy had been stuck with the guilt.

Winters would start his investigation by searching for similar crimes. Begin with the year in question and then branch out, moving forward and backward through time. The sort of thing that had been done to Sophia, a frenzy of savagery, was never a one-off. If Winters was lucky, he could find some guy doing hard time for a similar killing.

Go back to the D'Angelos, ask questions, dredge it up again. All the memories, all the pain. The same with her friends and her coworkers.

He wouldn't be a popular man around town, that was for sure.

He logged onto his computer to begin filling out a ViClas report. Start the wheels turning in an attempt to locate similar situations.

Having to reopen the case wasn't entirely bad: he needed something to do to keep his mind off what had happened to Eliza. His gut churned simply thinking about it. The art gallery had opened this morning. Margo had stopped by the house last night and, trying to smother her cough, said she was well enough to come back to work. Eliza was feeling better, but her face wasn't looking good. Winters knew from personal experience the third day was the worst. That's when the swelling started to go down but the colors came out in all their glory.

He remembered the first time he'd taken a punch to the face. He'd been a new cop, young, naïve, keen, still wet behind the ears. They'd been called to a bar where a big-time brawl had broken out. When he tried to separate two of the combatants, a third guy had come out of nowhere and delivered a solid punch to Winters' jaw. He'd been frozen in place for a moment, stunned and not quite understanding why someone would want to hit him. Fortunately, his partner had been a grizzled old guy who'd learned long ago that the uniform didn't give him immunity.

Winters had gone to his parents' house for Easter dinner two days later. His poor mom had almost fainted at the sight of his face. She hadn't been happy at him going into police work in the first place, and over the ham, scalloped potatoes, and green beans her conversation was all about the successful careers her friends' children were enjoying.

He'd learned over the years to avoid a punch when he could, and to roll with it when he couldn't. His blood boiled simply thinking of someone hitting Eliza.

Chief Paul Keller had walked into his office yesterday morning and told him Ray Lopez would be investigating the attack on Eliza, what was almost certainly an attempted rape. Winters was to stay out of it, to work on anything else that came up, and on the D'Angelo killing when he had the time.

No arguments. Keller had turned and walked out.

Winters went back to his computer. It didn't take long before he found a similar case to the

D'Angelo murder. It happened in Revelstoke, about three and half hours' drive from Trafalgar. In mid-November of 1990, two months before the death of Sophia, a twenty-five-year-old white woman with long dark hair left her job at a lawyer's office to walk the few blocks home. Her body had been found in a park not far from her house the following morning. Like Sophia D'Angelo, she had been penetrated with a sharp instrument and her throat had been cut. No one was ever arrested for that crime, and the case remained open to this day.

Winters searched for any mention of the Revelstoke killing in the files of Sophia's case, but found nothing. He leaned back in his chair. That was odd. Even twenty-five years ago, when they didn't have the computer systems they had now and police forces weren't as good at cooperating and exchanging information, someone should have noticed the similarities.

"How's Eliza?" Barb said from the doorway.

Winters blinked and rubbed his eyes. Barb's purse was tossed over her shoulder. "What time is it?" he asked.

"After two. I'm going out for a late lunch because the chief had some last-minute work to do on his speech for Rotary this afternoon. Do you want me to pick anything up for you?"

"A sandwich would be nice, thanks. Whatever

looks good." The day had passed without him even noticing. He leaned back and stretched. With a twinge of guilt, he realized that he'd been so engrossed, he hadn't given Eliza another thought. Eliza. Now that he was thinking about what had happened to her, at the same time as reading the D'Angelo file, he was getting angry all over again. There had been no sign of a knife threatening Eliza. He had to remember that. He couldn't afford to get the cases mixed up, even in his head.

"Barb, I've been going through the D'Angelo case files. I know the situation's upsetting to you, but if you wouldn't mind, I've got questions for someone who was there."

She gave him a tight smile. "Why don't I get those sandwiches and then we can talk? I'm happy to help, if I can."

"Good idea. And in answer to your original question, Eliza's okay. Nothing's permanently damaged, but her face looks worse than it is. She won't be leaving the house for a few days. Here." He dug in his wallet and handed her a green bill. "My treat."

"Be right back."

She brought him a baguette heavy with roast beef and a generous slather of mustard, and a ham and Swiss for herself. They unwrapped their sandwiches in silence. "You must know," Barb said at last, "people are saying Walter Desmond attacked Eliza."

"About the only thing Eliza and Merrill agree upon is that he was a young man with long dark hair. Never mind the hair, Desmond is not young, and certainly doesn't look it. Prison takes its toll."

"Ray went around to the B&B," Barb said. "To warn Walt about the gossip."

"How'd he react?"

"He said people have been saying worse things about him for a long time. I'd just wish he'd leave, John. He has to know he's not welcome here. Innocent or not."

"Tell me about Doug Kibbens. And be honest, please, Barb. Loyalty is a good thing, but our first loyalty has to be to the truth. Wouldn't you agree?"

She nodded slowly, chewed thoughtfully. "I started working here straight out of high school. Right from day one, I loved every minute. I loved being part of it. The excitement, the belief that we were doing good. My friends thought it was so thrilling, and although I never divulged any confidential information, I might have been guilty occasionally of letting them think I was more important than I was.

"Most of all, I loved the guys. They were all guys, men, back then. In the bigger cities women were starting to get ahead as officers, but not out here. I heard the occasional crack about women not being able to take it, and I agreed with them.

Being a police officer was all about being tough, about bringing down the bad guys." She smiled. "Now, I look at Molly and Dawn and see what great officers they are. Gentle and empathetic one minute and as tough as any of the old guys the next. The difference is, I think, that they know when to be kind and when to be hard. It's not all about bashing heads all the time. Rhetorically speaking, of course."

"I understand."

"Doug Kibbens was an old-time cop. This town was different back then, John. It was still a working-man's town, not the tourist place it is now. Not as affluent. The occasional hippie or band of New Age travelers wandered into town, and Kibbens and his men would take them aside and tell them they wouldn't like it here. So they left." She chuckled. "A lot of them went up the valley, and there they remain to this day. By the time of the D'Angelo murder, things were changing. And changing fast. More tourists, a greater variety of people moving here. A lot more money. The new chief came from Toronto and brought a much more cosmopolitan outlook on the world."

"How did Kibbens handle the changing times?"

"I thought he did okay, John. He did his job, got promoted to sergeant. He was a good cop. And I'm saying that because I believe it. I do."

"I checked his file. He died the year after the D'Angelo case. Car accident."

Barb's eyes slid to one side.

"What?" Winters said.

She let out a heavy sigh and put down her sandwich. "The accident report was doctored somewhat."

"What do you mean?"

"The line about going off the road in icy conditions? Not true. The road was dry and there'd been no rain or snow that day. It was a single-car accident. He went off the side of the mountain at the top of the pass."

"Suicide?" Winters knew that a substantial number of single-car accidents, heck even some multi-vehicle ones, were believed to be suicides. Hard to prove.

"Probably," Barb said. "No skid marks. No hazardous road conditions. Just a straight line through the guardrail and over the edge. One of the guys altered the Mounties' report to mention ice on the road, and the chief let it stand. Out of respect, really. It might not have been suicide. He might have swerved to avoid a moose or elk. The car burned, so there wasn't much evidence left, of the car or of Doug himself. Maybe he had a heart attack."

"Kibbens was alone in the car?"

"Yes, thank heavens. He was divorced by then,

and his wife had moved away. I forget her name. They didn't have any children."

"He was still working here when he died," Winters said. "Someone would have cleared out his desk. I don't suppose you remember what happened to his stuff?"

"As it happens, I do. I was the one who had to pack up the residue of his entire career. It wasn't a nice job. His ex-wife came back for the funeral, but she didn't want anything of his. It was boxed and labeled and sent to the city hall basement where I guess it remains to this day."

"What would you do, Adam?" Smith asked. "If you knew a cop had done something wrong, but no one else did?"

"Why are you asking, babe?"

"Hypothetical case."

"Geeze, Molly, don't try out for the movies, will you? You can't act your way out of a paper bag. Spill."

"I can't, Adam. If I tell you, then you'll be compromised. One of my colleagues did something. I should tell, but I don't want to rat him out. Or her. Him or her."

"No clues in that phrasing, Mol. Did he do something illegal or unethical?"

"Not illegal. I'd say unethical. Some might not agree."

"Harassment of another cop? Did someone say something to you? I'd break his freakin' neck, except you told me not to do that."

"It didn't involve me. I happened to see him, or her, in the act of disobeying a direct order."

"That's a hard one, but if it was me, I'd let it go. But it's not me, so you have to do what you think right. My advice, for what it's worth, is if he put anyone's life in danger, or interfered with evidence or something, you can't let that pass, but otherwise let Dave trip himself up."

"I didn't say any names."

"You don't have to, Molly. Even over at our office there's talk about Dave Evans. He cuts corners, takes shortcuts, throws his weight around. He'll hang himself, soon enough."

She let out a laugh that contained not a trace of humor. "Nice to know it's not just me who thinks he's a jerk."

Adam put his arms around her and held her close. He ran his hands up her back and his breath was hot on her neck. He whispered in her ear, "You'll do the right thing, because you're you. If you need me, you know I'm here. I'll always be here."

Norman barked his agreement.

Chapter Twenty

Walt Desmond flinched at the sound of the front door opening. He thought he'd be able to relax here at the B&B, a quiet house among friendly people. He'd been a fool. The cops weren't going to let him carry on as if nothing had happened—as if he were only another tourist, here for the mountain air and the great views.

A different officer, a detective, had come by yesterday, first thing in the morning. Asking him about some woman who'd been attacked in town the previous night. Oh, yeah, he made it sound as if he had Walt's interests at heart. "Thought you should be aware, sir, some people are saying it's not a coincidence this happened so soon after your return."

Some people. Meaning if folks weren't already thinking it, the cops would make sure they added two and two and came up with five. The guy had been friendly enough. Frankly, Walt would prefer dealing with the uniformed goons who'd threated him last night. Always better knowing exactly what you're up against, right off the bat. Another lesson he'd learned in prison.

Some of the tension drained out of his shoulders when he heard soft footsteps in the hall. Not the cops this time, but one of the women.

"It's a lovely day. You should be outside." Carolanne came into the common room.

"Just using the computer," Walt said. "Where's the rest of your gang?"

She threw herself into a chair. Her face was flushed with health and exercise, and her legs were brown from the sun. Her tight shorts showed muscles taut and sleek. "They have gone, hard as it is to believe, kayaking."

"Why's that hard to believe?"

Carolanne groaned. "We were on the water at eight o'clock. Every muscle I own aches. Muscles I didn't know I owned ache." She laughed, lifted her arms, took off her ball cap and ran her fingers through her hair. Her breasts were small and round. For some reason he thought of windfall apples. "All I wanted in the whole world was to finish the last run and get into the shower, and then Darlene proclaimed, 'I've got a great idea.' She's a maniac, that one. So off they've all gone to rent kayaks. Tomorrow's the open house down by the lake. We'll be having some fun," she made quotes in the air with her fingers, "races and taking interested people out for a paddle. You should come, Walt."

"I don't think I'd fit in," he said.

"Everyone fits in. That's the great thing about dragon boating. There are men's teams, women's teams, mixed teams, teams of young people, seniors' teams. All ages can do it. I have to admit that as exhausting as I'm finding my teammates, I'm glad I've gotten into this."

I'm glad you have, too, he thought but would never say.

She jumped to her feet. "I'm hitting the shower. Then I'm going to walk into town. Browse the shops, have a coffee."

"Have fun," he said.

She stopped in the doorway, hesitated, and turned back to face him. "Come with me, Walt?"

Panic crashed into his chest. "I couldn't."

"Sure you could. You need to get outside. If I might say, you could use some sun. Finish up what you're doing, and we'll go. I won't be long." She dashed off.

He stared at the space where she'd been. The air was full of the scent of her. Sweat, not the rancid scent of sweat generated by bitter, angry, violent men doing hard time, but something light, almost fresh. The sweat of a hard workout on the water under a hot sun. Good sweat on a clean body. The sweat of laughter and fun. Not of desperation and rage and hate.

He'd stayed in all day, afraid of running into more cops or some of his old neighbors, who might be also thinking it was not a coincidence a woman was attacked only hours after Walt returned to Trafalgar. They wouldn't bother him, surely, if he was with Carolanne. Yes, a walk would be nice.

He turned back to the computer to check the e-mail account Louise had set up for him. He logged onto G-mail the way her assistant had taught him. He had one message. He read it quickly, and leaned back in his chair with a low whistle.

Five million bucks. This morning Louise filed the papers to sue the government of British Columbia for five million dollars on his behalf.

Chapter Twenty-one

Eliza was one of those people who didn't eat when they were upset, so Winters had gone home after his sandwich with Barb to make his wife toast and a soft-boiled egg. She was a stoic, largely unemotional person, and even after having been married to her for thirty years, Winters couldn't always read her. She seemed to be doing okay. Concerned about her appearance, for sure. Her lip was cut, her left eye swollen, and the tender skin around it turning purple, black, and yellow. But no bones had been broken, swelling would go down, cuts would heal, and skin would repair. Her stomach held a bruise the size of a fist and she grimaced when she laughed, but again, no permanent damage had been done. Human bodies are resilient.

Eliza was resilient.

She greeted him with a kiss, then caught a glimpse of herself in the hall mirror. "I hope no one is saying the police made me invent an attack by a stranger to cover for you knocking me around."

"Don't even joke about it, Eliza."

She ran her fingers over his cheek. "Don't mind me. I know how upsetting this must be for you."

He couldn't help but give her a smile. "Look at you, trying to comfort *me*."

"I'm hoping to go into the store on Monday. I feel fine, a bit sore, but no worse than if I'd put in too much time at the gym after a long break. I'd go in tomorrow, but I think it's better to let the town's conversation die down a bit first. In the meantime, I can do paperwork here as easily as there. It'll give me a chance to get the September exhibit organized."

He didn't think she was feeling as blasé about the incident as she was pretending. But he gave her a kiss and didn't pry.

"I don't suppose you have any news?" she said.

"Ray's on it," had been all he could say.

Meredith Morgenstern ordered a glass of white wine. The man with her asked for a beer, and the waitress went to get the drinks.

"Thanks for seeing me," the man said. Meredith knew he was forty-two, but he looked a good deal older. He was several inches shorter than her five-foot ten, and considerably overweight. He still had a full head of thick black hair, but he peered at her through coke-bottle-bottom glasses.

Meredith smiled. "Thank you. You have a story to tell. I'm here to listen."

The interior of the Bishop and Nun was empty at this time of day. The few customers had taken tables on the small square of sidewalk out front. Meredith had chosen this place precisely because she knew they were not likely to be interrupted.

"My folks are getting old," the man said. "Dad wants to fight, but I'm worried it will kill him. Mom's got one foot in the grave already."

"Surely your parents understand they have nothing to fight *with*. Or against. The case is closed. Over. At least as far as Walter Desmond is concerned."

"It's not over for them. It will never be over. Not for me, either. Sure, I've been able to get on with my life, more or less, but they're stuck in time. Not a single thing has changed for them since Soph died, except their rapidly aging bodies and deteriorating health."

"What do you want me to do, Mr. D'Angelo?" Meredith asked. She kept her attention focused on his face. Her eyes were warm and soft, her expression one of sympathy and understanding. She'd practiced that expression in front of the mirror often enough.

"Call me Tony."

She nodded. "I'm happy to, Tony."

Tony D'Angelo, younger brother of the late Sophia, only surviving child of Gino and Rose, arrived in Trafalgar yesterday afternoon. He lived in Toronto, he told Meredith on the phone, but came home at this difficult time to be with his family. Friends of his parents had been in and out of the house constantly, bringing cakes and casseroles, paying condolences, digging for gossip, exactly as if there'd been another death in the family. To the D'Angelos there might as well have been. The man who'd murdered Sophia was not only out of prison, but he was here, walking the streets of Trafalgar along with decent, law-abiding people. Everyone said it was a disgrace. At least that's what they said to his parents' faces. What they said behind their backs was another matter entirely. A lot of people were saying Desmond was innocent after all. That the police had screwed up.

They were a pack of vultures, Tony thought, picking over the carcass, searching for the few last, juicy scraps. The people of Trafalgar had forgotten the D'Angelos and their tragedy a long time ago. They thought it was over when Walter Desmond went to prison. They carried on with their lives as Tony's mother and father sank into a premature old age. That Tony himself had fled the mourning-drenched home as soon as he was old enough, and over the years his visits had become increasingly infrequent, was something he tried not to think about. He'd overheard Mrs. Morgenstern (bearing a chicken casserole) breathlessly telling Father McIntyre, who had not been the priest back in Tony's childhood, that her daughter Meredith was home for a visit. Meredith had a very important job with a newspaper in Montreal, did Father McIntyre know? Meredith was doing very well for herself; she had a byline in the paper.

Tony's ears pricked up. He didn't know who Meredith was, but if she worked for a big paper maybe she could help him out. Someone needed to tell his family's side of the story. He'd later found her parents' number in the phone book and gave her a call.

He played with the beer mat on the table. He looked up, then back down again. "It's just…" He paused to stutter. Women liked that. "We're afraid my sister, the beautiful older sister who I adored, is being forgotten in all of this."

The waitress brought their drinks. "Want anything to eat?"

"No," Meredith said quickly. "Thank you." The last thing she wanted was Tony munching his way through the conversation. The waitress gathered up the menus and left. Meredith pulled a small digital recorder out of her bag and placed it on the table. "Do you mind if I record what you have to say? Helps me remember when I write up my article."

"Not at all." Tony sipped his beer.

"You're a good deal younger than Sophia," Meredith began.

"That's wrong," Tony said.

"I'm sorry. I thought you said..."

"She was born five years before I was. But I am much older than she will ever be."

Meredith dabbed at her right eye.

"I adored her," Tony said, "What was not to adore? She was beautiful, smart, and, above all, kind. She looked out for me. She taught me about girls, about the proper way to behave around them. My folks were pretty old-fashioned, they couldn't teach me much about dealing with modern women. I'll always be grateful that Soph was there to do that."

As he spoke Tony D'Angelo could almost believe himself. Sophia had never given him a minute of her time, and that had suited him just fine. One thing no one ever said about Sophia after she died was that she was a nasty-mouthed vindictive bitch. The first time he'd been interested in a girl, he'd been fourteen, awkward and shy, already wearing thick glasses and embarrassed about it.

The girl herself—he didn't even remember her name—had been all bones and angles and equally shy. The first time he brought her around to his house, Sophia, who at nineteen should have had better things to think about than ruining his life, whispered to her that Tony liked to masturbate with the door unlocked, hoping she'd walk in. He'd come back from the bathroom to find the girl gone, his confused mother holding a tray of pop and cookies, and Sophia with a self-satisfied smirk on her face.

That his parents had been old-fashioned was certainly true. He wondered now if part of the reason Sophia had turned out as mean as she was, was her way of getting out from under their control. Her curfew had been hours before her girlfriends', so she climbed out the bedroom window to head back to the party. She hadn't been allowed to date in high school, which meant she lied to the folks about where she was going and never brought her boyfriends home to meet them. Even he, the much younger brother, knew Sophia was a slut.

Everyone knew that.

Everyone but his parents.

Being a slut got her killed, Tony believed. She would have agreed to meet Desmond at the empty house. Probably said she needed to test out the bedrooms or even the kitchen floor before deciding whether or not to buy. And she ended up getting more than she bargained for. As for finding him creepy, the way her work friend had suggested? Ha, sweet little Sophia liked the creep factor, all the better to rub it into her parents' faces.

Although, try as she might, they never saw it.

He figured their old-fashioned ways caused her death. He'd told them so, on more than one occasion. He'd thrown it into their faces. They hadn't wanted her living in the big city, where she'd be away from their control, so they gave her money to settle in Trafalgar. If she'd stayed in Victoria, she would have settled down eventually. She would have married a nice Italian boy and had the pack of grandchildren his mother so desperately wanted.

"She was very popular at school," Tony said to Meredith. "All the kids loved her."

Well, the boys sure loved her. Not a word of that had come out after her death. Respect for the dead and all that. Tony had followed Walter Desmond's trial closely, his parents so wrapped up in their self-absorbed grief they didn't have a thought to spare for their surviving child.

He may have hated his sister. She might have been a slut and a thoroughly nasty person, but she didn't deserve to die; she didn't deserve to be murdered in the brutal way she was. At the hands of

Walter Desmond. Now Desmond was out of jail and, by all accounts, back in Trafalgar.

And every emotion, of hate for his sister, contempt for his parents, even a deeply suppressed guilt that as her brother he should have protected her—every feeling Tony D'Angelo had bottled up all these years was also back.

He felt something touch his hand. He blinked. Meredith had reached out and laid her fingers lightly on his. He realized his fists were clenched. Embarrassed, he pulled away. "This must be so terribly difficult for you," she said in her soft sympathetic voice. "I am in awe of the courage it must take to talk about it. I can see how deeply the pain still lies."

"Yeah," he said.

"Let me digest all this, and put down some ideas for my story. I think it might have national appeal."

"What does that mean?"

"I planned to write a little story for the local papers, sort of a tribute to Sophia. With Desmond getting off, there's potential for this to get attention all across the country, so I'm going to pitch it to my paper. People are interested in miscarriages of justice, but I'd like to remind my editors and the reading public that we mustn't forget the victim in all of this."

"The only *miscarriage*, as you put it, is happening right now. That man killed my sister and he's walking free."

"The appeal was very persuasive," Meredith said. "A witness was located who put Desmond far away from the scene of your sister's killing at the time it happened."

"Witnesses make mistakes. They can be bribed. They forget things. How come everyone's so quick to believe the cops screwed up twenty-five years ago, but this new witness must be on the level, eh? Tell me that."

Meredith backtracked as fast as she could. "I *totally* see what you're saying, Tony. Good heavens, that might be something to look into."

Tony saw the gleam in her eye. "Sorry. I shouldn't have shouted at you. I guess I get carried away when I think…"

"I understand." Meredith lifted her hand and indicated she was ready for the bill. "I'd love to have a picture of Sophia. The paper ran one the other day, but it was small and blurry. Do you or your parents have a nice one I can use? I can't promise to get it into the paper, you understand, but I'd like to know what she looked like. I'd like to understand her better."

"Sure." The bill arrived. Tony put up a token protest but, as expected, Meredith insisted on paying. "We can go around there now, if you like," he said.

"Your parents won't mind me dropping in unannounced?"

"They won't mind. We can walk. It's just a couple of blocks away."

They stepped outside and Meredith put on her sunglasses. "I haven't asked about you, Tony," she said. They walked up Elm Street and headed west on Front. "What do you do for a living?"

The sidewalks were busy with shoppers and those browsing and enjoying the day. The restaurant patios were full as people relaxed in the sunshine. The Mountain in Winter Gallery was open; the front window featured a single watercolor painting by Nelson artist Maya Heringa—sweeping strokes of blue and orange and green representing mountains and sky, trees and water.

"Did you hear what happened here Wednesday night?" Meredith said to Tony.

"No, what?"

"A woman was attacked in the alley. Thank goodness, a passerby ran him off, or who knows what might have happened."

"That's too bad," Tony said, not much interested. He stopped dead, the words caught in his throat. Up ahead a man and a woman were studying the menu outside a restaurant. The woman was middle-aged, tall and slim, but nothing worth a second glance.

The man, however…

If Tony D'Angelo had passed Walter Desmond in any other place at any other time, he wouldn't have given him a second glance. A lot of years had passed, and the man had changed. He was older, of course, but also much harder looking. His gray hair was cropped short and he was bigger than Tony remembered. Not bigger, as in fat, but in muscle.

"What's the matter?" Meredith asked.

"Will you look at that? As bold as brass. Walt Desmond himself."

"Heavens. I think you're right. Tony, don't do anything foolish."

He didn't hear her.

Chapter Twenty-two

Molly Smith was also watching Walter Desmond. Although she was trying very hard not to look as though she were. He was with one of the dragon boat women. They walked together like any long-time couple or two casual friends. They didn't touch, but kept in step and chatted. That is, the woman chatted, and her laughter drifted down the street, while Desmond looked around, wide-eyed. It made Smith think of herself the first time she'd been to Seattle on a visit to her grandparents. The child who'd always lived near a small town and grew up with the wilderness as her playground had been awed by the zooming traffic on the highway, the tall buildings stretching overhead. "Catching flies?" her older brother Samwise said, and she snapped her mouth shut. After sticking her tongue out at him first, of course.

She'd come out of the pedestrian walkway leading to the alley that ran behind the Mountain in Winter Gallery, thinking she could fry an egg under her Kevlar vest if she were so inclined, at the moment Desmond and the woman went past. The cops on the beat had been ordered to patrol the alleys and walkways regularly. That alley in particular was often used as a shortcut or as a place for shop employees to park. Not today. Today, everyone was spooked.

Most everyone, anyway. She'd run off a pack of teenage boys hanging around the back of the convenience store who said they were on guard. *Oh, great.* Fourteen-year-old vigilantes hopped up on testosterone and action movies. That was sure to end well.

The police had been ordered not to interfere with Walter Desmond in any way. Molly Smith had no intention of breaking that order. She hadn't seen Dave Evans or Jeff Glendenning since Thursday evening. She'd tossed and turned all that night (more like all morning, as she'd finished work as the sun was coming up) and eventually decided to say nothing about what had happened. Not to Evans or Glendenning or anyone. Glendenning was a sergeant and these days he was just filling in time waiting for retirement. Nothing she could do about him. But Evans was her contemporary, the same level as her, and they worked closely together. She'd be keeping her eye on him.

Desmond and his friend stopped at The Front Street Diner, where a section of the sidewalk had been marked out as a patio. Walt took off his hat and scratched at his short gray hair as they studied the restaurant menu displayed on a stand at the hostess desk. A couple, looking like they were back from a hike in multi-pocketed khaki pants and cotton shirts, thick socks, and solid boots, got up from a table, hefted their backpacks, and left. The hostess picked up menus and gestured to Walt and Carolanne to follow her.

Smith decided to head in the other direction. She'd cross at the intersection and walk back through town on the far side of the street. If she so much as looked at Walt Desmond sideways, he might think she was bothering him.

Before she could move, a man ran past, followed closely by, of all people, a worried-looking Meredith Morgenstern. Meredith caught Smith's eye and said, "There's going to be trouble."

The man grabbed Desmond's arm and spun him around. Desmond dropped his hat. "You bastard," the man yelled. "You murderous bastard."

Carolanne screamed. Passersby either leapt out of the way or gathered around to get a better view. Desmond had twisted out of the other man's grip and had his arm pinned behind his back before Smith could so much as blink, much less interfere.

Meredith had her phone out and held it up in front of her, snapping pictures.

"Break it up." Smith pushed her way through the crowd. "What's going on here?"

"That man," Carolanne yelled and pointed. "He attacked my friend for no reason at all."

The man struggled in Desmond's grip. With a single twist, Smith knew, Desmond could break his arm. The man looked at her. His eyes were dark, his hair black, his skin olive, living testimony to his southern European heritage. Smith's heart sank. This had to be the D'Angelo son. He looked a lot like his dad.

"Thank you, Mr. Desmond," Smith said. "You can let go now. There'll be no more trouble here."

Desmond stared at her for a long time. She did not look away. Then he shoved the man toward her. "I did nothing to him."

"Nothing! You call murdering my sister nothing? Arrest him," D'Angelo shouted at Smith, spittle flying, eyes red with rage. "He attacked me."

"Sir," Smith said, "you can't say that. I was standing right over there. I saw everything that happened. You ran at this man and you would have assaulted him had he not been faster than you. Is your name D'Angelo?"

"As I'm sure you know." He was considerably overweight, his face flamed red, and a vein pulsed in his forehead. Sweat dripped down his cheeks. He swiped his hand across his face.

Guy's a walking heart attack, Smith thought. "Why don't you come with me, Mr. D'Angelo? We'll go for a walk, let these people enjoy their lunch."

D'Angelo turned back to Desmond, who had pushed Carolanne behind him. Walt's face was perfectly calm: it showed so little emotion it might have been carved of granite. In contrast, Carolanne's eyes were wide with shock, her lip trembled, and her eyes filled with tears. D'Angelo clenched and unclenched his fists. He looked as though he might explode any second.

"Please, Mr. D'Angelo," Smith said, "if you attempt to continue this fight, I will have to ask you to come with me."

"You'd arrest me? And let that son of a bitch sit in the sun and have a drink?"

"Do you know his first name?" Smith whispered to Meredith.

"Tony."

"Tony, help me out here, please. Mr. Desmond has as much right to walk the streets as anyone else. Don't make an issue of it. Go home."

For several long seconds no one moved. Cars continued to drive by on the street, but a crowd was gathering. She heard whispers of "Poor Sophia" and "How dare he?" along with "Crooked cops." This could turn ugly in a flash. She touched her radio. Time to call for backup. Walter Desmond was clearly able to handle Tony D'Angelo, but she feared if it came to a fight, some of the men standing around might decide to jump in.

Tony pulled back his head and spat. A lump of phlegm landed at Walt's feet but he did not so much as flinch. He kept his expressionless eyes fixed on Tony.

"Stay out of my way, you murderous bastard." Tony turned and walked away. As he passed Smith he said, "Useless cops."

She looked at Walt. He nodded, ever so slightly.

"Okay, everyone, show's over. Break it up." People shifted their feet. They muttered to their neighbors. "Now!" she shouted. The back of the crowd began to peel away, and soon the street had returned to normal. Carolanne bent over and scooped up Walt's hat. She handed it to him, and he put it on his head without a word. On the other side of the street, Smith's mother stood in her shop doorway, watching. She held her phone in her hand.

Smith smiled to herself. She encountered plenty of problems policing in the small town where many of the residents had known her since she was a toddler, but there were advantages too. Such as Mom as backup.

"We'll pass on that lunch," Walt said to the hostess. "I've lost my appetite." He gave Smith a weak smile. "Looks like you've come to my rescue once again. Thank you." He walked away, head high, steps firm.

Carolanne hurried to catch up with him. Meredith took a step to follow but Smith glared at her. "Butt out, Meredith."

Meredith lifted one perfectly sculpted eyebrow. "Is that any way to talk to a member of the Fourth Estate?"

"Yes," Smith said.

"I'd better check to see if Tony's okay," Meredith said, making her retreat.

"About that lunch tomorrow," Smith called after her, "it's off." She'd been prepared to sit down with Meredith, talk about the old times, and catch up with their lives (not that she much cared what Meredith was up to). Seeing as how Meredith had managed to get herself involved in the D'Angelo/Desmond situation, no doubt digging for dirt to write a story, the more sensational the better, any gesture of friendship was not gonna happen.

Smith trotted after Carolanne and Walter. The woman had grabbed his arm. "Don't let them chase you away, Walt."

"Discretion," he said, "is the better part of valor."

Smith fell into step beside them. "Mind if I walk with you?"

"Not at all," he replied. "Happy to have you, in case I need a bodyguard."

The incident might never have happened. The crowd had dispersed as if into thin air, and no one was paying them any attention. No one, other than the young guy who dashed across the street the moment he caught sight of the uniformed officer heading his way, trailing the scent of pot behind him like a cloud.

"Why are you here, Mr. Desmond?" Smith blurted out without thinking. "You had to know feelings would be running high. That was Tony D'Angelo, Sophia's brother. What's he supposed to think, seeing you?"

"He's supposed to think it's a good thing an innocent man was exonerated. As is everyone else in this town."

"Are you that naïve?" Smith asked. "The D'Angelos have spent a lot of years hating you." The words spilled out, almost as if they were out of her control. It wasn't her place to editorialize on Walter Desmond's life decisions or on the psychology of the grieving family. "It's been the entire focus of their life for more than twenty years. They can't simply turn around and say all is forgiven, even if the courts can."

"But he didn't do it," Carolanne shouted. "Why can't people see that?"

"It's okay," Desmond said. "It was a mistake, coming here, to Trafalgar. I understand that now. My lawyers warned me against it. I'd liked it here. I'd been happy here. I'll be on my way tomorrow."

"No," Carolanne said. "Don't let them run you out of town. They'll forget soon enough and go back to minding someone else's business."

He smiled at her. "You have a good heart."

"I'll leave you now," Smith said. "Call us if you need us."

"Thank you," he said. "I didn't kill Sophia."

"I've read the summary of the appeal," Smith said. She wouldn't come right out and say she believed him, although she did.

"As I didn't do it, someone else did. Is your department going to be looking into that?"

"As far as I know, the case has been reopened."

"That's good," Carolanne said. "Soon as they catch the other guy, then everyone will know you're innocent, Walt."

Smith watched them walk away. They didn't touch, but it seemed as though they moved closer together.

She'd called Walt naïve, but that wasn't the right word. Hopeful, maybe. Carolanne, now, she was naïve. The chances of Winters finding the killer all these years later were pretty much nil. Without another man heading for prison, no one was going to let this go. And even if they were so inclined, Smith had recognized the look on Meredith's face as she snapped pictures of the two men facing each other down. She was determined to get the story, no matter how much trouble it churned up. Her pictures wouldn't look good on the front page of the *Gazette*. The muscle-bound ex-con and the much shorter, flabby man peering through his thick glasses.

Chapter Twenty-three

Detective Ray Lopez came into the office and tossed his jacket over his chair. "It's a scorcher out there, and they're calling for more of the same over the weekend. Getting anywhere with that?"

Winters rubbed his eyes. "Nowhere. What about you?"

"Might be. I had Merrill come in for a picture lineup, and showed her all the sex offenders we have on file. She didn't recognize anyone. I'm not surprised. Unlikely she got much of a look at him. Everything seems to have happened mighty fast. I also took the pictures around to your place to show them to Eliza. Hope that was okay," he mumbled. Lopez didn't have to ask. It wasn't up to John Winters, who had no role in this other than as husband of the victim, to object or not. "She couldn't pick out anyone definite either. However, I am hopeful about one thing," Lopez said.

"Yes?"

"I did a reenactment with Ron Gavin acting the perp, and it's possible, likely even, the guy put his hand on Eliza's car. He needed to brace himself to hold her in place. We got some good prints."

Winters smiled. Fingerprints from a car parked in a public place wouldn't be worth much in court, but it was a start, a good start, toward trying to identify the guy.

"Gavin's going to rush the prints. It helps that Eliza's car's so clean."

"She takes it to the carwash regularly. The drive-through, where not a human hand touches it."

"We also got some hairs off Eliza's shirt. She and Merrill both said the man had long hair. Longer than what's normal these days, anyway. I've sent them to the lab. I won't get the results as fast as the fingerprints, but they'll be worth more."

"Good work, Ray," Winters said. Eliza's hair was brown with caramel highlights. His, what he had left of it, was more gray than anything else and nothing anyone would call long. They had no pets, and Eliza wasn't ever inclined to stop and stroke a dog or cat on the street. When it came to people, she wasn't a hugger and it was highly unlikely she'd ever get close enough to any of her customers to transfer their hair to her. "They give you an approximation of how long it'll take?"

"To get the test results back? The fingerprints,

Ron's running them now. The hair, I'm hoping for within a couple of days."

Winters whistled. "That's fast."

"Attack on a cop's wife? Yeah, they can be fast."

"Thanks, Ray." Winters had no doubt his detective had pulled in a heck of a lot of favors.

Lopez glanced at the clock. It was after five. "Not my place to tell you what to do, but you should be off home. That case has waited twenty-five years."

"I appreciate the advice," Winters said. "I checked in earlier and fixed Eliza something to eat. She's resting, but her spirits are good."

"Glad to hear it. I'm going to type up my notes and then head off myself. Madeline's preparing a picnic supper to eat down by the lake. She says it reminds her of her childhood, before the days of home air conditioning, when the nights were hot and humid and her mother couldn't bear to be in the kitchen. Or even in the house."

"Nice memories," Winters said.

"Not really. Her mother always made fish paste sandwiches, soggy potato salad, and opened a can of fruit salad. To this day, Madeline hates fish paste and potato salad, and don't get me started on her opinion of canned fruit."

Winters laughed. "That's what family memories are made of. The good and the not-so-good."

"I can't imagine," Lopez said, "what it must be like for families like the D'Angelos where every memory gives nothing but pain."

"Got a minute?" Molly Smith appeared in the doorway. She'd taken off her Kevlar vest and was fanning herself with a piece of paper.

"Sure," Winters said. "Hot out there?"

"I might invent breathable bulletproof clothing. I'd make my fortune."

"I'll take a piece of that action," Lopez said. He moved to shut down his computer, but the e-mail program beeped to let him know he had a message.

"What's up, Molly?" Winters asked.

"Sophia D'Angelo's brother, Tony, attempted to assault Walt Desmond at the Front Street Diner this afternoon."

"Yes!" Smith and Winters turned at the shout to see Lopez leaping to his feet and punching the air. "Got him! The fingerprints on Eliza's car? A match. A known scumball by the name of Richard James Anderson. Anderson did three years in prison for sexual assault. He was released on parole six months ago. According to his parole records, his most recent address is given as…ta da…Trafalgar, British Columbia."

"Oh, yeah," Smith said. "We're aware of him. Makes my skin crawl just to look at him."

"I included a picture of him in the photo

lineup for Merrill and Eliza," Lopez said. "They didn't pick him out, but that's not surprising. Among other things his hair's a lot longer than when his mug shot was taken."

Good work." Winters got to his feet and reached for his jacket. "Let's pay a call on Mr. Anderson."

"I will pay a call," Lopez said. "You will stay here."

Winters dropped back into his chair. "Right."

"Looks like that picnic's going to be delayed. I'll let you know what Mr. Anderson has to say for himself. Molly, I need a uniform. Want to come along?"

"Wouldn't miss it."

"I want to hear what happened in town earlier, but there's no hurry," Winters said. "I'll be here for another hour or so. Fill me in if you get back in time, or give me a call at home."

"Will do," she said.

After Lopez and Smith left, Winters returned his attention to the old files.

Smith was back so soon, he knew they'd had no luck.

"Not at home. He has a basement apartment in a house that's been divided up. The landlady lives in one of the units and she was in. She said she hasn't seen him in a couple of days. We told her to call us soon as he comes back, but not to let him know we were asking."

"Think he's done a runner?"

Smith shrugged. "He kindly left his curtains open and so, with the landlady's permission, I took a peek through the window. All his stuff seems to be there. It's one heck of a mess, anyway. We've put a BOLO out on him and his car. Won't be long until we have him in our tender care, John."

He wasn't so sure of that. Some of these people seemed to be able to fly under official radar for a long time, particularly if they had friends of similar mind. He leaned back in his chair and ran his thumb across the surface of his watch. "Tell me about the incident earlier. Did they get into a fight? Walt Desmond and the D'Angelo brother? What's his name?"

"Tony. It wasn't much of a fight. Tony was so far outmatched it was almost funny. Walt swatted him away as though he was a pesky fly. Walt held him off, and that was all. I was no more than ten meters away, and saw the whole thing go down, so no one can get into a he said/he said game. I reported it, but it made me wonder if you're making any progress on Sophia's case."

"This sort of cold case is very time-consuming,

Molly. I have boxes and boxes of documents to wade through. I need to speak to the D'Angelos again, and I'm simply dreading it."

"My mom said something interesting about Sophia," Smith said.

"Go ahead." Winters often wished he could put Lucky Smith on the payroll. She wasn't a gossip, and she didn't interfere in people's private affairs, but she was a keen observer of human nature. She knew just about everyone in the Mid-Kootenays, and those she didn't know, weren't worth knowing. She was involved in many community groups and would be actively working for one side or another on just about any controversial issue that came up. She had a memory for people, and the things they said or did, as sharp as any he'd ever seen. Winters sometimes wondered how Paul Keller could keep up.

"Mom didn't know Sophia or her family, but she did know that not everyone thought Sophia was the paragon of virtue the papers painted her as. I've glanced over some of the reports. Everyone said what a nice person she was. That's normal in a high-profile case. I guess I'm just thinking if that wasn't true..."

"She might have had enemies," Winters said. A murder investigation was often about digging up the dirt. Uncovering hidden secrets. Secrets of the dead person; secrets of someone who might have wanted them dead; secrets, sometimes, of a great many innocent people. When a death was as brutal and widely publicized as this one had been, people believed it was important to show respect, not only for the deceased, but the grieving family. Anything, any rumor, any suspicion, which shone a bad light on the victim had to be buried deeply. It was an important skill for an investigating detective to be able to worm out dark secrets from a witness who might only be wanting to do what they saw as the right thing.

If there was one thing Doug Kibbens appeared not to have been it was a skilled interrogator.

"What are you thinking?" Winters asked.

"A boyfriend she ditched, maybe?" Smith said. "Someone's boyfriend she stole. Did you come across anyone like that?"

"The case was shoddy, Molly. And that's the problem. Kibbens questioned her current boy-friend. He worked as a bartender and was at home alone that afternoon. He had no alibi, but his clothes had no blood on them and his fingerprints were not found at the scene. He was soon elimi-nated from their inquiries. Then again, everyone, except for Walt Desmond, was eliminated almost immediately. There was, however, one point of interest. I passed over it thinking it wasn't signifi-cant, but you're reminding me. The boyfriend said he and Sophia had been going out for about three months, but he'd never met her parents. They, on the other hand, insisted she didn't have a boyfriend. She told her coworker her boyfriend had given her the missing bracelet, but her parents said Sophia had bought it for herself. There seems to have been no attempt, at least not that I can find, to locate any other boyfriends, either current or in her past. Sophia had been at university before moving back home in the summer, but it doesn't appear that Kibbens so much as attempted to contact anyone she might have known there."

"What about that boyfriend? Is he still around? Does he have anything to say?"

Winters shook his head. "I'd like to talk to him, but the file says he was from Australia. He left Trafalgar a few months after Sophia's death. The trail's going to be difficult to pick up."

"Here's an idea. The brother, Tony, was with Meredith Morgenstern when I saw them. She witnessed the altercation."

Winters groaned.

"That made me think. What about Tony or Gino D'Angelo? Were they ever considered suspects?"

"No. Tony was still in high school, and he was at basketball practice that afternoon. Gino worked for the city, he's an accountant, and was at his desk in city hall at the time his daughter died. Mrs. D'Angelo was home alone, but she'd phoned her mother to wish her a happy birthday at four, and the police have a record of the call. She used a landline. Not many people had cell phones back then."

"Sophia died on her grandmother's birthday? That's so sad. It was in January, right?"

"January 15." Winters sucked in a breath.

"What?" Smith said.

January 15. Where else had he seen that date recently? He swung back to his computer and scrambled through the files, while Smith watched with a questioning look on her face.

Sophia D'Angelo had been murdered on January 15, 1991.

Sergeant Doug Kibbens had died in a car accident, a suspected suicide, on January 15, 1992. Exactly one year later.

Coincidence? It could be. But John Winters didn't put much stock in coincidence. He opened the report on Kibbens' accident. He felt Smith's breath on his neck as she leaned over his shoulder to read along.

"That was the investigating officer?" she said.

"Yes." Kibbens' car had burned on impact but not been totally destroyed. A full forensic analysis of the wreck and the scene had been done. No evidence had been found pointing to any foul play or tampering of the vehicle. The brakes or brake lines did not appear to have been interfered with.

"Single-vehicle accident. Middle of the day. No witnesses," Smith said. "You think suicide?"

"Yeah. Barb says that's what they thought, too, but out of respect they covered it up in the report. No one can say for sure. He might have had a heart attack behind the wheel. There wasn't much left of him for the autopsy. It's the date that interests me. And it interests me a great deal. Anniversaries are important things. A year is nothing other than one more ride around the sun, but people remember dates. Birthdays. Weddings. Deaths. Sometimes deaths most of all."

"Why would Kibbens have killed himself on that day?"

"Precisely the question, isn't it? He was an experienced cop. He'd seen a lot. He'd spent some time in Edmonton and in Calgary. Big city, big-city crime. The D'Angelo scene was ugly and messy, but any cop who's attended at a traffic fatality has seen worse."

Smith grimaced.

"There was nothing about that case that should have bothered him so much he'd kill himself a year later. Unless…"

"Unless," Smith finished the thought, "he killed her himself."

Chapter Twenty-four

"You're sure you want to?" Walt asked. "I'll understand if you're tired."

"The wine's in the fridge. The team's not back yet. Let's have at it." Carolanne smiled as she tried to calm her pounding heart. She and Walt had come straight back to the B&B after the young policewoman left them. Walt had walked beside her, with little more to say than a casual comment about the weather and how long the heat wave might last. If she hadn't been there, if she hadn't been witness to that whole scene, that hideous fat man, the things he said, the horrible, horrible hostile crowd, she'd think nothing at all out of the ordinary had happened to Walt. If he didn't want to talk about it, she wouldn't make him, but she hadn't wanted to leave it hanging between them either. When they got in, she told him Darlene had put a bottle of nice wine in the fridge.

"I'll be right down," he said, and she ran to get the wine.

Mrs. Carmine was in the kitchen, sitting at the island in the center of the room sipping tea and reading a magazine. As Carolanne came through the door, silent in her running shoes, a look of pure irritation crossed the landlady's face. It was covered instantly, but not before Carolanne read a world of complaint. Mrs. Carmine hated running this B&B. She hated her guests and she hated her life. She put on her fake smile. A smile, nothing more than an upward twist of the lips, Carolanne realized, can hide a whole lot of hurt.

"Can I get you anything, dear?"

"No. No, thank you. I'm looking for the wine. Don't get up. I can get it."

"Is everything all right, dear?"

"Perfectly fine, thank you." Mrs. Carmine might hate running a B&B, but she and Carolanne had something in common: Carolanne hated staying in them. Give her a nice hotel, the more stars the better, any day. A place where the staff didn't poke their noses into your business or expect you to make conversation over the "home-cooked" breakfast with people in whom you had not the slightest interest. The team had booked the Glacier Chalet without any input from her, and Carolanne figured it wouldn't be so bad. With her friends staying there too, it would be more like being in a dorm than a stranger's house. She rummaged in the small fridge set aside for guests and found the bottle. Not even room service or a bar.

"I didn't hear the girls coming in." Mrs. Carmine put her magazine aside, making sure Carolanne realized what a great sacrifice it was. "I'll get some treats out for you."

"They're not back yet." Carolanne held up the bottle. "It's just for me. I mean for Walt and me."

Mrs. Carmine's right eyebrow rose. "I noticed you two going out for a walk earlier. Now, I never pry into my guests' lives, but are you sure it's wise to make friends with him, dear?"

"It's never a mistake to be kind," Carolanne said.

"So true. But, well, you must realize that he has a…difficult past."

"I know he went to prison for a crime he didn't commit."

"Didn't he? Oh, yes, he got out over some technicality…"

"Hardly a technicality. The police were found to have screwed up royally."

"Not for me to judge. But they haven't arrested anyone else, have they?"

"No," Carolanne admitted.

"That in itself should tell you something, dear. I hate to say it, this is such a peaceful town, at least it always has been. But you might not have heard about the unfortunate incident the night before last."

"What sort of incident?"

Carolanne could pretty much read the woman's face. Mrs. Carmine was torn between wanting her guests to feel safe, and thus not rush back to where they came from, and the desire to spread gossip. The latter won out. "A woman was attacked. She was in a back alley by herself and it was after dark, so I'm sure no one has anything to worry about. Not if you and your friends keep your wits about you."

"You mean it was her fault?"

"I didn't say that."

"She was alone after dark. Perish the thought."

Mrs. Carmine bristled. "You're twisting my words. All I'm doing is giving a word to the wise. Perhaps you don't want to be *alone after dark* with your new friend. I wonder where he was Wednesday evening. Have you asked him? Come to think of it, that was the day he arrived in town, wasn't it, dear?"

Carolanne walked out of the kitchen. What a nasty foul-mouthed old bat. For a moment she considered going up to her room and packing. She should leave, check into a hotel. No, if she did that, Mrs. Carmine would assume Carolanne was taking her advice and getting away from Walter.

"Here, let me take that." He reached for the bottle. "Everything okay?"

"Fine," Carolanne smiled. While she was getting the wine, Walt had run upstairs to use the bathroom. Hopefully, he hadn't heard any of that conversation. She studied his face. He smiled back at her. His eyes were warm and brown. How anyone could think that a man with eyes like that could do something so vile…

"I'm sorry about what happened earlier." He found glasses and poured their drinks. "I'm not the most popular guy around here."

"Forget her," Carolanne said.

"Forget who? Did she…" he jerked his head toward the kitchen, "…say something? I was talking about what happened in town."

"Oh, that. It doesn't matter."

"It doesn't matter to me, but I shouldn't have involved you. Constable Smith was right. I shouldn't have come back. I didn't…" he hesitated.

"You didn't what?" Carolanne said.

"I didn't expect to meet someone whose opinion about me I care about."

Carolanne glanced away, feeling heat rush into her face. She took a gulp of her wine.

"I'll leave in the morning," Walter said.

"No! I mean, no you can't let them run you out of town. Tomorrow's our open house. Come with us. Try out the boat. You'll have fun. When was the last time you were on the water? Oh, sorry, bad question."

He didn't seem to mind. He twisted his glass in his hand and studied the pale yellow liquid. Carolanne glanced outside. The windows of the common room gave a view over the garden. This was a big property, with an immaculate lawn and well-maintained flower beds lining a patch of deep woods. The grass had been mowed earlier, and birds hopped about searching for bugs or seeds blown in on the wind.

"The last time I was on the water?" Walt said. "Buddy of mine had a sailboat and he took Arlene and me out on the lake now and again. I liked it. He was a good guy. One of the only ones who stood by me even after I went away. He wrote for a few years, but then the letters got fewer and eventually stopped altogether. I'd love to come and see your boat, Carolanne." He looked up and gave her an enormous smile in a face full of joy.

Carolanne's heart leapt. And she realized she was falling in love.

Chapter Twenty-five

It was a great day for a festival. The sun shone in a cloudless sky and although it was still extremely hot, a soft, welcome breeze was blowing off the river. The park lining the riverfront was set up for a fair. Artists and craftspeople had erected tables and tents to display their goods, local farmers offered fresh produce, the library had a tent decorated with brightly colored balloons, designed to attract children. Smith spotted her mom, staffing the Women's Center booth and handing out pamphlets. The display was about childhood nutrition. Better for today, Smith thought, than the one they sometimes dragged out about domestic abuse. At the RCMP tent a community services officer was chatting to passersby. Their exhibit concerned safety on the water.

"Adam and Norman are doing a shift later," Smith said.

"You mean at the booth?" Solway replied.

"Yeah. Children love meeting the dog. Norman's a complete and total ham. He loves it almost as much as the kids. Adam would rather go to the dentist."

Solway grinned. "I bet a whole bunch of high school girls, and some of their mothers, will suddenly find a renewed interest in the importance of boating safety."

Adam did look mighty good in his uniform. At six-foot four and two hundred well-muscled pounds, with deep brown eyes, chiseled bone structure, and perfect teeth, he might have been a poster-boy for police recruitment.

"It's probably none of my business," Smith said, "but I've been wondering—"

"Why Francesca hasn't been around lately?"

"Uh, yeah."

"She found a new job, and her plans to move to Trafalgar got sidetracked." Francesca was Dawn Solway's girlfriend. They were unofficially engaged and had plans to marry when Francesca, an American lawyer, got through the paperwork to move to Canada and start looking for a job.

"Oh," Smith said. They walked on.

"I could point out that one of the partners in her new firm is responsible for the sidetracking. It's over between us."

"Sorry to hear that. Are you okay?"

"Thanks, Molly. I'm okay. Just as well. The relationship was getting more complicated than I was happy with anyway."

Judging by the wistfulness in Solway's voice, Smith doubted it, but she kept her opinion to herself. If Solway was looking for a shoulder to cry on, she knew Smith would be there for her.

They made their way through the happy crowds and down to the water. Two of the long, thin brightly decorated boats were pulled up to the dock, and several others were out on the river. Low, sleek and fast, they sliced through the water to the beat of the drum and shouts of the women.

"They sure can pack a crowd in those boats," Solway said. "If one capsizes it'll be a heck of a rescue operation."

Smith counted. Each boat had between fifteen and twenty women in it. As well as the two rows of paddlers, one person was sitting in a chair (a chair!) at the bow, facing backwards, beating a big drum and occasionally bellowing, and another was at the back, standing up to steer.

Each boat had an ornate, fearsome-looking dragon's head attached to the front. Smith and Solway headed for boat number three, the one crewed by the women staying at the Glacier Chalet. The sides were decorated with green decals representing dragon's scales; the creature's eyes were wide and his teeth displayed in an open mouth.

One of the women spotted them heading her way and hurried over to greet them. "Nice to see you, Officer. Are you here to try it out?"

"I'd like to. Please, call me Molly. This is my friend Dawn. It was Dawn's idea to come."

"Nice to meet you, Dawn. Welcome. I'm Darlene. Have you paddled before?"

Smith and Solway nodded in unison. "Kayaked anyway," Smith said. "A lot when I was young, not so much these days. Hard to find the time."

"You have to make the time, don't you? That's the great thing about being part of a team. No excuses allowed."

"Your boat's beautiful," Solway said.

Darlene couldn't have looked prouder if Solway had admired her firstborn child.

"Is the drum, like the dragon's head on the front, only for show?" Smith asked. "It looks mighty impressive."

"The drummer keeps the pace, which is important with so many people working in unison. Some coaches don't like them, though. They think a good team doesn't need external aids to work together."

"Like me. Hi, I'm Laura. Welcome."

"Laura's our coach," Darlene explained, "and she *really* doesn't like the drum."

"It adds unnecessary weight," Laura said. "For nothing but show. We're a highly competitive sport, not here to paddle in circles and splash each other."

Smith glanced at a boat pulling into the dock. As well as the team members identifiable in their matching shirts, it contained several teenage girls who were doing just that, laughing and splashing. And clearly having a lot of fun with it.

Laura grinned. "Don't mind me. I'm just an old curmudgeon. If people are interested in our sport, that makes me happy. Darlene why don't you get these two suited up?"

"I'll be the drummer," Smith said. "That way I'll get a comfortable seat."

Darlene laughed. "Oh, no you don't. Come on, I'll find you two life jackets and paddles. We'll be pushing off in a few minutes."

"Almost everyone who's been here today has some familiarity with boats," Laura said. "It's nice to see."

"That's Trafalgar," Solway said.

Laura studied Smith and Solway, and then she turned to Darlene. "These two look like they can handle it more than most beginners. Why don't you gather the team and take them out for a real paddle?"

Darlene grinned. "Good idea." She raised her voice. "My team! Everyone, let's line up."

Laura reached into the jumble of orange and black vests and pulled out two. "These should fit, give them a try." She tossed them to Smith and Solway, who slipped them on.

"Seems like I've been hearing about dragon boats a lot lately." Solway adjusted her straps.

"It's becoming huge," Laura said. "Not only in North America but all over the world. We're going to Italy for a big race in the fall."

"Wow, that's impressive," Solway said. "Can anyone put together a team and participate?"

Laura shook her head. "There are races at all levels, pretty much everywhere, but to compete in the international ones you have to qualify. We've done that."

"Congratulations," Smith said. "Quite an accomplishment."

Laura beamed. "Modesty forces me to add that we've qualified in our age group, the over fifties. Which is one of the great things about dragon boat racing. Anyone can find a team. Not everyone's here right now, but we have enough to take you out."

Something over Smith's shoulder caught Laura's eye and she shouted, "There you are. We're going out, get in line."

Carolanne was ready for a day on the water

in a ball cap, sunglasses, and her team uniform. A few people openly stared at the man with her but most minded their own business. Smith leaned over and whispered in Solway's ear. "Walter Desmond. Heading our way."

Solway muttered under her breath. "Why do you suppose he's still hanging around? Is he looking for trouble?"

Carolanne said something to him and pointed to the boat. He smiled at her and nodded. Almost reluctantly, she left him standing alone. "Hi. I'm glad you came," she said to Smith. She half-turned and glanced back at Walt, watching her. He gave her a reassuring wave and she smiled.

Smith and Solway exchanged glances. "I guess we know the answer to your question," Smith muttered.

"Are you both right-handed?" Laura asked.

"Yes," Solway said.

"I can paddle either," Smith said.

"Okay, in that case you can be together in the back." She eyed the women who'd fallen into two neat rows, all of them holding paddles and putting on their life jackets. Laura told a couple of them to switch places, and then said, "Let's go." The women walked out onto the dock and Smith and Solway fell in behind. "Here," Laura said, "you'll want these." She handed them each two small padded orange cushions. "Those seats get mighty hard. I'm going to steer today, although Nancy usually does it, and I'll keep an eye on you two. We can do without the drummer."

The women slipped off their shoes and climbed into the boat. Holding carefully onto the gunwales, Smith and Solway stepped cautiously down the length of the boat to the backseat. The paddle felt comfortable in Smith's hand. She dipped it into the water and pulled a stroke. The sun was hot on her head and sunlight danced on the water. People had gathered on the banks to watch them. She waved, although she didn't know who she was waving to.

"Reverse slowly," Laura called. The boat began to move. They backed away from the dock and Laura said, "Hold the boat." They thrust their paddles into the water, holding them down. "Let's go. Slowly."

They headed to the middle of the wide river. Laura said, "Half speed," and they glided forward. They moved over the calm water much faster than in a single-person boat. Churned up by the women's paddles, the water was moving swiftly by the time it got to Smith. All she had to do was paddle. Unlike in a canoe or kayak the steering was done by the person standing at the back. All the paddlers did was provide the power.

"Eighty percent," Laura called. The women dug in and they skimmed over the water.

"This is a heavy boat," Laura said. "We only have fourteen people on board. A full complement is eighteen paddles, so each person is doing more." Smith threw a glance at Solway. Her face was intense as she moved with the rhythm.

"Full forward," Laura yelled, and the paddles picked up their pace. "It's as much about backs and hips as shoulders and arms," Laura said. "Swing those hips. Ribs touching thighs."

Smith watched the women seated ahead of her. They lifted half off the seat with every forward movement and bent far over. They moved in unison, arms and bodies and paddles, forward, back, over, and up. The boat skimmed across the surface of the water. She felt exhilarated, part of something bigger than herself. She hadn't been out on the water at all this year, and knew she'd be feeling this workout tomorrow.

They paddled under the big black bridge leading out of town, to where the river widened even more. They passed a blue dragon boat that was heading back, and the women booed each other with much laughing and good-humored jeers. They approached an orange buoy, and the boat began to turn, keeping close to it. Smith glanced over her shoulder. Laura stood in the stern, feet firmly planted apart, arms pulling at the tiller, her face set in concentration. She caught Smith watching her and grinned.

"Enjoying it?"

"It's great. How long's a race?"

"Two hundred and fifty meters, five hundred, or two thousand." The first two would be about speed, the latter endurance. "The two kilometer races have several turns, lots of chances for collisions in the turn. All part of the fun."

They paddled up and down the river several times, then Laura called for them to take it easy and she steered the boat toward the dock. They tied up and everyone got off.

Solway was almost glowing. "That was great. Thanks for taking us out."

"My pleasure," Laura said. "Glad you enjoyed it."

They found their shoes and slipped them on. It had been fun, Smith thought, lots of fun, but she didn't think dragon boating was for her. She preferred the solitude of kayaking. Being alone in the boat, maybe with one other person. Kayaking, to her, was about the wilderness, the peace and quiet, the solitude, the chance of seeing a bear fishing or a moose tugging at water weeds. Not people lining the shore cheering you on or twenty women packed together, working as hard as they could.

Dawn Solway, clearly, didn't agree. "I'm a convert. Let's do it, Molly. I wonder how much one of those boats cost? Probably not a lot, no engine or moving parts. We can put together a police team. It'd be great for teambuilding, the chief's big on teambuilding these days, and some of the guys, no names mentioned, are in need of a good workout."

"We only have twenty officers," Smith pointed out. "And we can't all be out in a boat at the same time. We'd need the entire force and some of the civilian staff. Can you see the chief and Barb putting their backs to it?"

"We can ask the Horsemen, too. Or maybe call it an emergency services team and invite fire and the paramedics. It would be great to have Adam on. Do you think he'd like that?"

No, Smith thought, but didn't say. "You could teach Norman to do the drumming. I can't see him handling a paddle."

Solway laughed and Smith smiled at her friend. When Dawn Solway got an idea into her head, she didn't let it go. The Trafalgar Emergency Services Dragon Boat Team would be a reality before the end of the summer. Smith wondered how the heck she was going to be able to get out of it.

As Solway predicted, a crowd of women of all ages had materialized at the RCMP booth. Norman sat proudly beside the table, resplendent in his police vest, accepting praise and admiration. Adam shifted awkwardly in his big boots and tried not to look as though he'd rather be just about anyplace else. Catching sight of Smith and Solway watching him, he broke into a huge smile and waved enthusiastically. They waved back.

"Wanna go over and say hi?" Solway said.

"Nope. Let him suffer. I'm starving. Let's get something to eat."

"Good idea."

They made their way across the park to the food stands, where they deliberately avoided the truck offering freshly prepared organic salads and rice bowls in favor of the barbeque line.

Smith happily added the full arrangement of condiments to her hot dog and was taking her first big bite when she noticed Walt and Carolanne studying the food truck menu. A man came up to Walt, and Smith lowered her hot dog, hoping she wouldn't have to intervene. Instead, the man stuck out his hand. Walter looked genuinely surprised, and then he took the offered hand in his. They exchanged a few words, the man slapped Walt on the back, and he walked away. Carolanne beamed from ear to ear.

"Not everyone wants to see Desmond run out of town," Solway said.

"No," Smith said, "but those who do are not going to be happy as long as he's here."

Walt and Carolanne ordered rice bowls and carried them back to the boat dock.

"Gotta run," Solway said, wiping mustard off her hands onto a napkin. "Afternoon shift." She tossed the napkin into a trash container. "Will you look at that? There's something I never thought I'd live long enough to see."

"What?"

"Over at your mom's booth."

Smith choked on the last mouthful of bun.

Trafalgar's Chief Constable Paul Keller, dressed in jeans and a tee-shirt, stood in front of the table under the Trafalgar Women's Center banner. He handed out brochures to women and men pushing strollers, smiled at babies, and discussed the benefits of early-years nutrition.

"I wondered how much longer he could resist getting involved in Mom's activities," Smith said.

"Think he'll be campaigning for marijuana legalization soon, or for an end to fracking?"

"If Mom has anything to say about it, he will," Smith said with a laugh.

Chapter Twenty-six

John Winters threw the newspaper onto his boss' desk.

"I saw it," Keller said. "I danced the jig when that woman left town. She's back, is she?"

"Meredith's parents live here," Winters said. "Natural enough for her to visit. Just our bad luck the Desmond story broke at the same time."

The front page of Monday's *Gazette* contained a color picture of a pretty young woman. It was a university graduation photo, the woman smiling shyly from beneath the flat-topped hat, a blue robe draped across her shoulders, proudly clutching a diploma tied in red ribbon. Winters had seen the original of that photo a couple of days ago. In the D'Angelo living room. Sophia.

The story consisted mostly of Tony D'Angelo's memories of his sister, accompanied by a sidebar that was nothing more than a rehash of the old case updated with the news of Walter Desmond's appeal and pardon.

"Could have been worse," Keller said. "Although we don't need people seeing this picture and then looking out their window to see Walt Desmond stroll by."

"It is worse," Winters said. "Meredith works for a tabloid in Montreal. They ran the same story yesterday, only that one was heavy on police incompetency."

Keller groaned. "We can pick our poison. Everyone who believes the police did their job will want to string Desmond up. His defenders will be baying for *our* blood. You getting anywhere?"

"Friday afternoon, I came across an interesting tidbit." Winters explained about the circumstances around Doug Kibbens' death and the significance of the date. "I have his case notes, sparse as they are. I want a look at any personal items he might have left behind. I've got someone down in the dungeons of the city hall basement searching this morning. His ex-wife didn't want any of his things, so Barb tossed the contents of his drawers into a box and had them put into storage."

"What do you hope to find, John?"

Winters shrugged. "I'd like to know what he was thinking. Maybe get some clue into why he killed himself. If he did. This morning, I'm going out to talk to Jack McMillan again. He won't like it, but I have questions about Kibbens."

"It's got to be done," Keller said. "We knew they were close. At work and as friends."

"I debated all weekend about the best way of approaching the D'Angelo family again. Sophia's father Gino is nothing but hostile and, to be honest, I'm afraid of him having a heart attack and us being blamed for haranguing them.

"Did you see Molly's report on an altercation between Tony D'Angelo, Gina's brother, and Desmond on Friday?"

Keller's face was grim. "I did."

"I want to talk to him. A brother's more likely to know what was happing in his sister's life than the parents were. I don't want to go to the house. I'm going to call Tony and ask him to come in later today."

Keller nodded. "I saw Desmond at the park on Saturday."

"What was he doing there?"

"Nothing but what everyone else was. Having a good time. No one bothered him, and I saw a couple of guys around his age talking to him, without trying to take a swing. He spent most of his time with a woman in a dragon boat team uniform. Mid- to late fifties, tall and slim, brown hair. You know anything about her?"

"Molly's report on the altercation with Tony

mentioned Desmond was with a woman at that time. Might be the same one."

"I just wish he'd leave. If the rest of the media pack picks up Meredith's story, they'll be descending on us like the plague of locusts they are. We can handle questions about the case. I want to get to the bottom of it myself, but having Desmond here raises everyone's emotions." Keller rubbed his eyes. "At times like this, retirement is looking mighty good. How's Eliza?"

"She's planning to go into the gallery this afternoon. Her spirits seem good and no lasting physical damage was done."

"You don't sound entirely sure of yourself, John."

"I'm not. I suggested we do something yesterday, get out of the house, maybe go for a hike or drive to Nelson for lunch, but she said she'd rather stay home and read, which is unusual on a nice summer's day. I offered to drive her into work this afternoon, and she laughed me off. I wonder if she's dealing with it as easily as she thinks she is, or mentally shoving it under the carpet. I've tried to talk it over, and she gives me a little laugh and says all's well that ends well and finds some excuse to leave the room."

"Do you think Victim Services might be able to help?"

"I suggested it. She refused outright."

"She hasn't led a sheltered life, as you well know, John. Maybe she can handle it in her way. If you need any time…"

"Thanks, Paul."

Barb's head popped around the door. "I just got a call. Rose D'Angelo's been rushed to hospital. They suspect it's a stroke."

"That can't be good. She's had one before," Keller said.

"She went to the mailbox and got the day's newspaper. Opened it to see Sophia's picture on the front page. Her son says she cried out and dropped on the spot."

Keller shook his head. "It never ends. Not for them. Keep me posted, Barb. John, ask Ray to come in, will you? I want an update."

"He's got his eye on a known offender by the name of Anderson. But Anderson seems to have gone to ground."

"He'll pop back up soon enough. They always do. You'd better take a uniform with you to call on McMillan. He won't be happy to see you."

"What a dump," Molly Smith said. The truck jerked and buckled as it bounced over potholes in the yard. "McMillan can't be short of money; he must be on full pension. You'd think he could fix the place up."

"Takes more than money," Winters said. "Takes interest too."

"Nice piece of property, though," Smith said. At the end of a little-traveled road, nestled into the slope of the mountain, surrounded by thick forest, this could be a dream home for an escapee from the city. Too bad about the crumbling house, the bare dusty yard, the weed-choked driveway, and the piles of junk everyone. "Can't imagine the people in that nice big house we just passed are happy being next to this eyesore."

"I can't imagine McMillan cares whether they're happy or not."

The door of the house opened, and two dogs ran out, barking and snarling. "Wait," Winters said. "I don't think he'd be stupid enough to set those dogs on us, but accidents do happen, don't they?" He rolled down the window. Smith left the engine running.

Jack McMillan sauntered onto the porch. He stood watching, while his dogs leapt against the sides of the truck, barking and showing their teeth.

"I'm not playing this game," Winters said. "I'm getting out." He unzipped his jacket. "Shoot if you have to."

"Careful," Smith said.

"I mean shoot the dogs, not McMillan."

"I got that, Sarge, thanks."

Winters opened the passenger door. The dogs stepped back, but they continued barking. "Call them off, Jack," Winters shouted. He put a foot on the ground.

McMillan whistled. These were two well-trained animals. They ran straight to their master, the older one limping slightly. McMillan gestured for them to go into the house, and he closed the door behind them. Smith got out of the truck. Together she and Winters walked across the yard to meet McMillan halfway. Dust rose at their feet and the sun was hot on their heads.

"Can't be too careful these days," the old cop said. "You never know what sort of lowlife will come snooping around." He dug in his shirt pocket and pulled out matches and a pack of cigarettes. He lit up. He looked at Smith, stared too long to be polite. She forced herself to not look away.

"Cops need girls these days to protect them?" he said at last.

"I want to talk to you about Sergeant Doug Kibbens," Winters said.

McMillan took a long drag. The eczema on his right hand was bad. "Good officer. Good man. Steady. Loyal." Another look at Smith. "Tough as nails. Not like the ones you get these days. You've mussed your lipstick, sweetie."

She said nothing. She didn't wear lipstick on duty or off. McMillan was trying to bait her, plain and simple. She wouldn't give in. His world was fading fast, and they were all better for it.

"Hot out," Winters said.

"Suck it up," McMillan replied. "You step one foot in my house and my dogs'll rip it off."

"Sergeant Doug Kibbens died in a car accident a year after the D'Angelo killing."

A shadow passed behind McMillan's eyes. "Yeah, he did. Musta slipped on a patch of ice, went through the barrier and over the side of the mountain. Not much left of the poor guy once he hit bottom."

"That's not true," Winters said. "And you know it. It was middle of winter but the road was bone dry. No skid marks. I'm wondering why the department covered it up."

"What the hell does it matter to you? He had a heart attack. Maybe he tried to avoid a moose. Maybe he dropped a lit cigarette into his lap and lost control. You ever lose control, Sergeant? Must be easy to lose control working around chicks all day. You always obey orders, Constable?"

"Fuck you," Smith said, immediately wishing

she could take back the words. No need to play straight into his misogynistic, mean-spirited hands.

McMillan laughed. "I like ones with spirit, too."

"I get the point," Winters said. "You don't want women on the job. I'm guessing you don't want anyone who doesn't have the same color skin as you either, but that's not why we're here. Tell me about Sergeant Kibbens. You said he was a good cop. I've read his service record. It's a good one. He had a good career."

Smith said nothing. She'd also looked up Kibbens' record. Undistinguished, was the word that came to mind. Nothing detrimental, either.

"You got that right at least," McMillan said. "Doug knew how to get things done. He got results."

"Was he the sort to worry about how he got those results?" Winters asked.

"By the time Doug died, things were changing. More rules, what they call more 'civilian oversight.' What I call a bunch of busybodies interfering in what's none of their business." Another glance at Smith. "Standards slipping. I was in Vancouver couple of months ago. Saw a cop out on the street. Guy musta been about five four. I thought he was a kid playing dress-up at first."

Jack McMillan was nothing but a seething

mass of resentment. What on earth, Smith thought, did it matter to him, or to anyone, if a police officer was short? She'd known short guys with black belts and tall husky ones who tripped over cracks in the sidewalk. McMillan wasn't any older than her mom or dad, were Andy still alive. There were lots of things Lucky and Andy liked about the modern world—human rights, for one thing—and lots they didn't. Even Lucky had been heard to say kids these days were rude and self-absorbed. But she took the good with the bad and got on with her life.

Smith glanced around the yard. The dark forest closed in around them. No potted plants, no flowers. Just dust and weeds, rusting machine parts, and collapsing outbuildings. McMillan sat up here on his mountain at the end of the road, alone with dogs he'd trained to be as mean as he was, and seethed.

What a waste of a life.

"Look, Jack," Winters said, "level with me. You must have wondered about Doug's death. Was he having problems, money problems, maybe? Anything happen to upset him or anything to be depressed over?"

"You don't get it, do you, Winters? Men like Doug didn't get depressed. They had a problem, they took care of it. End of story."

And that, Smith thought, was the problem in

a nutshell. When they couldn't take care of it, or talk to anyone about it, they fell apart. And they ended up swallowing their gun or sailing over the edge of a mountain.

"Did he take care of it?" Winters said. "Was Sophia D'Angelo a problem for him?"

Smith might have expected McMillan to lash out at Winters. But he didn't. He just looked away, into the woods, and scratched at the rash on his hand. Inside the house the dogs had stopped barking. Birds sang in the trees at the edge of the forest, otherwise all was quiet. "You got nothin' Winters. Nothin'. The case was over. The man arrested, found guilty, put in prison where he belonged. All you're going to do is blacken the name of a good cop. Attack a man who can't answer for himself. Forget about it."

"You know I can't do that. If Walt Desmond didn't kill Sophia," he put up his hand, "and I'm not saying that's what I believe, I'm saying that's what the courts say. If Desmond didn't do it, someone did. The case is open, and it's on my desk. If you can help me, I'd appreciate it. That's all."

"I can't help you. I said it all at the time. Doug's death has nothing to do with that case. There are three hundred, sixty-five days in the year. That he had his accident on that particular day means nothing. Now, get off my property."

"If you remember anything…" Winters said.

"You'll be the first I call. Yeah, right."

Winters gave Smith a nod. They turned and headed back to the truck.

"Sorry to hear about the wife," McMillan called after them. "They say she wasn't badly hurt. That's what you get when the police can't run troublemakers out of town because they're afraid of hurting someone's feelings."

Chapter Twenty-seven

Eliza thought she didn't look too bad. Careful application of makeup hid the remains of the bruises on her face and after a lifetime on the catwalk she knew how to walk without showing pain or discomfort, no matter how bad it might be.

And, compared to some of the clothes and shoes she'd had to wear over the years, this wasn't bad at all.

She'd driven toward the alley at the back of the gallery as she always did, but as she approached her parking space, her heart rate sped up, and a tightness filled her chest. She circled around to Front Street and found a place close to the gallery. If she got a ticket for overstaying the time limit, too bad, she could afford it. Assuming the bylaw officer would even ticket her. No doubt they all knew her car. Ray Lopez had returned the BMW, after doing whatever he needed to do with it to gather evidence.

Evidence. They'd wanted her to go to the hospital. Get checked out. She'd refused. She did not want them touching her, collecting their evidence. Her body was not a crime scene.

It had been once, a long time ago. Never again.

It happened before she met John. She'd been a wide-eyed innocent, fresh from small-town Saskatchewan, plunged almost overnight into the glamorous world of high-fashion and modeling. She'd gone on a date one evening with a man she'd met at a party. A nice meal in an expensive, hugely popular new place, and then a walk in the park after dinner. He was in his fifties, and said he could do great things for her career. Her agent had told her to be "nice" to men with influence. She'd been trying to be nice.

He'd raped her in a quiet patch of woods. He hadn't so much as attempted to seduce her. He'd simply knocked her to the ground, torn at her clothes, and had sex with her. Then he'd gotten to his feet, adjusted his trousers, and said he'd drive her home now.

She called the police. They took her to the hospital where her body had been treated as a crime scene, and nothing else. Embarrassed, humiliated, the only person she called was her agent. The agent arrived, absolutely furious. Furious at Eliza for reporting the incident to the police. The officers themselves hadn't seemed to much care. A detective went around to the man's house. He told them Eliza had led him on, hoping he'd find her modeling gigs. What was he to do? What would any red-blooded man do? They'd had a look at her, hadn't they? Looks a heck of a lot older than eighteen, doesn't she?

She hadn't been there, of course, but she could imagine the chuckling and elbow-nudging and winking that went on. His word against hers, the detective told her. She could insist on pressing charges, but how would that look, her name dragged through the courts?

Her named dragged. As though she herself were the criminal.

She'd tried, and largely succeeded, in not thinking about it over the years. She saw the man occasionally, at industry parties, business meetings, on photo shoots. He'd tried to talk to her once, and she'd turned and walked away. He'd been killed in a car accident a couple of years later, and she'd surprised herself at how delighted she'd been to hear the news.

Things had been so different the other night. The police treated her with respect. They believed (or pretended to believe) every word she said. They respected her wishes, and asked her what she wanted to do. No one had so much as suggested that she'd wandered out her back door and decided on the spur of the moment to have sex with a passing stranger before changing her mind and crying rape.

Why was that? she wondered. Why so different from the other time? Was it because this was a small town, and they all knew her. Or knew, more to the point, knew her husband? Was it because she was older and had money and influence? Or was it because times really had changed? And that one of the biggest changes was that one of the officers at the scene had been female?

Eliza sat in her car and studied the street. People passed by, many of them smiling and chatting, no one in a hurry, most dressed in colorful, comfortable summer clothes. A young couple walked hand in hand, the girl in a long flowing skirt made from patches of mismatched fabric, and a tight tank top that showed full breasts, and arms and shoulders covered with colorful tattoos; the boy with a scraggy unkempt beard, baggy pants, and a tee-shirt advertising a motorcycle company. A tall black woman, her head of curly hair dyed pure white, pushed a baby stroller, and chatted with a white woman with multiple piercings and hair too black to be found in nature, holding an excited little boy firmly by the hand.

Two men, one of whom was dressed in a dark

business suit, the other in ironed trousers and an open-necked shirt, stepped out of the way of a group of middle-aged women in yoga gear, carrying mats under their arms and coffee cups in their hands.

Eliza sat in her car, her hands on the wheel. On one side of her art gallery the patio at the Front Street Diner was full, on the other side patrons streamed in and out of Crazies Coffee. From where she was parked, she could see down the hill to the river. The water wasn't blue but green, reflecting the steep mountainside filling half the sky. She lived on that side of the river, partway up that mountain. She could go home, just drive away. Go home and bury herself in her duvet and pillows.

An elderly couple, their clothes speaking of money to spend, stopped at the Mountain in Winter Gallery. They studied the Heringa painting in the window. The woman said something, and the man nodded. They went inside. Eliza could see Margo crossing the floor to greet them.

She'd told Margo she'd be at the gallery in time to relieve her for the afternoon. No doubt Margo had made plans for her time off. She'd be expecting Eliza. If Eliza didn't come, she'd phone John.

Eliza took a deep breath. She peeled her hands off the steering wheel, one at a time. John had offered to drive her to work today. She'd told him not to be silly. She wished he were here now.

She opened the door of her car. She put one foot on the pavement, and then the other. She got out. She closed the car door. She breathed. No one was paying her any attention at all. She told herself she was in Milan, about to go on the catwalk for Versace's spring show. Two weeks ago, she'd been in Paris, enjoying a few days off. She'd gone bike riding along the Seine with a couple of friends. She'd swerved to miss an elderly man who'd stepped into her path and she'd fallen, tumbling over the handlebars of her bike. She'd broken two ribs. The pain had been excruciating. It still hurt like heck, but she had a job to do. She was a professional.

Eliza Winters smiled and sailed into her art gallery, head up, back straight, steps firm and sure.

Chapter Twenty-eight

To his considerable surprise, Walt had had a lot of fun on the weekend. On Saturday, he'd gone with Carolanne to the dragon boat fair because it was important to her. It had been nice to stand in the sun, to watch families chattering and children playing. He would have loved a hot dog from the barbeque cart, but Carolanne went straight to the food truck and he'd been happy to follow. People looked at him, some openly staring, some glancing quickly away, but he was getting used to that. A few people came up to him to say hi, and a couple of guys even shook his hand and said they were glad he was back. He hadn't recognized them, but he'd pretended to. When he saw the police tent, he'd been about to turn away, walk in the other direction. But then he realized the dog was paying him not the slightest bit of attention, and neither had the big cop. Probably because he'd been far more interested in observing the progress of the pretty young policewoman who'd come to Walt's aid the other night.

Walt watched Carolanne in her boat with her teammates. She glowed on the water. Her bronzed skin, her brown hair streaked with gold, her long legs and strong arms. She'd enjoyed taking people out on the water, showing them how to get in and out of the low boat, how to paddle, to listen to the beat of the drum telling them what to do.

That night, she'd gone out with her friends for dinner, but he declined to join them. He'd had enough of being outside for one day. Walking the streets, standing on the soft green grass of the park, eating what and when he wanted, going where he wanted. It was all a new experience for him, and he found it exhausting.

The team had relaxed on Sunday. What they called relaxing, anyway. Several of the women shopped for a picnic and then went hiking in the mountains. Walt and Carolanne stayed behind and spent a quiet day, reading in the shade of the garden, going for a walk into town. He'd kept an eye out for Tony D'Angelo and anyone else who might be up to causing trouble, but the day passed without incident. From what Walt could tell, the mood in town was shifting in his favor, probably as people were reading up on the case and the results of the appeal. Still, he knew never, never to let his guard down.

Monday was the final day of the dragon boat training. Carolanne and her team had their last race this afternoon, and they'd be leaving in the morning, heading back to their regular lives.

Time for him to be going, too. But he had no regular life to go back to.

Would he ever?

Louise was confident the government would settle. The payout was likely to be substantial, maybe as much as the five million she'd asked for.

He'd come to Trafalgar determined to find out *why*. But now, he wasn't so sure it mattered anymore. Knowing why Kibbens and McMillan had worked so hard to convict him wouldn't turn back the clock. It wouldn't bring Sophia D'Angelo to life, or put Walt back in his chair in the real estate office, or give Arlene the will to keep on living. Spending time with Carolanne and her friends had reminded him that life could be about simple pleasures. Maybe he could have a life after all.

Five million bucks was more than enough to give a man a new life.

Would that life include Carolanne?

Walt shook his head. No. The cloud of all that had been done to him, of the years he'd lost, of the years Arlene had lost because of him, would hang over him always. He couldn't...he wouldn't...ask Carolanne to share that burden with him.

Chapter Twenty-nine

Waves of rage radiated out from John Winters. Smith maneuvered the truck around the potholes in Jack McMillan's yard and down the steep, crumbling mountain track. She hit a particularly big depression and felt the jolt run up her spine.

"Do you think…?" she said, summoning her courage.

"No, I don't think McMillan had anything to do with the attack on Eliza. He wouldn't dare, for one thing. He was only trying to get my back up. He certainly succeeded in that." Winters took a deep breath. "I've been told conscious breathing helps control anger."

"It does," Smith said.

"Another sign of how soft police officers are these days," Winters said, taking another breath. "Okay, anger over."

"Waste of time," Smith said.

"Anger or that visit?"

"Both, I guess."

"I'm not so sure. He made one extremely interesting comment. McMillan remembers the exact date Kibbens died. He remembers it so well, he mentioned it. Which means that he thinks about it, and he thinks about it a lot. All these years later he's still thinking about it. The date's so important to him he had to make a point of telling us that it wasn't important. Let's make a stop at Big Eddies, Molly. I think we deserve a drink after that."

They got their drinks, coffee for him, tea for her, and Winters walked the one block back to the office, while Smith took the truck out on patrol. The only call she got all morning was an out-of-control bicycle careening down the steep mountainside streets. A parked car ended the bike's journey before it could go over a cliff. The woman riding the bike broke her arm and left for hospital in the back of an ambulance.

Smith headed back to the station for lunch. She parked the truck and was coming in the back when Dave Evans walked out. She hadn't seen him since that incident in the alley on Thursday, and had been glad of it. They eyed each other. She waited for him to speak.

"I was expecting to be called into the chief's office," Evans said at last.

She shrugged.

"You didn't report it?"

"Do you think I'm a rat?"

"Maybe I did," he said. "Thanks."

"Jeff will be retiring soon. He doesn't have much to lose if he has a black mark on his record. But you? Why would you do something like that?"

"I said thanks, Molly. Doesn't mean I have to explain myself to you."

"You interfere with Walter Desmond again, and I will report it."

"That's always assuming you find out about it." He pushed his way past her. "I'm on the street today. Call me if you need backup."

She watched him go. Another swaggering macho jerk.

"Joanne found what she thinks you're looking for," Jim Denton said from the dispatch desk as Winters walked in with his coffee. "She put it on your desk. You might want to wear a mask, all the dust that trailed in behind it. Probably full of spiders and dead bugs, too."

"I'd ask if you're always so cheerful," Winters said, "but I know the answer to that one."

Denton chuckled.

"Are you getting any calls about Walter Desmond?" Winters asked.

"You mean other than the CBC wanting to interview the chief?"

"TV or radio?"

"Both. The cameras will be here at three."

"Too bad I have an appointment at the hairdresser at that time," Winters said, rubbing his short salt and pepper hair.

"A couple of calls, yeah. One or two asking why we haven't run him out of town, and a couple assuming that I'm interested in their opinion of a miscarriage of justice and the incompetence of the TCP. Why's he here, John? Do you think he's trying to make some sort of statement?"

"I haven't even met the guy, so I have no idea. Eventually, I'm going to have to talk to him about what happened that day and I'm taking bets he's not going to be happy about that. I'm trying to get all my facts organized before I meet with him."

The desk phone rang, and Denton reached for it.

Winters stuck his head into Barb's office. "I have an appointment with Tony D'Angelo in ten minutes. Once that's finished, do you have time to go through Kibbens' effects with me? You might see something I'll miss."

"Sure. Give me a buzz when you're ready. The boss has a TV interview this afternoon. I don't know why they're bothering to send someone all this way to hear him say he cannot comment on an active investigation."

"Perhaps they're hoping for a shot of you in the background, Barb."

"Aren't you the charmer," she said, trying not to look pleased.

The box squatted in the center of Winters' desk. It was covered in a layer of dust and sealed with tape. *Sgt. D. Kibbens. Jan. 1992* had been written on the top and sides in thick black marker.

Winters studied it. It wasn't much larger than a shoe box and looked as though it hadn't been disturbed since it was packed away all those years ago. He was tempted to open it and have a quick peek, but held himself back. Better to have the first look with Barb beside him to answer any questions he might have.

A few minutes later his desk phone rang. Denton informed him that Tony D'Angelo had arrived, and Winters went to the lobby to meet him and take him to the witness interview room.

The meeting did not go well. Tony was hostile, and almost openly rude from the very beginning. "This has to stop. It's killing my parents. My mother's in the hospital, again."

"I'm sorry to hear that. I…"

"A stroke. A bad one this time. The doctors won't say how bad. I don't know how my father's going to manage if Mom isn't able to take care of him and the house. I can't drop everything and…"

"Mr. D'Angelo, you have my sympathies. Truly. You must be aware that I can't stop investigating your sister's murder…"

"Investigating! The police got the man who killed Sophia, and all you're doing is opening old wounds, digging it all up again, like some sort of ghoul. This is literally going to be the death of my parents."

"I am sorry for what your family is going through, Tony. But justice has to be done, doesn't it?"

"Justice was done. This is just a travesty."

"Indications are strong that Walt Desmond did not kill your sister."

"So you say." Tony was considerably overweight and peered at Winters through thick glasses. Beads of sweat were forming on his brow although the air conditioning in the station was turned higher than Winters liked it.

"So the court says. If Walt didn't kill her, then someone else did. Do you want him to get away with it? Even all these years later we still have a chance of finding him." Winters did not add, *an extremely poor chance.*

"I was seventeen years old. I was at basketball practice after school when Soph was murdered. I scarcely remember anything about it." His eyes slid away, and Tony studied the painting on the wall. It was a nice picture, of a child in a sun-kissed, flower-filled meadow. It had been deliberately chosen to be calming and pleasant in this room where things discussed were rarely pleasant and never calming.

"Were you and your sister close?"

"We were five years apart. A lifetime at that age. She was a great girl. I really looked up to her." Tony's eyes were dry, but he plucked a tissue out of the box on the coffee table. He twisted it between his fingers.

"At the time she died, she had a boyfriend, an Australian by the name of Leonard Fitzpatrick, right?"

"So they said."

"Said? You didn't meet him?"

Tony shrugged. "Like I told you, big age difference."

Winters knew the D'Angelos had claimed their daughter didn't have a boyfriend, whereas she did. He'd wondered why she'd kept him a secret from her family. It seemed as though it was even more of a secret than he'd assumed. "Fitzpatrick was never considered a person of interest in the original police investigation. I'd like to talk to him, but a lot of years have passed and it's going to be difficult to track him down. You can't tell me anything about him?"

"Never even heard of the guy until Soph died…was murdered." The tissue was in shreds now.

"Was she seeing anyone else at the same time?"

"Why would I know? I mean, I was just a kid, right? She was a grown woman. Worlds apart. Not that we weren't close, though," he added quickly. The sweat was running freely down his face. He grabbed another tissue.

"What aren't you telling me, Tony?"

"Next you'll be saying Soph had it coming."

"I won't ever be saying anything of the sort."

"She was a nice girl. She was a good sister. She was!"

"Tony, I am…"

"I've had enough of this. I'm leaving."

He struggled to get out of the comfortable chair and then headed for the door. Winters could do nothing but follow.

He stood at the window, watching Tony D'Angelo hurry down the hill toward town. Despite the heat and his weight, he was almost running.

Running, Winters thought, *from what?*

He had learned far more from what was unsaid than anything Tony had to tell him. Tony was consumed by guilt about something. That something might not have anything to do with the murder of his sister, but he'd been carrying it around all these years. Secrets, always secrets. And in a twenty-five-year-old case, secrets had a lot of time to fester. Kibbens had interviewed Tony's basketball coach. The coach said Tony had been at practice between four and five that day, and the boy couldn't have left for so much as a bathroom break without him noticing.

Winters suck his head in Barb's office. "Ready?"

She pushed back her chair. "Ready."

They studied the grimy, dust-covered box on Winters' desk. "Looks like it hasn't been disturbed," Barb said.

"Let's see what was important to him." Winters touched the yellowing tape and it came away with little more than a gentle tug. He opened the box and began taking out the contents. Three framed photographs of groups of men displaying their catch were on the top. Two had been taken on the lakes or rivers around Trafalgar and one in what was probably a charter boat in the Caribbean. Only one man appeared in all three pictures.

"He was a keen fisherman," Barb said. "I'd forgotten that. He would have gotten on well with Paul."

Kibbens had been a carrying more weight than he probably liked. He was average height with thinning hair. He wore sunglasses in all the pictures, and he was not smiling. Winters looked down through the years and studied the man's face. He could read no secrets hidden there. "You recognize any of the guys with him?"

Barb tapped one of the shots with mountains in the background. "Pete Hill. A really nice guy. He died of cancer before the D'Angelo case, very sad. Here's Jack McMillan."

Winters picked up the picture. Hard to believe this was the same man now living up on the mountain, drinking and smoking his days away, with nothing to do and no one but two dogs for company. "He was a good-looking guy, back in the day."

"Oh, yes. Jack was popular with the ladies. Until they got to know him better. I probably shouldn't have said that."

"That's why we're here, Barb, sorting through a man's effects."

"Doesn't seem right, somehow."

"It's got to be done. Sophia D'Angelo deserves as much."

He put the photos to one side. Next was a small desk calendar, a month per page, illustrated with photographs of fish. A few of the white squares had notes jotted in them. January 16, the day after Doug died, said, 1:00 Dentist.

"This is all personal stuff, looks like. I don't see any court dates."

"He might have kept a separate calendar. If so, it would have gone to the law clerk so she could sort out what was supposed to have been his schedule."

Winters quickly read three months' bank statements. Normal amounts of money going in and coming out, leaving a small but consistent balance at the end of every month. He flicked through the cancelled checks. Nothing made out to anyone more interesting than the electric or phone companies or a menswear store with an address in Trafalgar but a name he didn't recognize.

"Funny to think how things have changed," Barb said. "I haven't had a letter from my bank in years. I do everything online now."

There wasn't much else in the box. An old copy of a fishing magazine. Some notices from the union and memos about the day-to-day running of the police department. An invitation to a retirement party.

Before long the box was empty except for a plain white envelope with nothing written on the outside. Winters picked it up. It had no bulk, so anything inside wouldn't be more than a piece of paper or two. It was sealed, but the glue had weakened. He slipped the envelope open and took out the contents. One photograph and a small white slip of paper. He studied the slip first. A gas station receipt. The ink was faded, and he handed it to Barb while he searched for his reading glasses.

"I remember this place," she said. "Near Winlaw. We used to stop for gas there sometimes when we went to visit my sister in New Denver. It closed down a long time ago."

"What's the date on it?"

"September 12, 1991."

Eight months after the murder of Sophia D'Angelo and four months before the death of Doug Kibbens. One single gas station receipt kept in an envelope in the bottom of a desk drawer. Winters turned over the photograph. He put on his glasses and Barb leaned closer to see better.

"What do you suppose that is?" Barb said. "Looks like a bracelet."

It was a bracelet. A slim gold bracelet inset with fake diamonds. He sucked in a breath. This could only be a picture of Sophia's missing bracelet. The one that had never been found. Not on Walt Desmond, not in the house where the woman had died or in the Desmond car or home. The one her work colleague admired the day Sophia died; the one the police insisted Desmond had taken off her body and thrown away in a panic before his arrest. The bracelet in the picture was lying on a forest floor among a mound of decaying leaves, small broken twigs, a scattering of pine cones.

A hand lay on the ground beside it, the wrist stretching beyond the edge of the picture so Winters couldn't tell if it was attached to an arm or not. The hand was palm up, the fingers curling inward. It was white, a man's hand almost certainly, the palm square, the fingers thick and short. The grooves were lined with dirt, the nails broken, the pads of the fingers rough with callouses. No rings and no indentations that Winters could see. The tip of the index finger was missing down to the first joint, but the injury had been old, fully healed, when the photo was taken.

"What does all this mean, John?" Barb said.

"I have absolutely no idea," he replied. "But I'll venture to say it means a heck of a lot."

Chapter Thirty

She had not enjoyed the afternoon at work. As soon as the elderly couple left—without buying anything—Margo had fussed over Eliza until she snapped at her to stop. And then she had to apologize, and explain she was perhaps still a bit under the weather, but nothing to worry about. And Margo began fussing again. Did Eliza want to sit down? Was she sure she was okay to be in the store alone this afternoon? Did she want a glass of water, or maybe a coffee? Eliza had smiled and said, "No, thank you. Don't let me keep you."

She'd been relieved the moment the door shut behind Margo. And then, a moment later, she'd had to stop herself from running into the street begging Margo not to leave her all alone.

For the rest of the day, Eliza jumped every time the chimes over the door sounded. She'd not dared to answer a knock at the alley door, and the delivery man had to come all the way around to the front to drop off a parcel. She hadn't wanted go to the bathroom, afraid of being trapped in there if someone came after her.

One of her busybody neighbors had come in earlier, under the pretext of wanting to talk about the end-of-summer sidewalk sale. She studied Eliza's face, while trying not to, looking for signs of the attack, and made cloying remarks such as, "You must have been so frightened." She dug for details with questions like, "Does your husband have any suspects, dear?" Eliza had gritted her teeth as long as she was able and finally asked the woman to leave because she had a shop to run. The woman had pointedly looked around, noticing the total absence of customers, and left. Not that Eliza cared what her fellow shop owners thought of her. Most of them didn't like her much anyway.

Thank heavens it was Monday. She closed at six on Monday. She needed a bath, a long hot bath. And then she'd wrap herself in a heavy robe, heedless of the weather, and crawl into bed. She'd be okay in her own bed in her house high up the mountainside. She'd be safe there.

It was almost five o'clock, and she was counting the minutes until she could close. It was her gallery, she could go home whenever she wanted, but she was determined to wait until six.

The chimes over the door tinkled merrily and

a man came in. He was in his mid-thirties, tall and thin, with light brown hair, three-day stubble on his jaw, and a bobbing Adam's apple. "Hi. I saw that painting in the window and want to ask about it. I'm looking for something for my mom's retirement gift. Uh…are you okay, Ma'am?"

Eliza ran behind the counter. Her chest heaved, and her breathing was coming in sharp gasps. "I'm…we're closed."

"Oh, okay. Can I come back tomorrow?"

"No. I mean, yes, fine. Tomorrow."

"Do you need help, Ma'am? I can call someone, if you like."

"No. Just leave. Please. Now."

He almost ran out the door. She flew across the room and turned the lock. Her legs collapsed beneath her, and she lay on the floor weeping.

Chapter Thirty-one

It had been a great week. Even better than Carolanne had expected. She stole a peek at Walter, relaxing and reading a book in a comfortable armchair on the far side of the room. As though he felt her eyes on him, he looked up. He smiled.

She smiled back.

They'd had their final race earlier today, a five hundred-meter, against longtime rivals from Kamloops. Carolanne's team won by a large, highly satisfying margin, making the perfect ending to the week.

Tomorrow they were off for home. The women back to their jobs and families and lives and more training for the big race in Italy in September.

Walt? He hadn't said what he was going to do. Carolanne knew he had nowhere to go. She hoped he wouldn't stay in Trafalgar, not on his own.

She'd seen the article in the paper this morning. They all had. Mrs. Carmine had made a point of laying it out on the buffet next to the coffee and yogurt and fresh fruit. The headline said, "A Brother Remembers," and letters almost as big on the top of the sidebar said, "Desmond Returns to Trafalgar."

Carolanne had pointedly ignored it. She stirred her coffee and poked at her eggs Benedict while her stomach churned. Darlene picked up the paper and glanced at the article. When she heard the tread of a man's feet on the stairs, she stuffed the paper into the trash. "No need for gossip disguised as news."

Later, after the breakfast dishes had been cleared away, when Walt had gone back to his room and the women were either sitting in the garden reading or had gone for a walk, Carolanne slipped downstairs to the breakfast room. She pulled the paper out of the garbage and read it. To her infinite relief, the article didn't accuse Walt of anything. It just said that after many years in prison he'd been exonerated and released from prison when new evidence had come to light. The piece on the dead girl, Sophia, had been touching. Her brother painted a picture of an older sister he adored and who he still missed every day. Carolanne thought back to meeting the brother. That fat, angry man. The vile things he'd said.

Still, she couldn't really blame him. The family believed Walter had killed his sister, Sophia. The police and the courts had said so. It must be a heck of a lot to deal with, now that Walt was back in town and found not to have done it. The article quoted the chief of police as saying the investigation into the murder had been reopened. A lot of time had passed. For everyone's sake, Carolanne hoped the truth would finally be uncovered. She put the paper back into the garbage and slipped upstairs to her room.

Now, they were resting in the common room after dinner. Tomorrow would be their last breakfast here. Carolanne and her friends would say good-bye to Walt. Would he want her phone number or her e-mail address? If he didn't ask, should she ask if she could contact him?

Did she want to see him again? He had a complicated life right now, and a lot of issues to deal with. Yes, she thought when he smiled at her, she did.

Darlene came into the room, hiking shoes on and a light sweater tied around her waist. "I'm going for a walk. Anyone want to join me?"

"Not me," Carolanne said. The other women murmured no and Darlene left. They heard the door slam behind her.

Walter closed his book. "I'm going up. I hope I'll see everyone at breakfast before you leave."

"Sure," the others said.

"Good night then," he said. "Good night, Carolanne."

She watched him walk out of the room, heard his footsteps climbing the stairs. She fought back a sense of disappointment. Surely, she hadn't been hoping he'd make some sign or gesture asking if he could visit her in her room later?

What a silly idea. He was just a nice man, terribly lonely and in need of a friend. That was all. They'd go their separate ways in the morning, and she'd never give him another thought.

She was ready to turn in herself, but didn't want to go upstairs immediately after Walter. That might look like she was hoping for a nocturnal rendezvous. She stared at her own book for about five minutes, before deciding enough time had passed. "I'm off. Night all."

"Sleep well, Carolanne."

Loud banging on her door woke her. She opened sleepy eyes, thinking she must have overslept. The team planned to get up early, have breakfast, and be on the road by eight. She blinked and realized it was still dark. "What?"

"It's Nancy. Open up."

Carolanne threw off the covers, switched on the bedside light, and stumbled to the door. She hadn't locked it. Maybe she had been subconsciously hoping for a nighttime visitor.

Nancy was in cotton summer pajamas, her short gray hair sticking up all over the place. "Is Darlene here?"

"What? No, of course not. What would she be doing in my room? What time is it?"

"It's past three. I woke up to go to the bathroom and saw that her bed hasn't been slept in."

"She went out for a walk earlier. Did she come back?"

"Doesn't look like it. I went to bed right after you. I left the bedside light on for her and fell asleep. The light's still on."

"Have you tried calling her?"

Nancy held up her phone. "No answer. It rings a couple of times before going to voice mail. I'm worried."

"Maybe she stopped in at a bar, ran into one of the other teams and they asked her to join them."

"It's three-thirty, Carolanne. The bars are long closed and you know as well as I do that our crowd aren't the sort, or the age, to stay up this late."

"Have you checked to see if her car's still here? Maybe she got a call about an emergency at home."

"That might be it," Nancy said, "although I can't imagine she wouldn't phone me from the road. I'm going to get the others up. You ask Walt if he's seen her and then run down and check on the car, will you?"

"Why do you think Walt would know anything?" Carolanne protested.

"Maybe I should have asked him before waking everyone up. You know Darlene's having a hard time in her marriage these days, don't you?"

"She wouldn't... I mean, Walt wouldn't..."

"Gee, Carolanne. The guy's been in prison for twenty-five years. He must be desperate for sex. With a woman, I mean."

"You can't say that!"

"Check on the car. I'll ask him." Nancy ran down the hall and hammered on Walt's door.

Carolanne snatched her iPhone off the bedside table and headed downstairs at a rapid clip. If Darlene was with Walt, she didn't want to see them together, flushed and embarrassed at having been caught. She threw open the door and stepped outside. A light breeze on the night air, still warm with the heat of the day, carried the soft scent of the surrounding woods. She didn't have a light, but she didn't need one. Streetlamps illuminated the pathway. The parking lot was at the back of the house.

In her haste Carolanne hadn't bothered to search for her shoes, and sharp stones dug into the bottoms of her feet. She skipped across the gravel to the grass and rounded the house. A strong light shone over the back door, shining onto the group of neatly parked cars. All were where they should be. She pushed down a touch of panic. There was no conceivable reason for Darlene to be out so late.

Nancy tried to phone Darlene and no one had answered, but Carolanne thought it might be worth another try. She held her breath while the call went to wherever phone signals go. She heard a ring on the other end. Three rings and then Darlene's cheerful voice said, "Hi! It's Darlene. I hope I'm having too much fun to answer my phone right now. Leave a message and I'll call you back. Bye."

Carolanne hung up. She turned to go back to the house, not knowing what she feared most: that Darlene had been found safely tucked up in bed with Walt, or that her friend was still unaccounted for. She stopped, held her breath, and listened to the night. A car drove past. A dog barked. All fell silent.

She phoned again. This time she hung up in in the middle of the third ring and strained her ears to listen. There it was: a faint sound that lingered in her ears. Opera music. A soprano, wailing her heart out to the accompanying crescendo of a full orchestra.

Carolanne wasn't a classical music fan, and she didn't know the name of the singer or the piece, but she recognized it as Darlene's ringtone. The music was cut off mid-note.

She dialed again, and this time she held her own phone away from her. The music started, faint but recognizable. From somewhere in the trees a phone was replying. The bright bulb above the back door cast a pool of yellow light. Bugs swarmed around it, and beyond its reach all was dark. Carolanne fumbled for the flashlight app on her phone and switched it on. She played the beam across the yard. Beyond the gravel parking area, the lawn stretched to the patch of thick dark woods surrounding the property. Darlene must have dropped her phone when she was out for her walk. That, however, didn't explain why she hadn't come back.

Carolanne focused the beam of her flashlight on the ground in front of her and pressed redial on her own phone. She headed toward the music in the distance, getting louder as she approached. Now, the beam from her iPhone was the only light.

Brown hiking shoes. Bare legs. Black biking shorts. A body, lying on the ground.

Carolanne screamed.

Chapter Thirty-two

"Some people's idea of fun," Molly Smith mumbled.

"Weren't you young once?" Dave Evans replied.

"I was young. I am still young. I was never that stupid." She might have added that she'd never been a boy, but that didn't seem like a good idea at the time. Monday night and she'd pulled another double shift. She'd been about to head home, when Sergeant Peterson called her and said that not only was one officer still off sick, but Brad Noseworthy had phoned to say he'd been throwing up all afternoon. Smith grumbled, but agreed to stay on. Adam was working tonight so she had nothing to go home to (except for some much-needed sleep) and it didn't hurt to stay on Peterson's good side. Besides, she could always use the overtime money. She and Adam had one night in Toronto before their flight home, after the canoe trip with the kids. She'd started checking into luxury hotels.

They'd needed two cars and three officers to break up the fight in the Potato Famine. A pack of barely legal boys had been drinking steadily all night and decided they didn't want to leave at closing time. The bouncers tried to show them the door, punches were exchanged, a full brawl broke out, and the police were called.

The four worst miscreants had been escorted to the police station to sleep it off in the city's finest jail cells. They'd be up before a judge in the morning. It had been a bad fight: one of the bouncers had broken his arm, and a waitress who'd gotten in the way of a flying bottle might require stitches to her hand.

When the young men were locked up and processed, Smith headed upstairs to make herself a cup of tea and check if anything remained in the box of homemade cookies the law clerk had brought in earlier. Evans followed her and tossed coins into the pop machine.

Their radios crackled. "Two-Four and Five-One."

"Here," Smith said. "As in right here, in the lunchroom."

"A 911 call from 1894 Victoria Street. Suspected sexual assault on a female. Ambulance has been notified."

Smith and Evans exchanged a glance.

"Whatdaya know? The Glacier Chalet," Evans said. "Walt Desmond."

"You don't know anything about it," she said.

"Then let's go and find out." Homemade cookies, cans of pop, and boiling kettles forgotten, they ran through the station and out the back. Smith had the keys to the truck, and she jumped into the driver's seat. She slapped on lights and sirens and they tore out of the parking lot and through the sleeping streets.

The Glacier Chalet *again*. Smith would think another riled-up citizen had attacked Desmond, except that dispatch had said a woman. That might be a mistake, and it was also possible for women to be vigilantes. But what if it wasn't? Desmond had done time for a horrific sex crime as well as a murder. Could he possibly be stupid enough to return to the scene of his crime and attack again? Within weeks of being released?

She'd learned her first week on the job that no one was ever too stupid.

All the lights were on in the B&B and the front door stood open. Smith pulled to a stop half on the sidewalk and jumped out. Mrs. Carmine stood on the porch, wrapped in a dressing gown. Walt Desmond was on the sidewalk, waiting for them. "This way," he called. "She's back here."

Smith and Evans switched on flashlights and

followed Desmond around the house and across the lawn. A group of women formed a circle at the edge of the woods. Flashlight apps threw a maze of beams across the scene. A woman lay on the ground in the circle of light. Carolanne was crouched beside her, rubbing her hand.

The watching women stepped back as Smith and Evans reached them. "She's okay. She's okay," Carolanne said. She was dressed, as they all were, in an assortment of nightclothes. Everything from a frilly satin and lace gown to shorty cotton pajamas with yellow cartoon figures.

Evans shone his flashlight directly into the face of the woman lying on the ground. Darlene blinked and groaned. She struggled to sit up.

Smith dropped to her haunches. She put her hand lightly on Darlene's chest and said, "Lie still. An ambulance is coming."

"I'm okay."

"No, you are not. That's quite a cut you have there." Drying blood matted Darlene's hairline and fresh blood dripped down the side of her face. Her bottom lip was cut and her mouth was swelling.

"She was unconscious when I got here," Carolanne said. "I called 911. When I touched Darlene, she began to wake up." She started to cry. "I thought she was dead."

Walt Desmond took a step toward her. Dave

Evans thrust his arm out. "Don't make a move, buddy." Walt glared at the younger man, but said nothing.

Darlene's tee-shirt was pulled up to her shoulders, her sports bra along with it. Her bike shorts were twisted down past her buttocks, but her panties seemed to still be in place. Carolanne saw Smith looking, and tugged at her friend's shirt.

They heard a shout as the paramedics arrived. Carolanne got to her feet to give them room to work.

"What happened here, Darlene?" Smith asked. "Do you remember?"

"I went for a walk. Coming back. I…" her eyes rolled back, her head slumped.

"We'll take it from here, Constable," the paramedic said. "Out of the way, please."

Smith stood up. She pressed the button on her radio. "Five-one. We need a detective here."

"Ten-four."

"The forensic unit as well."

"Ten-four."

Evans stepped into Walt's space. He poked the man in the chest with one finger. "Wanna tell us what went down here, Walt?"

Walt blinked. He looked, Smith thought, terrified. He made no move to step back. The circle of women turned away from the activities of the paramedics to watch the men. Walt looked at them. He glanced at Smith, then his eyes passed over her and settled on Carolanne. "I didn't..." he said.

"You can tell us down at the station," Evans grabbed Walt's arm. "Let's go."

"What the hell?"

The women whispered to each other. Mrs. Carmine had followed the ambulance crew. She gasped and lifted her hands to her mouth.

Carolanne stepped in front of Evans, hands on hips, eyes blazing. "That's crazy. Walter didn't do this. Let him go."

"Please don't interfere, Ma'am," Evans said, very politely.

"He... he was with me. In my room. For the past hours. Isn't that right, Walt?"

Smith swung her flashlight toward him. For the first time Walt showed a flicker of emotion, and his eyes filled. Then he blinked and the tears dried.

Although, she thought, it might have only seemed to have been tears in the harsh white glare of her Maglite.

"It's all right, Carolanne," he said. "Don't worry about me. Please."

Evans pulled his handcuffs off his belt. The watching women gasped.

"Can I have a word, Constable Evans?" Smith said.

"Later," he said.

"Now. Mr. Desmond, can I trust you to remain here?"

"Yes, Ma'am," he said. "You can."

Smith walked a few yards into the deep shadows of the woods. Evans followed. "Are you outta your freakin' mind?" she said, trying to keep her voice low.

"What's your problem, Smith? The guy's a sex offender. A sex crime's been committed here. Or at least attempted. I'm taking him in."

"According to the law of the land, as of right now, he has no criminal record. I'll remind you of that, Dave. For God's sake. Maybe he did it, maybe he didn't. For what it's worth, I don't think he did. You can at least wait for Winters or Lopez to get here. Desmond's not about to attack anyone while we're watching."

"I am following procedure, Smith." She couldn't see his face, but she could hear the handcuffs swinging in his hand. His words were clipped with anger. This, she realized, was personal. Nothing to do with Walter Desmond or even Darlene and the dragon boat women. It was all about Dave Evans and Molly Smith, and it had been coming for a long time.

She glanced back at the circle of activity. The paramedics were loading Darlene onto their stretcher. One of the women held Darlene's hand. Walt Desmond had put his arm around Carolanne's shoulders. A tall figure was tiptoeing toward them across the lawn, watching her footing in the dark.

"Are you aware that Walt's suing the Province of British Columbia and the Trafalgar City Police for five million dollars?" Smith said.

"What?"

"A CBC crew came into the station this after-noon to interview the chief. They asked him for his reaction. He said he had no comment except that Walter Desmond is free to enjoy the hospitality of Trafalgar, the same as any other visitor. What do you think the chief's gonna say when you arrest Desmond without cause, and over my objections? You think he doesn't have a heck of a high-powered lawyer behind him to have mounted a claim like that? I can see the suit going up, substantially, if they can now claim harassment. The town will take it outta your hide, Dave."

Evans hesitated.

"Do what you think you have to do," she said. "I see Meredith Morgenstern has arrived. She'll be wanting some good pictures."

Evan snapped the cuffs onto his belt. He marched across the lawn, walked past Walt without stopping, and went to greet Ron Gavin, the RCMP

forensic officer who was lugging his bags of equipment toward them.

Ellie Carmine approached Smith. She
clutched a tattered dressing gown, faded pink cloth
and ragged hem, around her although the night
was warm. "Moonlight?"

"What?" Smith almost snapped. "I mean, yes
Mrs. Carmine, how can I help you?"

"I can't have him here anymore."

"Who, Mrs. Carmine?" Although Smith knew
full well.

"That Walt Desmond. I…it's not safe. Look
what's happened here. I can scarcely believe it. We
might all have been attacked."

"Do you know who did this, Mrs. Carmine?"

"Well, I mean, isn't it obvious?"

"It's not obvious to me, Mrs. Carmine. Are
you wishing to make a formal statement? If you
know something, I'll call Detective Lopez."

"Can't you arrest him, Moonlight? Without
making a fuss, I mean. That newspaper girl is here.
I don't want it mentioned in the papers that the
Glacier Chalet is the sort of place that attracts guests
of…that sort."

"Mrs. Carmine, if you are uncomfortable
having Mr. Desmond in your home and business,
you are allowed to ask him to leave. But please,

don't be making accusations you can't support. Now, if you'll excuse me."

Carolanne and Walt had moved into the shadows. They were standing close together, alone under a red cedar, watching the activity. Meredith spotted them and headed their way. Time for Smith to intervene.

Chapter Thirty-three

Ray Lopez looked up from his computer when John Winters came into the office.

"You look like you've been up all night," Winters said, noticing the red eyes, mussed hair, and trace of stubble.

"Pretty much. A woman was attacked at the Glacier Chalet last night."

"She okay?"

"She will be. She regained consciousness at the hospital, and I was able to talk to her."

"Happen inside or outside?"

"Outside. You know what that property's like. Plenty of space between the house and the one next door. That patch of woods at the back. The woman, one Darlene Michaels, a guest at the B&B, says she went for a walk before turning in. She was coming back around ten, when she saw what she thought might have been a fox running around side of the house. She was curious, went to have a look. She was hit from behind, pushed to the ground. She says she was knocked unconscious, which is probably the case as she appears to have fallen hard and hit her head on a rock. One of her friends found her hours later."

"Sexual assault?"

"An attempt, but no more. Her clothes had been interfered with, but that's about all. I suspect when he realized she'd passed out, he thought he'd killed her, panicked and took off."

"Did she see him?"

Lopez shook his head. "Not a glimpse. A total sucker punch. The doctor who examined her found a very large bruise on her lower back."

Winters sipped his coffee. "Same guy who went after Eliza?"

"At a guess, yeah. Can't see there being two of them acting separately. Same MO. Come up behind them, no hesitation in using his fists to subdue them."

"You getting anywhere with it?" Winters' gut churned. He tried not to let it show. Eliza had phoned him from the store yesterday, crying so hard he could barely make out the words. He thought she'd been attacked again, but when he said he was sending an officer, she said no. She was having a difficult day, she wanted to go home.

He went to the gallery, found the door locked,

her red-faced and weeping. He wrapped her in his arms and held her for a long time. Then he half-carried her into the small restroom where he splashed water on her face and her wrists. When the crying finally stopped, and she tried to force out a weak smile, he took her to his car and drove them home. A hot bath, and into bed with a cup of tea, plenty of sugar added, and a piece of buttered toast. When she was resting comfortably, he went downstairs and made a couple of phone calls. Victim Services first, and then Margo. Margo was willing to put in extra hours at the gallery as needed, and Eliza had an appointment with a counselor this morning.

He blamed himself for the breakdown. Eliza was nothing if not stoic and unemotional. He'd allowed himself to forget that a lack of emotion on the outside didn't mean suffering was not happening on the inside.

"Eliza," Lopez said.

Winters blinked. "What? Sorry, Ray, I missed that."

"Everything okay at home?"

"It will be. Last night Eliza realized she needs help dealing with the trauma of what happened to her. I've set up some appointments for her."

"If she needs anything, Madeline would be happy to help."

"Thanks," Winters said. "I'll keep that in mind. What were you saying?"

"Still no sign of Anderson, the guy whose fingerprints were on Eliza's car. We have a watch on his house, and the landlady's a longtime Trafalgar resident. She won't give him a heads-up that we've been around. I collected some hairs from last night's victim's clothes and they're on their way to the lab. No chance of fingerprints, though. It all happened outside, in the trees and on the grass."

"Last night's attack was at the Glacier Chalet. Isn't Walt Desmond staying there?"

"Yup. And isn't that exactly what we need? Meredith Morgenstern showed up. When I find out who called her, I'll have his guts decorating my coatrack."

"Probably some kid listening to the police radio," Winters said. "It's no secret Desmond's staying there."

"He's not anymore. He went to a motel. Ellie Carmine was flapping about, making a heck of a scene, all while saying she didn't want a scene. She pretty much accused Desmond of the assault and demanded he be arrested. Desmond wisely said he didn't want to cause any trouble. One of the women guests waited while he got his stuff and drove him to the Mountain View."

"All while Meredith was watching, no doubt."

"And making copious notes. Mrs. Carmine did say one interesting thing to me. She demanded to know why, and I quote, that young man hadn't taken Desmond away after arresting him."

"What did that mean?"

"Molly said they had no reason to arrest Desmond and ordered Ellie to go inside and let forensics do their work. Molly pointedly avoided looking at me."

"Meaning…"

"Dave Evans and Molly answered the 911 call. When I got there Molly was alone at the scene, other than Ron Gavin, trying to calm Ellie down, trying to get the women to go inside, to get rid of Meredith, protect Desmond from any vigilantes who might arrive, and help Ron secure the scene. Dave was on the sidewalk out front, supposedly keeping curious passersby away. Although, at four a.m., there weren't any."

"Something must have happened. I'll talk to Molly."

"Unlikely she'll tell you," Lopez said.

If Evans had wanted to arrest Desmond, already suing the TCP in an extremely high-profile case, with no grounds, and Molly stopped it, Evans was darn lucky. Evans was a hothead. Everyone knew it. He was fonder of the authority that came with the gun and the uniform than Winters thought healthy. He always figured Dave Evans would screw up one day, and get himself kicked off the force. That would be his problem, but if he screwed up and the fallout landed on the TCP, that would be everyone's problem. Winters made a note to have a word with the chief. Nothing they could do, unless Molly laid a complaint. And she wouldn't. A police officer, more than almost any other job, had to be able to count on colleagues to be at their back. Lives depended on it. The police union wouldn't let them fire Evans because John Winters had a suspicion he might have done something he shouldn't.

Winters' phone rang, cutting off all thoughts about his junior officers.

"Morning, John. Steve Barrington here. I got your message. What's up?"

Yesterday Winters had put a call into the RCMP detachment that looked after the area closest to where the gas station receipt he'd found in Doug Kibbens' effects had come from. They exchanged greetings and news for a couple of minutes and then Winters said, "I'm looking into a cold case, and came across something you might know about. I haven't got much, but I'm trying to locate what is likely a deceased from 1991. A white male."

"And…"

"Not much to go on, I know. I don't have a

picture, I don't have a description. But I do know he was missing the first joint of an index finger. I have reason to suspect he was either killed or dumped after death in the forest near Winlaw. I don't even know if his remains have been located."

"Lots of forest around here, John."

"This is a heck of a shot in the dark, I know."

"Let me see what I can find. I'll call you back."

"Thanks." Winters was about to say there was no hurry, but he bit the words back. As long as Walt Desmond insisted on hanging around Trafalgar, he'd treat this case as urgent.

It wasn't long before Winters' phone rang. "That was quick," he said.

Steve Barrington chuckled. "Not hard to find. In 2001 human remains were discovered near a hiking trail not far from Winlaw. The doc estimated they'd been there for about ten years, maybe a few more, not much less. The skeleton was virtually complete. He guessed that the body had been well buried, but recent excessively heavy rains washed part of the mountainside away and uncovered it. Male, thirty to fifty years old, Caucasian. That's about all he could determine. The few scraps of clothes found on him were mass-produced. The one distinguishing feature of the deceased was a neatly severed portion of the index finger on his left hand. Cut with a sharp object, not chewed by animals post-mortem. The body was never identified or claimed."

"They able to determine the cause of death?"

"Marks consistent with passage of a bullet were found on the ribs and one bullet was still resting in the skull cavity. The round was from a single-shot hunting rifle. Not an uncommon weapon."

"Could that have happened by accident? A hunter out on his own?"

"The autopsy report says foul play was suspected, and I'd say suspected is an understatement. One shot could possibly be an accident, unlikely two. But I doubt he stood up, dusted himself off, and decided to dig himself a grave."

"That we can be sure of. I'm particularly interested in a piece of jewelry. A woman's bracelet."

Winters heard keys tapping. "Nothing found on or around the body," Barrington said. "No wallet, papers, anything. Certainly no bracelet. I'm guessing the bracelet was a shiny thing, right?"

"Yes."

"Even if he did have it on him when he was buried, when the remains were uncovered a bit of jewelry's likely to be something the first passing bird would pick up. A nice pretty trophy for her nest."

"I want to have this guy sent for another autopsy. Okay with you?"

"Have at it."

"Thanks." Winters hung up. A body had been discovered fifteen years ago and never claimed. Which means the deceased had no one who particularly cared about him or was searching for him. It had been buried for about ten years prior to being uncovered. That put it precisely in the time frame of the murder of Sophia D'Angelo, but that came as no surprise to Winters.

He called Barrington back. "One more question. The reason I'm asking is that it might have to do with a cold case the TCP handled. Is there any sign of TCP involvement?"

"Nope. We contacted you guys, of course. There seems to have been a sudden interest, thinking it might be the body of some guy who'd disappeared from Trafalgar, name of Nowak, but it turned out not to be him. Dental records were a total mismatch."

"Thanks again."

"Any time."

Doug Kibbens had kept a picture of the hand of an apparently dead man with Sophia's bracelet. Rather than report the discovery of the body and a piece of costume jewelry everyone was searching for, Kibbens had shoved the photo deep into his desk drawer.

Had Kibbens buried the body himself? Had he

taken the bracelet with him, or left it to be picked up by scavengers?

Or had Kibbens found the photograph and for some reason not turned it in?

Why would an unidentified and unclaimed dead man have Sophia's bracelet? Winters could think of only one reason. He'd killed her and taken the jewelry as a souvenir.

Why on Earth, if that was the case, would the investigating detective not have reported finding it?

Curiouser and curiouser.

He started the paperwork necessary to have the remains transferred to the morgue in Trail for Dr. Lee to have a look at. Probably not much she would find that the original autopsy hadn't, but you never knew. His phone rang again. Jim Denton on the dispatch desk.

"I got a call from the Mountain View motel. A bunch of men have shown up and are demanding to speak to Walter Desmond. Desmond declined to speak with them, and they say they are not leaving. I've sent a patrol car."

Winters groaned. *What was this? The Wild West?* "I'll go."

Chapter Thirty-four

"You don't want to do this, Carolanne," Walt said.

"I think I do."

"I'm nothing but trouble. You saw what happened last night. That stupid cop was going to drag me off in handcuffs. He didn't need evidence, he didn't need proof. If that policewoman hadn't been there, I would have had an accident in the back of the cruiser."

"All the more reason," she said, "that you need me around."

He smiled at her. "To keep me safe?"

She smiled back. "Yes."

He turned away. Poor Carolanne; she had no idea what she was getting into. This motel room was cheap and nasty, but it was the sort of place where a man could show up at four in the morning and be given a room with no questions asked. He couldn't offer her a chair, so she perched awkwardly on the edge of the small, hard bed.

"How's Darlene?" he asked.

"She's going to be fine. They want to keep her in another night, for observation. I said I'll stay and help out. I called my office and told them I won't be back tomorrow as planned."

"Doesn't she have family?"

Carolanne glanced away. "Her husband's coming. But, well, I thought she might like to have a friend around."

And they were back where they started. If nothing else, Walter thought with a smile, Carolanne was a loyal friend.

A knock sounded on the door. He groaned. The cops. More questions. More probing. More harassment.

Carolanne got up and went to the door.

He'd phoned Louise this morning to tell her what had happened last night. He could almost hear her rubbing her perfectly manicured hands together in glee. An associate of hers, she said, would be on the next plane out of Vancouver. If the TCP twitched in Walt's direction, they'd sue the police and the town of Trafalgar for every penny they had.

Louise was not a friend. She was most definitely not loyal. Unless her loyalty was to justice, which she knew was not always the same thing as the law. If she so much as suspected Walter had put a toe over the line, she'd drop him and his suit in a second.

Still, he was darn glad she was on his side.

"Time we had another talk, Desmond," Gino D'Angelo said from the open door. His son stood on one side of him, a hefty young man on the other. They were not brandishing weapons, not that Walt could see anyway, and there were no mysterious bulges beneath their summer-weight trousers and tee-shirts. But the unknown guy looked like he knew one end of a fight from another almost as well as Walt did, and whatever happened, Walt would not defend himself against a tired old man as wrapped in his grief today as he had been twenty-five years ago.

"I have nothing to say to you."

Gino looked at Carolanne. "Get lost, woman."

She slammed the door in his face and twisted the lock. She spun around to face Walt, her eyes wide and frightened. D'Angelo hammered on the door.

"Shall I phone the police?" Carolanne said, her voice low.

"That would be a good idea." Walt sat on the bed next to her while she made the call. He took her hand. The pounding on the door continued. Someone, probably the desk clerk, arrived and asked what was going on. He said he was calling the cops. Tony D'Angelo yelled at him to go ahead.

It was time, Walter realized, for him to be on his way. Louise's associate was due to get into town any minute. He'd leave with the lawyer. Go someplace where no one knew him, where they wouldn't stare when he passed or try to get the police to arrest him because some bitter relative wanted to start a fight. Somewhere where he didn't have to watch out that the cops themselves weren't about to nudge him into an alley.

Sirens. Coming their way. Pulling up next to his door.

"What's going on here?" a woman called.

"That man," Gino D'Angelo said, "he killed my daughter. He's out of jail and he's assaulting women and you people don't care."

"We care very much," the woman said. "But right now I care that you are disturbing the peace. Please, go home, sir."

Walter let go of Carolanne's hand and went to the window. He pulled back the curtain and took a peek outside. A policewoman, not the pretty blond who was Andy Smith's daughter, but another one, shorter, squarer, stood between Gino and the motel room door, trying to reason with him. A sizeable crowd had gathered. He studied their faces, but could see nothing other than mild curiosity. That, he knew, could change in an instant.

A truck, more rust and dust than metal, pulled to the side of the road. The window rolled down. A light flared as the person inside lit a cigarette.

Walter's gut tightened. Jack McMillan. He didn't get out of the truck but he didn't need to. Walt knew who it was. He could smell him; could feel him. McMillan had haunted his dreams for a long time. He lifted his arms, put them into position. Sighted down the length of his right arm. Took a beading on the fat head, the ugly face. If he had a rifle, he'd use it. If he could blow the bastard's head off, he'd go back to jail a happy man.

Involuntarily he glanced toward his backpack, in which were all his worldly possessions. *No. Not here. Not in front of Carolanne.*

"Walt," Carolanne said. "What's happening?"

He lowered his arms, turned his back to the window, took a deep breath, and tried to smile at her. "Don't worry. The police are here."

When he checked outside again, a van was parking close to his door. The man who got out was in his fifties, face well-lined, hair mostly gray. He sported a neat although unfashionable salt-and-pepper mustache, and was dressed in jeans and a blue shirt under a light jacket. Nothing about him, not the way he looked or the way he walked or the way he held himself, said cop.

But Walter Desmond knew that was what he was.

"Go home, Gino," the man said.

"I will not, Sergeant Winters. Not until you arrest that man."

"You can't tell us what to do, Winters," Tony said. "It's a free country."

"It is that, but the owner of this private property has called us saying you're making a disturbance. Looks like a disturbance to me. If the person in that room, whoever that might be, doesn't want to talk to you, you can't bash down the door."

"The doctors are saying my mother will never recover. You don't care about her. You don't care about my sister. You don't care...."

"This is getting tedious," Winters said. "Go home. Constable Solway, please ask the onlookers to disperse. Anyone who refuses, arrest them."

"Forget about my sister, then. Forget about the man who killed her. What about the women of this town today? What about the crimes he's committing now?"

"Your own wife, for God's sake man!" Gino shouted.

"The women at Ellie Carmine's befriended him," Tony said, his voice rising as he approached hysteria. "He thanked them by attacking one of them."

"That's right," someone shouted. "I read it in the paper this morning."

Constable Solway was having no luck getting people to move. The crowd was growing and Walter could hear whispers passing from person to person. The mood was getting ugly. Solway spoke into the radio at her shoulder, and threw a glance toward the motel room window.

"Walter Desmond did not commit the attack in Trafalgar on Wednesday, and not last night either," Winters said. "An arrest is imminent."

"Is that true, John?" a man shouted.

"I don't believe you," Tony D'Angelo said.

"Mr. Angelo, I am not going to stand here in the street and lay out my case in front of the public. I am telling you, all of you, that we have evidence we will be bringing before a judge in due course and that evidence has nothing to do with Mr. Walter Desmond."

"Good enough for me," the man in the crowd said. He headed for his car, and several people followed him. Another police car pulled up to the motel. A spotlessly clean yellow Ford Explorer pulled into the motel lot.

"Go home, Mr. D'Angelo," Winters said in

a low voice. "Please don't cause any more trouble. Tony, leave. Now."

"I don't..."

"It's all right, son," the old man said. "We've tried. It's between him and his God now." Gino threw a look at the motel room window one last time, and then turned and shuffled away. His head was bent and his steps were heavy.

"Are you going to see your father safely home?" Winters said to Tony.

Tony hesitated. He glanced at the other man who'd come with them, who merely shrugged.

"Or are you going to make your dad walk all the way by himself?" Winters asked.

Without a word, Tony left. His friend followed.

Walt opened the door. "Thanks," he said.

Winters stuck out his hand. "I'm Sergeant John Winters. Trafalgar City Police. I'm investigating the Sophia D'Angelo murder. I've been wanting to ask you some questions. Seems now's as good a time as any. Can I come in?"

"I hope you're not planning on ordering me not to leave town. That would be ironic, don't you think?"

"You're more than welcome to do as you please. But if you are referring to last night's incident, I'm not investigating that."

The Explorer pulled into a parking space next to the cruiser. Solway moved as if to tell him to keep on going, but Walt took a guess at who this might be and said, "He's with me." The pickup truck drove away with a puff of exhaust and rattling of the muffler.

Walt watched it go, and then he stepped back. "Come on in. My lawyer's arrived. Good timing." The man hurrying toward them clutching a briefcase to his chest was so young, Walt wondered if he shaved yet.

"Mark McMaster. What's going on?"

Handshakes all around. Sergeant Winters nodded to Solway, indicating she could leave.

Carolanne stood beside the bed. She said nothing. All the time, while the crowd gathered outside and the tension built, Walt had been aware of her, standing at his side. In prison he'd learned to smell fear. He had smelled it on her, but she had made no move to leave him.

He didn't much care what happened to him. He'd been through the worst the world could throw at him. He'd survived. Sometimes he wished he hadn't. But responsibility for another person, that was different altogether.

"Leave us now, please, Carolanne," he said.

"I'd like to stay."

"I want you to go."

Her eyes were wide, traces of fright still lingered. "I…" her voice broke. "I have to go home tomorrow. I have my job and…things to do."

She picked up her purse and dug through the contents. She pulled out a pen and a scrap of paper. "If you need anything, Walt, here's my number." She scribbled quickly and placed the paper carefully on the nightstand. She walked out of the room. Sergeant Winters shut the door behind her.

Chapter Thirty-five

Walt could tell Winters nothing he didn't already know from reading police reports and legal documents from the time of the original crime and fresh evidence presented at the appeal. The lawyer, he'd quickly come to understand, was here to "protect Mr. Desmond's interests." Which Winters interpreted as meaning they'd slap another lawsuit onto the TCP, given half a chance.

Between Dave Evans and Tony D'Angelo, they might well get it.

If Walt Desmond hadn't killed Sophia D'Angelo, Winters wanted to know, then who did? As to that, Walt couldn't help him.

He hadn't known the young woman. He hadn't met her before she came into the real estate office saying she wanted to buy a house. He'd shown her some properties and taken her for coffee a couple of times to talk over the details of what she was looking for and what she could afford.

Nothing eventful had happened. They'd toured several houses, seen what there was to see and left. She'd been pretty and friendly, maybe borderline flirty, and he'd enjoyed her company. That was all. He got the impression she wasn't really interested in buying and he'd feared she was wasting his time.

As for who might have killed her, he had no idea. Not a one. "And believe me, Sergeant, I've had a heck of a lot of time to think about it."

McMillan, a patrol officer, had been first on the scene in answer to Walt's frantic phone call, followed by Kibbens, the detective. Winters gently probed for details of any contact Walt might have had with the police before the fateful day.

Nothing. He'd never spoken to either of the men before they showed up at the house where poor Sophia's bloody body lay sprawled across the kitchen floor. He knew who they were, of course. Most people did in a town this size. He'd seen Jack McMillan coming out of Arlene's shop on one or two occasions, and he'd been in the audience when Kibbens had given a speech to the Rotary Club in the fall.

Winters left, feeling more frustrated than ever. The killer of Sophia D'Angelo had gotten away with it for almost thirty years. Looked like he was going to keep getting away with it. Winters had phoned Ryan Smethwick, the man in Alaska who'd claimed to have helped Walter with his flat tire at the time Sophia was being slaughtered. The guy had repeated his story, and Winters had no reason not to believe him. He had no police record, no known contacts in the criminal world, no ties whatsoever to Walter Desmond, the D'Angelo family, or anyone in British Columbia, by the looks of it.

As for Walt himself, it didn't matter what Winters thought of him, but he couldn't help but think the guy had gotten a mighty raw deal. He looked like the lifer he'd been: all muscle, stony expression, wary eyes. Except when he looked at that woman, Carolanne. Then the expression relaxed and the eyes softened. If only for a moment, before he snapped the veil of self-control back down.

Carolanne. And Jack McMillan. Winters had seen McMillan's truck pull up to the motel. Someone had obviously alerted him as to what was going on. When Walt talked about McMillan and Kibbens, still struggling after all these years to understand why they would have wanted to ruin his life, his self-control slipped again.

McMillan would be wise to keep his distance.

Winters got into the van and was about to switch the engine on when his phone rang. Lucky Smith.

"I hope I haven't got you at a bad time?"

"Not at all, Lucky. What's up?"

"Paul and I want to invite you and your wife around to my…our house on Saturday. Nothing special. We're going to have a small barbeque."

"We'd love to come." So, Paul was moving in with Lucky, was he? He hadn't said anything about selling the condo. Maybe he was going to rent it out. No surprise that they would live in the house Lucky had shared with Andy, where they're raised their children. It was a sprawling home on a fabulous piece of wilderness property nestled next to a meandering branch of the Upper Kootenay River. Winters couldn't see Lucky moving into Paul's soulless modern condo close to town.

"Three o'clock," she said. "Bye."

"Hold on, Lucky. As you probably know the Sophia D'Angelo case has been reopened. I'd like to talk to you about it. You were around back then. I wasn't. I'd like your opinion on what was going on in town at the time."

"If you think I can help, I'd be happy to talk to you, although I don't know anything. I haven't thought about it in years, but it's coming back, seeing as it's pretty much all anyone is talking about these days."

"I'll be there in five minutes. If you have time, I'll treat you to a coffee."

Lucky was waiting on the sidewalk in front of her store when he arrived. They walked the two blocks to Big Eddies Coffee Emporium, which had a nicer patio than the closer Crazies Coffee. Today was definitely a patio day. Not quite as hot as it had been but pleasantly warm and sunny.

"How's Eliza?" Lucky asked.

"She's doing well. She's been advised to get some counseling to help her deal with what happened, and I'm happy to say she's taking the advice."

"I'm glad," Lucky said. "I volunteer at the women's center and we do a lot of work with abuse victims. No one needs to go through it alone, not anymore. I heard, of course, about a woman being attacked last night at Ellie's place. The same man?"

"Unofficially, yes."

He got the drinks—black coffee for him, a chai latte for her—while she searched for a table on the patio. When he came outside, carefully balancing two cups, she was sitting at a table in the corner, her face lifted to the sun, her wide colorful skirt spread around her. He grinned.

He was an old-time cop, although not too old-time he hoped, and she was an old-time hippie and still an energetic activist. They were too different to be close friends, but he liked Lucky a great deal. Her passion for her causes came from genuine goodwill and, dare he say it, love. Knowing her, and coming to understand her, had made him, he hoped, more sympathetic. As for her, she was the sort of left-wing activist who never had anything good to say about the police, but he'd sensed her melting over the years he'd known her. Maybe sympathy and understanding went both ways. First her daughter became an officer, then she made friends with John Winters, and lastly Lucky found herself dating none other than the police chief himself. Winters wondered if he could congratulate himself on being a matchmaker.

"You look pleased with yourself." She gave him a bright smile.

"I'm thinking it's a nice day. The boys and girls in uniform will be happy the heat's broken."

"We're supposed to get some rain tomorrow. We need it desperately. When it's been this hot and dry, it doesn't take much for the forest to ignite."

Winters grimaced. Living out of town, with their own house surrounded by woods, he and Eliza had an escape plan drawn up and a box of supplies in the garage, ready to be loaded into the car with next to no notice. He sipped his coffee. "Dawn Solway has decided what we need is a police dragon boat team. Last time I saw Paul, he was nipping into the men's room. The one place she can't follow him to sign him up."

Lucky laughed. "Poor Paul."

She'd found a table in a corner, tucked into a nook against the stone wall that kept the hillside from tumbling into the coffee shop. Flowers and trailing vines covered the wall and above their heads a small fountain tinkled merrily. A line of expensive strollers was parked outside, and a group of young mothers, wearing running gear and bouncing babies on knees, had pulled two tables together. They were far enough away, and their laughter loud enough, Winters was confident he and Lucky could talk in private.

Lucky didn't have much to tell him about Walter Desmond, a man she'd barely known. She knew his wife slightly better, more as fellow shop owners than as friends. She hadn't known Sophia D'Angelo at all, although, Lucky said after some prodding on his part, she had reason to believe Sophia wasn't as universally loved as the newspapers made out after her death.

"Meaning?" he said.

"Meaning that girls of her age, the ones who knew her, didn't like her. 'Conniving bitch' was the phrase I overheard. Along with 'butter-wouldn't-melt-in-her-mouth.' It means nothing, John. Hearsay, gossip. High school resentments still festering."

He wasn't so sure. One of the biggest factors in Walt Desmond's conviction had been testimony that Sophia was a "stickler for the rules." Witnesses said she would never have gone into the house without the real estate agent letting her in, even if she had found the door unlocked. There'd been no sign of forced entry to the house or defensive wounds on Sophia herself. That, the Crown prosecutor told the jury, indicated Sophia had not been grabbed on the street and forced inside. She had gone willingly in the company of her killer, been taken by surprise, and overcome.

"Do you know any of those girls?" Winters asked. "Any of them still around?"

Lucky's eyes narrowed. "You are not going to try to say Sophia was responsible for her own rape and murder, I hope, John. If you are, this conversation is over."

"The character of a crime victim is totally irrelevant to any question of guilt or innocence, Lucky, and I hope by now you know me well enough to know I mean it. However, character does affect attitude and movement. A murder victim has no privacy and no right to their secrets. Someone killed her and they had a reason to do it, even if that reason is something you or I can't comprehend."

Lucky nodded. "Okay. Tina Osgood was one of the girls I overheard talking about Sophia back then. She's called Tina Bowman now, and she still lives in Trafalgar. I see her regularly because she works at the tourist information center. We've stopped offering guided hiking and kayaking daytrips since Andy's death, but the tourist center sends visitors our way who need topographical maps or equipment."

He sipped his coffee. "Did you know Jack McMillan or Doug Kibbens?"

Lucky snorted. "Jack McMillan put the pig in cop. No offense intended, John."

"None taken."

"Doug was okay, I thought. A perfectly pleasant man whenever I interacted with him, which was mainly over the time a purse-snatcher had been working Front Street. He was polite and professional and spoke to me as much as to Andy. I always maintain that says a lot about a man."

"But McMillan…" he nudged.

"Hard to believe now, but he was a very handsome man in his youth. He knew it too. I never liked him. I don't mean he ever tried anything with me or gave me reason to think he was on the take. I simply didn't like him, although some of my friends thought he was quite the guy. He'd spend his rounds popping in and out of the shops playing the charmer, letting the women know he was there to protect them, should they need it. Some women used to like that sort of thing. Many still do, come to think of it. He never came into my store." She barked with laughter. "Not since the time I was demonstrating against…I don't remember what right now…and I called him a fascist pig to his face. He said something ungentlemanly in return.

"When Doug died, whispers said he'd crashed his car deliberately, although that was hushed up. But that was only a rumor and I can't say if it's true or not." She sipped her drink. "The whole thing was a tragedy all round. Sophia, her family. Not to mention Walt and Arlene. And then Doug Kibbens dying only a year or so later. And now I hear Rose D'Angelo's had another stroke. So sad."

"Murder does that," he said. "Like a stone dropped into the lake. Waves and waves emanate out forever. Arlene was Desmond's wife, right? She's dead now, I've been told."

"Yes. We were told it was cancer, but rumor around town said she killed herself, poor thing. She died a few years after Walt was sent to prison. She was one of the shop owners Jack McMillan liked to visit during his rounds. Her store was where Eliza's gallery is now, did you know that? Almost directly across the street from mine. I was telling Moonlight the other day that I was, frankly, surprised at how devastated Arlene had been when Walt was arrested and convicted. I hadn't thought they had a good marriage. Not on her part, anyway. She was the sort of wife always making minor insults and throwing sideways digs at her husband. He never paid much attention, though." Lucky laughed. "Men can be oblivious sometimes. Present company excepted, of course."

John Winters froze, his coffee cup halfway to his mouth.

Oblivious.

He walked Lucky back to her store and, after being reminded about the barbeque on Saturday, he carried on down the street to the tourist information center. He knew Tina Bowman. She lived with her husband and two children not far from the center of town. They'd had a break-in at their house a few months ago. Garbage tossed around, drinking glasses and plates broken, small electronics taken. The case had not required all of John Winters' highly toned detective powers. A trail of footprints in freshly fallen snow led directly to the door of a neighbor against whom the Bowmans had laid several noise complaints.

Tina was seated at the reception desk when he came in. She gave him a smile of recognition. "Sergeant Winters, nice to see you. Are you interested in tourist brochures? Planning a nice romantic getaway with your wife? If so, you've come to the right place. I was sorry to hear about what happened to her, but they say she's doing fine."

"She is, thanks. I want to talk to you, Tina,

and not about tourism. Do you have a couple of minutes?"

"Sure." She waved her hand in the air. Other than the two of them the room was empty. The building was new, all tinted glass and deep red wood. Sun streamed through the wide windows; maps and colorful posters depicting the spectacular beauty of the Kootenays hung on the walls; display racks overflowed with brochures and pamphlets.

"You've lived in Trafalgar a long time," he said.

"Born and raised. God's country. Why would I ever want to live anyplace else?"

"Why, indeed. You were at school with Sophia D'Angelo."

Tina's eyebrows rose. "Wow, so that's why you're here. I heard the guy they put away for killing her didn't do it. I guess you guys are wondering who did, eh?"

"That we are."

"Yeah, I knew her back in the day. She was my age, went to the same school."

"Tell me about her."

"She was really nice…."

"Is that true?" Winters said.

Tina glanced at the stack of brochures on her desk. She ran a finger across the cover of one. An alpine meadow, masses of flowers, the sparkling blue lake far below, snow-topped mountains in the distance. "What do you mean?"

"Away from the press, away from the courts, I'd like to hear about the real Sophia, not the image of her given at Desmond's trial or in the papers. Tell me honestly, Tina. Please."

She sighed. He let the silence linger and eventually she looked at him. "Okay. After her murder and during the trial, it was like they were talking about different person. Not the Soph I knew. She was a wild one. I don't mean she ever did anything illegal, but she was the sort who wanted what she wanted when she wanted it, and God help anyone who got in her way. Her parents thought she was a little angel and they treated her like she was ten years old or something. She had some really mean things to say about them. I think she got a kick out of pulling the wool over their eyes.

"We were the same age, so in a lot of the same classes all through school. Back then, I didn't think much about why she was the way she was, but now I'd guess it had a lot to do with her parents. They were totally old-school, and brought Soph up as though she was a Victorian maiden or something. She couldn't go to dances or sleepovers or activities like that. She wasn't allowed to date. So she became sneaky. She did all those things, just lied to her parents about it. She had boyfriends, all right, lots of boyfriends. Sometimes even more than one at the same time. I'm not saying she was promiscuous, Sergeant Winters, no more than any other girl in our age group," Tina laughed. "She didn't have a reputation for that."

She gazed out the window for a long time. Winters let her think. "Now that I'm remembering her, from the vantage point of all these years later and the benefit of my years of maturity, I feel sorry for her. She had to lie to her parents. She had to break their rules all the time. Lying and sneaking around was simply the way she went through life."

"At the trial she was described as a stickler for the rules. What do you think about that?"

"Sergeant Winters, if there was a rule, as far as Soph was concerned, it was there to be broken. Maybe she changed after high school. I don't know. A bunch of us went out for dinner one night in the fall after she moved back to Trafalgar. She was talking about how her parents wanted her to stay in town. She'd taken the job at the bank but that was only temporary as far as she was concerned. She had plans. She was saving to go to Australia with some guy she'd met. I never spoke to her again."

"Thanks, Tina. I know that was hard, but you've been a big help."

"It's been a long time, Sergeant. I have a daughter and a son of my own, they're teenagers now. I've been determined to raise them both the same. I want them to have freedom, and be able to explore, but to know there are boundaries. It's not always easy. Maybe watching poor Soph had more of an influence on me than I thought."

"Is he in?" Winters asked Barb.

She took off her glasses and rubbed her eyes. "Gone for the day. He has a presentation to give to the town council tonight."

"I need about half an hour of his time tomorrow morning, first thing."

"I'll put you down." Barb turned back to the computer. She didn't ask what it was about. If Winters wanted to tell her, he would.

"I have good news and less good news," Ray Lopez said when Winters walked into the detectives' office.

"What?" Winters said, not in the mood for word games.

"DNA results on the hairs found on Eliza have come in. And we have a match. One Richard Anderson."

"Same slime-bucket whose fingerprints were found on her car?"

"The same. And, as we had hair from last

night's incident at the Glacier Chalet ready to be compared, they ran those as well. Same guy."

"I assume that's the good news. Now for the less good?"

"We can't locate him. He hasn't been around to his place for at least a week, although he doesn't seem to have moved out. His rent's paid up and all his stuff seems to be there. We have a BOLO on him and his car, and I have feelers out to persons of his acquaintance, so I'm confident it won't be long before I can have a little chat with him."

"Let's hope he doesn't do any more damage in the meantime," Winters said. "He's had two failures, if we assume rape was his intention. He's going to be very angry."

Chapter Thirty-six

Why? Over all the long years that was the one question Walt couldn't get away from. *Why*. Why had McMillan and Kibbens been so determined to prove he'd killed Sophia? Walt had understood he was the most likely suspect. He'd been found beside the body, covered in Sophia's warm blood. But surely the investigation should have spread out from there?

After all, someone killed Sophia.

Walt knew it hadn't been him. He had clung to that knowledge all those years, although it wasn't always easy. Sometimes he'd even doubted himself. In the dark night of the soul, when he lay awake in the narrow, uncomfortable cell cot, in the strange never-dark of a maximum-security prison, listening to the steady tread of the guards' boots, and the grunting, farting, snoring, and sometimes weeping, of men who had nothing left to lose, he'd wondered if he'd done it, after all.

Were they right, the forces of law and order, the police, the prosecution, the judge and jury? Were they right, after all, and he had killed her? Did he just not remember?

But then, as the weak light of day touched the edges of his cell and the prison awoke to another mindless, broken, soul-destroying day, he knew he had done nothing of the sort. Over the long years, he'd seen men, men who had raped and murdered, committed horrible crimes, confess, seek rehabilitation, beg forgiveness. And be released on parole. Sometimes they were back a few months later.

There had been no chance of parole for him. Not unless he confessed and "accepted responsibility" for his crime. One of his lawyers advised him to go ahead and confess, admit to it, just so he'd have a shot at parole. But Walter couldn't do it.

And so he sat in prison for twenty-five years, and wondered *why*.

Doug Kibbens was dead, but Jack McMillan was not. Yesterday Walt had been about to leave town, to admit to himself that some questions would never be answered. But then he'd seen McMillian watching him, and he'd known that he would never be able to rest until he knew. He'd pay a call on McMillan and ask. Ask outright: Why?

The fresh-faced young lawyer from Waterston and Gravelle wouldn't approve of the idea, so Walt had no intention of telling him. The lawyer had gone into town to check into the Hudson House. Clearly this rundown motel wasn't exactly to his liking. He arranged to meet with Walt tomorrow for breakfast, to talk over what had been happening, before deciding on a further course of action.

Walt didn't much care what "course of action" they took. All he wanted was for people to leave him alone.

But first, he wanted to know *why*. He needed to know why.

He checked that no one was hanging around outside lying in wait for him, and then went to the motel office. The clerk was behind the desk, punching buttons on his phone. He had *that* look, and Walt knew the man had spent time inside.

"I'd like to use the computer," Walt said, very politely.

"Not for guests. There's computers at the library in town. Go there."

"I don't have a car at the moment."

The clerk shrugged. "Not my problem, buddy."

Walt had come prepared. He pulled a pink fifty-dollar bill out of his pocket and held it up. "Won't be long."

The clerk eyed the money. "Can't get porn. It's blocked."

"I'm only wanting to look up a map. You

can watch if you want. As long as you keep your distance."

"Five minutes." He snatched the bill out of Walt's fingers. Walt walked behind the desk and settled himself into a chair. The clerk leaned over his shoulder and typed in the password. He smelled of tobacco and clothes that needed a wash. Walt almost smiled. It hadn't taken long in the company of women for him to be offended by men's smell.

"Step away," Walt said, and the clerk went back to his phone.

It was easier than Walt had thought. He found the name and address he wanted on Canada411. com. The man was getting sloppy. He typed the address into Google Earth, and up came a picture taken from a satellite. Walt traced the route from Trafalgar, down the highway for a couple of miles, up a twisting side road into the mountains. At lower levels houses lined the road, but inhabitation thinned the higher the road went. The pavement turned to gravel, and the gravel to dirt. And there it was. A house in a clearing.

Wasn't modern technology marvelous? Things sure had come a long way while he'd been inside. Good thing he'd always tried to keep up with what was going on in the world. Imagine, someone had photographed almost every house on every street in North America, and if they hadn't been physically driving up and down the street with a camera mounted on a car, they'd taken shots from satellites.

Walt closed the map program and got up from the chair. He knew he was leaving a clear trail for the cops to follow if they thought to check this computer. But he didn't care.

It was time.

It was long past time. It would end tomorrow. One way or another.

He'd seen a convenience store a few blocks from the motel when Carolanne had driven him here after he'd been kicked out of the Glacier Chalet. He walked there now and bought two packages of sausages, some granola bars, and a couple of chocolate bars. Then he went back to his room, where he checked the contents of his backpack and tossed out things he wouldn't need up on the mountain. Clothes, toiletries, an extra pair of shoes, his books. He checked to ensure what he needed was there, and added the food.

It was still daylight outside, but he slipped off his shoes and lay on the bed fully clothed. He set the alarm on the clock radio beside the bed for four a.m. Walt didn't have a car, and he couldn't rent one because he didn't have a driver's license. No problem. He was fit enough for a good long hike.

He'd ask McMillan *why*. If McMillan wasn't

in the mood for talking, Walt didn't have anything left to lose.

He closed his eyes and although he fell asleep almost immediately, sleep didn't come quite fast enough: an image flashed across his mind. Carolanne. Her lovely face, her wide smile, her kind eyes, her determined expression when she said she would stay with him.

He was glad something good had come into his life. Even if only briefly and at the end.

Chapter Thirty-seven

"Tell John I'm out back," Smith said to the dispatcher.

"Ten-four."

Rain had started to fall in the early hours and it was coming down hard now. The people at the fire centers and in the lookout towers would be breathing a collective sigh of relief today. This was exactly what they needed: a proper soaker, one that would drench the tinder building on the forest floor and nourish and protect the dehydrated branches and the dry, parched leaves. Her windshield wipers struggled to keep up with the deluge.

She didn't have long to wait before Winters came out of the station, running fast with his head buried into his collar.

She'd been on patrol, cruising through the quiet, peaceful morning streets of Trafalgar when the radio squawked to tell her she was needed to accompany Sergeant Winters on a call.

He climbed into her truck and shook water off like a dog emerging from a lake before doing up his seat belt.

"I've spoken to the chief, and I have his permission to pay a call on Jack McMillan. I don't expect things will turn nasty, Molly, but I need you to be on alert."

She didn't bother to point out that that went without saying.

"Jack McMillan and Doug Kibbens knew who killed Sophia D'Angelo. They covered it up, and framed Walter Desmond."

"What the…?"

"They took care of the killer on their own. Whether they knew he'd murdered Sophia either before or after Walt went down, they kept their mouths shut. And Walt served twenty-five years."

"Are you serious?"

"Yes, Molly. I am perfectly serious. And I intend to tell Jack McMillan that I know what happened."

"If we're bringing McMillan in," Smith pointed out, "you might want more backup than just me. He's unlikely to come willingly."

Winters shifted in his seat and looked at her. She could find not a trace of what she would have expected to see in the depths of his eyes. She saw no triumph, no satisfaction. Just weariness.

"We're not arresting him?" she said.

"I have not the slightest scrap of proof, Molly. I don't even have enough to bring him in for questioning, let alone lay charges with any hope of a conviction. Too much time has passed. Memories have faded, evidence is lost. My main witness, Doug Kibbens, is long dead."

"Kibbens would have been a witness then? Not an accused?"

"I don't know exactly how it all went down, but I'm convinced Kibbens killed himself out of guilt. He took the coward's way out, rather than manning up and confessing to what they'd done."

"You're hoping McMillan will do that? Confess, I mean?"

"Molly, I don't know what I'm hoping. The chief agrees that my reasoning's sound and gave me the okay to go ahead. Who knows? Maybe McMillan will tearfully break down and confess all."

She couldn't stop the expression from crossing her face. Winters gave her a tight smile. "Yeah, like that's gonna happen. Best-case scenario, he'll leave Walt alone."

"Do you think Walt knows this? Knows he wasn't convicted because of sloppy police work and a poor defense. That they knew he didn't do it, but didn't tell anyone. And why would McMillan and Kibbens do that, anyway?"

"I have my theories," Winters said. "Let's see what McMillan has to say."

She put the truck into gear and pulled into the street.

"Dave Evans was in the constable's office doing paperwork when I walked by. I considered asking him to come along."

Smith kept her eyes on the road. The windshield wipers moved in a steady rhythm that made her think of the dragon boat women, all those individual bodies moving as one. She drove with extra care. The streets were busy with people heading for work or tourists getting a start on the day, every one of them with heads down or umbrellas up, watching for puddles at their feet rather than approaching cars.

"Do you wonder why I didn't?" Winters said. "Ask Dave, I mean?"

"No."

"Should I have?"

She took her eyes off the road and glanced at him. "No," she said. Her heart was pounding. She didn't know what she'd say if Winters asked outright. If he asked, and she refused to answer, he'd be angry. If she did answer, she'd…She'd what? Not be doing anything more than telling the truth. Evans didn't like her now, and he certainly wouldn't like her any more if she squealed on him. Tough call.

Evans wasn't a bad cop, far as she knew, not on the take or open to turning a blind eye. He was just an entitled, arrogant prick who figured he knew better than everyone else. She might well need him someday to save her life.

"Want to tell me why?" Winters said.

"No."

"Your call, Molly. If you ever need to talk in confidence, I'm here."

She glanced at him again. "Thanks, John. Uh…nothing in particular, you understand, but I sometimes think Dave's too much influenced by Jeff Glendenning."

"Is that so?" he said.

She drove slowly up the mountainside, glad she was in the truck and not a car. Rivers that hadn't existed yesterday cascaded down the hill onto the rough road, and the big tires threw up waves of muddy water. She had the windshield wipers on high and strained to peer between raindrops into the gloom. "I don't suppose we'll get lucky and McMillan will invite us inside," she said.

"I don't want you to say anything. Just stand there and look imposing."

Despite herself she grinned. "Imposing. I suppose I can do that."

"Call dispatch the moment we get there." He pulled his cell phone out of his pocket.

The truck bounced as it left the paved road and turned onto the gravel. The wheels spun seeking purchase in the rapidly forming puddles and wet gravel slipping away under the torrent of water. Then the gravel road became dirt, and the wheels dug into the mud.

"That's not him, is it?" Smith said.

Winters looked up from the phone in his hand. "Who? Where?"

"Thought I saw someone. He's gone now." She had seen someone, a man probably, walking on the road. He'd glanced quickly behind him as the truck rounded the corner, and slipped into the trees. He wore a dark jacket and a wide-brimmed hat that covered his face. They were almost at McMillan's place, so she thought for a moment it might have been him. But it couldn't have been. The man she'd seen was too tall, too thin.

Strange to see someone out for a walk in weather like this. Might have been a dog-walker. She hadn't seen a dog, but that didn't mean anything. This far out of town not many dog owners kept their pets on a leash.

She turned into McMillan's property and stopped the truck in the center of the yard. She notified dispatch they'd arrived and then said, "What now?"

"Give him a minute. See if he comes out. If not, we knock."

They waited. All that moved was the falling rain, the wind in the trees, and the windshield wipers on the truck. Back and forth, back and forth.

"Let's go," Winters said. He got out of the truck.

Smith hesitated for a fraction of a second, and then she pulled her cell phone out of her pocket. She pushed buttons, put the phone away, and jumped to the ground. Her boot sunk into a couple of inches of muddy water. Rain dripped down the back of her neck into the collar of her shirt as they splashed their way across the yard.

No dogs barked and inside the house nothing moved. Winters unbuttoned his jacket. They climbed the steps as the rotting wood creaked under their footsteps, and by the time they were on the porch, Jack McMillan stood in the doorway, his dogs at his side. The dogs' ears were up, their tails moved slowly back and forth, and the muscles in their haunches quivered. Smith felt the solid weight of her gun on her hip but she didn't reach for it.

"All my years on the job, I never had the time o' day for do-gooders and layabouts bellowing about police harassment if I so much as looked at them sideways. I figured we never harassed anyone who didn't need it. I might have been wrong. I'm thinking of laying a complaint myself."

"Feel free," Winters said. "You're welcome to call a lawyer and we can talk down at the station."

"What do you want, Winters?" McMillan hadn't so much as glanced at Smith.

"To ask you a few questions, Jack. Mind if we come in?"

"Yes, I do mind. Say what you've come to say and get the hell off my property."

"Can you put the dogs inside?"

"No."

"Put the dogs inside," Winters said. "They look tense to me, and we don't want any misunderstandings here. Do we?"

McMillan stared at Winters for a long time. Winters said nothing, and Smith tried not to shift her feet. At least the porch was covered, although the wood was cracked and rotting in places, but they were protected from the worst of the rain.

McMillan snapped his fingers, growled, "Go!" and pointed to the house. The dogs looked as though they didn't want to obey, but McMillan snapped again and, with one last snarl at Smith, they turned and walked into the house. McMillan pulled the door shut and she was glad of it. She had absolutely no desire to shoot a dog, but she knew of more than one occasion when things had gotten out of control and an officer had been forced to kill a dog that attacked him.

McMillan crossed his arms and stared at Winters.

Around five a.m. the rain began to fall. He didn't mind. This was a warm rain, a summer rain. It blew on the wind and brought the scent of freedom with it: fresh air, healthy growing vegetation, leaf mulch, and good clean earth. He took his hat out of his pocket, pulled it onto his head, and kept walking. He munched on granola bars and chocolate and didn't think about much; he'd learned how to do that over the long years—a useful skill in prison. He enjoyed the walk; he still couldn't get enough of the luxury of time spent alone to do nothing but whatever he wanted to do. Once he left the highway and started up the mountain, quiet settled over him and the dark wet forest closed in. As the sun began to rise behind the heavy clouds, a few cars drove past, all of them heading down the mountain. A couple of dogs barked from the few houses on this road, but no one was out for a walk on a day like today, and no one so much as took their eyes off the road ahead to have a look at Walt.

He checked his watch. Coming up to eight o'clock. He'd always had a good sense of direction and of distance, and he hoped he hadn't lost it over twenty-five years of long straight corridors and high, enclosing walls. He'd left the paved road about five minutes ago, and knew there was half a kilometer of gravel before reaching the dirt lane that ended at Jack McMillan's place. Almost there. He'd been walking on this road not for a couple of hours but for twenty-five years. The journey was about to end.

One way or another.

He put his hand in his pocket and felt the solid weight of the Smith & Wesson 36. He'd bought the revolver in Vancouver from the brother of one of the few friends he'd made in prison. "When you're out," his friend had said, "if you need anything. Anything at all…" It was illegal, of course, and he'd be in trouble if the weapon was found on him. But he figured he could make a good case for needing to protect himself. Look at that mindless mob at the motel yesterday.

The revolver had come with an adequate supply of bullets. Walt threw most of them in a storm drain, keeping only three. The cylinder carried five rounds at a time, but he wouldn't need that many. One for McMillan, a spare in case he missed the first time, and one bullet for himself. It was very possible McMillan owned a rifle, but he wouldn't be likely to carry it on him, not when outside doing daily chores around his property. Walt would wait in the trees until the man came out of the house. He probably had a dog or two, and Walt had tossed the sausages into his pack in case the animals got curious. He'd crouch in the trees and wait. Walt had plenty of experience of waiting, of doing nothing.

When he heard the sound of a powerful engine coming up the hill, he slipped into the cover of the trees and tangled undergrowth crowding the crumbling edges of the road. He glanced over his shoulder as the vehicle came out of the bend. A truck, white, with Trafalgar City Police written on the side in colorful letters, kicking up mud and water. The truck passed without slowing.

Maybe he should have brought the extra ammunition after all.

Chapter Thirty-eight

"Doug Kibbens killed himself one year to the day after the murder of Sophia D'Angelo," Winters said. "I can't believe that's a coincidence, so I have to ask why."

McMillan shrugged. "Case was a tough one, even for experienced guys. I guess something happened to make him remember."

"Perhaps," Winters said. "Or perhaps guilt finally got the better of him."

McMillan's gaze was stony, his eyes blank. A vein twitched in his forehead, and he scratched at the rough red skin on the back of his right hand. "You better not be going around town slandering the name of a good cop and a good man, Winters. Doug didn't kill that girl."

"I know he didn't. I know you didn't, either."

McMillan let out a bark of laughter. "Now we got that straight, why don't you get the hell off my property?"

Smith kept her face impassive. What was Winters playing at? He was clearly onto something. And McMillan knew it. The crude comments designed to put Smith into what McMillan thought of as her place, were gone, as was the macho swagger and the tough-old-timer routine. The retired cop didn't so much as look at her, all his attention was focused on John Winters. He tried to keep the sneer on his face, but he couldn't do it, and Molly Smith saw traces of what might have actually been fear. He scratched faster.

"Her killer," Winters said, "has spent the last twenty-five years in an unmarked grave up near Winlaw. No name, no identify. No one to mourn him."

The vein in McMillan's forehead beat harder. "What's that got to do with me?"

Winters reached into his jacket pocket. He pulled out two pieces of paper. Smith's eyes just about popped out of their sockets as she tried to get a look without appearing interested enough to turn her head. Rain beat steadily on the roof of the porch.

Winters passed the pictures to McMillan. The older man sucked in a breath, but he didn't make a move to take them. "Thought you'd be interested, Jack." Winters held one up. "I took these pictures yesterday, in front of a room full of witnesses. The originals are now in the evidence locker. One's a photo of a photo, as you can see, of a man's hand. Constable Smith," Winters showed the picture to her, "do you notice that the tip of the index finger is missing?"

"Yes, sir."

"Do you see the bracelet in the photo?"

"Yes, sir."

"Recognize that bracelet, Jack?"

McMillan coughed. "Cheap piece of costume jewelry. Dime a dozen probably."

"Maybe. But it does have some considerable importance to this case, doesn't it? Constable Smith, you may not be aware of this, but even though her colleague testified Sophia was wearing a new bracelet the day she died, it was never found."

"Is that so, sir?" she said. "I'd say that's very interesting."

"Therefore, you might be wondering why a bracelet apparently exactly the same as Sophia's is lying beside the hand of what appears to be a dead man."

"Give it up, Winters. You got nothin'. A hand, a piece of junk jewelry you bought at some five and dime. Might even be your own hand, doctored up a bit, photoshopped. What do you want me to say? Oh, my God, it's Great Uncle Ralph. Always wondered what happened to him." McMillan spat.

"I also found this," Winters produced the

second photo. "The original is, of course, now in custody, but I took a couple of pictures."

It looked like a receipt to Smith. Just an ordinary receipt.

"From a gas station near Winlaw that's no longer there. The date is September 12, 1991."

Smith had to bite her tongue to keep from saying, "So?" A gas station receipt from eight months after the murder? What possible relevance could that have to do with anything?

"Date mean anything to you, Jack?" Winters said.

"Not that I recall."

"What makes it mean something to me is where I found the receipt and the original of this picture. A very interesting place," Winter said, calmly. "Want to know where that might have been, Jack?"

"No," McMillan said. But he made no move to go inside his house or to order them off his property. That would be all he'd have to do, and Smith and Winters would have had no choice but to walk away. His eyes flicked between the photos Winters was holding and the sergeant's face.

A branch broke in the trees close to the side of the house. Smith's eyes moved, but she could see nothing and it didn't happen again. She gave it no more thought. An animal, seeking shelter from the driving rain.

Walt broke into a trot as he followed the police truck. He kept to the cover of the bush, not wanting to be seen if the driver checked the rearview mirror. According to the map, this road ended just up ahead. And, according to the satellite view from Google Earth, McMillan's house was the last one. The police truck slowed and made the turn into McMillan's driveway. The property was unkempt and overgrown, and the wild forest crowded in. For once, Walter thought with a grim smile, luck was on his side. He could get close without being seen. He stood quietly next to a pine tree, heedless of water dripping onto his hat, soaking into his shoes, and waited. For some reason, the cops were waiting also.

Then the truck doors opened and they got out.

He expected to see the young cop and the overweight older one, instead it was Sergeant Winters first and then Constable Smith. Walt watched them cross the yard. They walked cautiously, checking out their surroundings, moving with care.

It was obvious they were not welcome guests. Interesting.

The two police officers climbed the steps to

the porch. The door of the house opened and Jack McMillan came out, two dogs at his side. The dogs barred their teeth and growled. Walt had seriously underestimated McMillan's dogs. These weren't pets that could be bribed into ignoring an intruder by a handful of meat and a friendly pat. Again, his luck held. The rain-soaked wind was blowing from the east, away from the house, and the dogs' attention was fully occupied by the two people on the porch.

Walt edged around the yard, keeping to the shelter of the trees. He couldn't hear what was being said, but it was easy to tell by the posture of everyone involved that this was not a friendly visit. The dogs moved. They went into the house, and McMillan shut the door on them. Walt let out a sigh of relief.

An equipment shed, moss-covered roof, cracked and rusty hinges, rotting doorframe, was set a few feet back from the house, at the side closest to the front door. He slipped through the woods and emerged from the shelter of the trees at the rear of the house. He crept forward, keeping himself between the house and the shed. Here, the wind was cut off and he could hear the men talking.

"Doug Kibbens killed himself," Winters was saying, "one year to the day after the murder of Sophia D'Angelo."

So, Walter thought, Winters was investigating

the case, not just going through the motions. Good for him. Man was a fool, though, if he thought McMillan was about to confess to murder. Over the years Walt had considered that McMillan himself, either alone or with Kibbens, had killed Sophia. He'd dismissed the idea. McMillan had arrived only minutes after Walt called the police. His uniform had been clean, as had Kibbens' when he showed up. The killer had to have gotten some of the woman's blood on him. Walt couldn't see them, try as he might, having a full set of protective clothing in their cars and being able to get cleaned up and changed fast enough without anyone noticing.

The police would be finished here soon. If his luck held, McMillan would stand on the porch and watch them leave. Then, before he could let his dogs out, Walt would suggest they have a long-delayed talk. He mentally settled down to wait.

"Are you interested in where I found these items?" Winters said.

"No," McMillan replied. His voice cracked and he cleared his throat.

Chapter Thirty-nine

Smith certainly was interested. "Why don't you tell me, sir?" she said.

"Happy to, Constable," Winters replied. "When Doug Kibbens died, his desk was cleared out. Standard procedure. His ex-wife wasn't interested in taking anything so it was put in a box and the box sent to storage. It's sad, I think sometimes, how little we leave behind and how quickly we can be forgotten. All the legacy of a man's life and career fit into one small office box. I'm surprised you didn't take some of his stuff, Jack. Or at least have a look through it."

"Make your point, Winters."

"My point," Winters said, "is that it mustn't have so much as crossed your mind that Kibbens would leave evidence behind. If an officer familiar with the case had gone through his desk, he would have found it and known it was important. Instead, they got a junior clerk to do it, and she didn't even open the envelope. Just packed it all up and sent it away. The man with the missing finger joint dead in the woods. Sophia's bracelet beside him. A gas station receipt from Winlaw. Not hard to put the pieces together. Did you know, Jack, that a body was found in the bush near Winlaw a number of years ago when a major storm washed away part of the mountain? A man with part of his finger missing. Never identified. Never claimed. He had been properly buried, deep enough that passing animals wouldn't dig him up. I wonder who would do that?"

"Biker gang, probably," McMillan said. "No loss to anyone. I'm surprised you'd spend your time on that, Winters. Got nothing better to do?"

"Better than exposing corrupt cops? You owe a lot to Doug Kibbens, Jack. His conscience got the better of him. It must have been pretty bad for him to end up killing himself. Too bad he took the coward's way out, though, rather than confessing. But he did leave a confession of a sort, didn't he, Jack? In his desk drawer for someone, for me, to find all these years later."

"Sorry to hear that," McMillan said. "Imagine, Doug hiding evidence. I wonder what made him do something like that."

Winters' story should have brought a burst of

justification to Walt. But it didn't. He'd known all along McMillan and Kibbens had concealed evidence that would have cleared him. Was Winters saying the two cops had killed Sophia's killer and dumped his body in the woods? In that case, more than ever, Walt's only question was why. It made no sense.

McMillan wasn't about to talk, and Winters didn't appear to have anything to charge him with. The sergeant was only here to satisfy his curiosity as to what had happened. Walt, however, didn't much care what had happened. He only cared why. He wiped rain water from the back of his neck, touched the gun buried deep in his jacket pocket.

"Tell me about Arlene, Jack."

"Who?"

"Don't give me that. You know perfectly well, who. Arlene Desmond. Walter's wife."

"Who?" McMillan said. He tried to sound disinterested, but Smith could tell he knew exactly who Winters was talking about. The blood drained from his face, and the vein in his forehead picked up its rhythm. His eyes flicked to Smith. He saw her looking at his right hand, scratched raw. He wiped his hands on the seat of his pants.

"Walter Desmond's wife, Arlene."

"Yeah, now I remember her. She died, I heard."

"That's right. She died. Most people think she killed herself. Heartbreak and despair will do that to a person, won't they? People in this town have long memories, Jack. Understandably, they remember Arlene and Walter Desmond in particular. Natural enough, wouldn't you agree? I've spoken to several witnesses who tell me you were having an affair with Arlene Desmond prior to the killing."

McMillan threw a hard look at Smith. "That Lucky Smith, I'll bet. She always was a poisoned-tongued bitch."

Smith just about swallowed her own tongue, trying not to react. And not at the insult to her mother, either; Lucky had heard worse. This was news to her. Lucky had specifically said she didn't know anything about the state of Walter and Arlene's marriage.

But this wasn't a court of law. Winters was free to draw all the conclusions he could, no matter how flimsy the evidence.

"Interesting isn't it, Jack, how things have changed in the past few years? These days the gossip would be all over Twitter: the arresting officer had been sleeping with the wife of the accused. Back then, people kept mum about things like that. People, some people, maybe most people, had more respect for the police than they do now.

Even in Trafalgar, they believed whatever we said. If Desmond had been arrested, then, ergo, he was guilty. Case closed, right? Sadly," Winters' voice turned hard and he bit at the words, "things have changed. And that has a lot to do with cops like you and your pal Doug, doesn't it? Cops who'd lie in court, pursue a personal vendetta against an innocent man. Cover up a crime for your own ends."

"No comment," McMillan said.

"Was it a shock to you when she didn't give up on her husband? When she insisted on his innocence, no matter what you said? She sold everything they had to pay his legal bills, moved away from Trafalgar to be near him. And then she died. A broken woman. Was she broken because of what had happened to her husband, Jack? Or because she understood that she was partly responsible for all that had happened?"

"Now you're stretching, Winters. You're outta your mind if you think Arlene killed Sophia."

"Don't be a total fool, McMillan," Winters snapped. Smith couldn't help taking a peek at him. He'd played it calm and cool up until now, reciting the facts in a bored just-between-us-guys tone. His composure was cracking. If there was one thing Winters hated, Smith had come to realize, it was police officers who put all the rest of them in a bad light. "Arlene didn't kill Sophia, and neither did you or Kibbens. But you were quick to take advantage of the murder to get rid of Arlene's husband. I don't know what you did to convince Kibbens to go along with it, but you're as responsible for his death as you are for Arlene's and for the waste of Walt Desmond's life."

"This conversation's over, Winters. If you and your girl aren't off my property in one minute I'm letting the dogs out."

Smith's eyes twitched toward the house. The dogs stood behind the screened door, looking out. They hadn't barked, not once, but their ears were up and they fixed cold, unblinking stares onto her. She liked dogs, a lot. Good or bad, dogs were what people made them. It wasn't their fault if these dogs were trained to be vicious, but they still made her skin crawl. Rain pounded on the roof and trickled between the cracks.

"Now, I have to wonder," Winters said, "if Arlene was in on it all along, and only when it was too late did she realize what she'd allowed to happen?"

"No," McMillan said, his voice very low. "She was a good woman. Better than I realized. Better than I deserved."

Chapter Forty

Blood roared in Walter Desmond's head. He didn't believe it. It couldn't be true. Arlene? He'd been framed and sent to jail so Jack McMillan could continue an affair with Arlene?

He walked around the corner of the house.

"You're lying."

The two cops whirled around. They had their guns out before Walter even realized he was holding his own in his hand.

McMillan stepped back and pressed himself against the wall of his house, his eyes wide and his hands up.

"Put the gun down," Smith said.

"Mr. Desmond, nice to see you," Winters said. "We were just talking about you."

Walt was surprised that his hand could be so steady. He kept the gun pointed at McMillan. The two cops carried Glocks, more powerful weapons than his. He didn't care. He'd shoot first; all he needed was one shot. McMillan was no more than four feet away.

"I'm sorry you had to hear that, Walt," Winters said, "But it's true. Jack and your wife were having an affair. I don't know all the details, but I've pretty much figured it out. When Sophia was murdered, Jack got the call and found you at the scene. He realized it was his chance to get rid of you and have Arlene."

"No."

"I don't know why Kibbens went along with it, but he lived to regret his part in the whole nasty business. Or rather, I should say he died to regret it. It's all long over, Walt, and nothing can be changed. Put the gun down and let Constable Smith drive you back to town."

"Good idea," Smith said.

"You stole my wife. You destroyed my life."

McMillan laughed. "I hardly had to steal her. She was willing enough. Desperate, actually. Desperate for what you weren't giving her. I've never known a woman to want it so much."

Walter stared at the man he'd hated all these years. Was it true? Yes, it was, he knew that. He'd probably always known it. When the whole horrible mess started, before he was arrested, before he came to fully realize they weren't going to turn around and apologize, saying they'd made a mistake, he'd almost thought it was a good thing. Arlene had turned loving, caring. The night Sophia died, to his surprise, and his intense shame, he'd been hungry for intimacy, and Arlene had been eager and willing. They'd made love for the first time in almost a year, and it had been powerful and good. He hadn't hated his wife; his emotions weren't strong enough toward her for hate. He'd simply had no time for her, for her bitter tongue, her snide comments at his increasing inability to perform, her open flirting with other men.

Jack McMillan. He probably shouldn't have even been surprised. McMillan was the sort of macho idiot Arlene ridiculed Walt for not being. McMillan strutted his stuff around town; he dangled his power in front of anyone and everyone. And Arlene, poor sad, desperate, lonely, Arlene had fallen for it. But even Arlene had seen through it eventually. Seen McMillan for what he was, and not wanted anything more to do with him. She'd stood by her husband when it mattered. Because of shame, because of regret, in atonement? He'd never know.

He lifted the gun.

Chapter Forty-one

Smith and Winters exchanged glances. He gave her a barely recognizable nod, and she stepped onto the top stair. The rotting wood creaked under her weight. "You don't want to do this, sir. Please put the gun down." She didn't know if Walt even heard her. His eyes were on McMillan, and his hand was steady, but his gaze seemed very far away. She wondered if he was on drugs. Then she realized he was on something far stronger than any drug. Revenge. A force so powerful it swept away all thought of self-preservation.

"You don't want to go back to prison, do you, Walt?" Winters said. Winters remained on the porch, watching McMillan as much as Desmond. If McMillan moved, if he tried to get behind Smith or Winters, this could turn into a bloodbath.

"Please, Mr. Desmond," Smith said, "put the gun down." The moment it looked as though Desmond was about to fire, she'd have no choice but to shoot. Frankly, she'd just as soon go back to the truck and drive away. Let him shoot McMillan. He deserved his revenge, and if McMillan died, well, too bad. No loss to anyone.

Unfortunately, that wasn't what the law would say.

One of the dogs growled. The other joined him. If McMillan made a move for the door, he wouldn't make it.

She took another step. She held her gun in both hands, but lowered it slightly so it wasn't pointed directly at the man. "Has Carolanne gone home, Walt?"

His eyes flicked toward her, but the gun remained steady. "What?"

"I liked her. She was nice. I think I could get into that dragon boat racing stuff, Walt. My mom's keen on it, too." She was babbling like a fool, but she wanted to remind him that there were good things in life. Lots of good things. Kind women, and warm, sunny days out on the water.

"This isn't a pajama party, you stupid bitch," McMillan yelled. "Shoot the fucker before he kills us all."

"He's not going to do that, are you Walt?" Winters said.

Walt gave Smith a slow sad smile. "Thanks for reminding me, Constable. He's not worth dying for and sure not worth making a good cop do something she'll always regret." He grabbed the barrel of the revolver with his free hand, turned it, and passed it toward her, butt-first.

She took the remaining steps quickly, accepted the gun, and whispered, "Thanks." Only then did she dare to breathe. She put her Glock away and cracked Desmond's gun open. Three cartridges fell into her hand. She looked at him. "Two empty places?"

"I thought the bastard might need two bullets," Desmond said.

She nodded, understanding the purpose of the third bullet. She dropped them into one pocket and the Smith & Wesson into another.

"Don't take another step," Winters said. His gun remained out and it was pointed at McMillan.

"I'm getting my dogs. That man's a dangerous lunatic. I have the right to protect myself."

"Fortunately for you, Constable Smith and I have a sworn duty to perform that task. Mr. Desmond threatened you, and you have a right to have him charged. Do you want to do that? Constable Smith and I will, of course, have to testify to the entire conversation preceding the threat, if the case comes to court."

McMillan spat.

"I thought so." Winters put his Glock away.

"Constable, we'll give Mr. Desmond a ride back to town."

"Yes, sir. Will you come with me please, Mr. Desmond?"

"Don't let those dogs out until we're gone," Winters said. "Unless you want me to lay a complaint."

"Fuck off, Winters."

"Happy to."

"That's it?" Smith said, once they were in the truck and she was maneuvering it down the slippery mountain road. Walt sat in the back, but Winters had told him he was not under arrest, and they'd drop him wherever he liked.

"That's it?" Walt echoed Smith. "McMillan goes on with his life, never mind what he did to me? To Arlene?"

"I'm taking what I have to my boss, Walt, but you have to understand that we have no real proof. The things I found in Kibbens' envelope don't relate to McMillian in any way. I'm sorry, but I have not a single scrap of usable evidence. I didn't know for sure McMillan was having an affair with your wife. No one told me, but several people said McMillan was often seen going into your wife's store, and everyone agreed he was a good-looking man, who liked to play the big shot around town. I had nothing but a handful of pieces, and I threw them on the table and let McMillan put it all together for me."

Pieces, like how men could be *oblivious* to what their wives were up to.

"Poor Arlene. We didn't have a good marriage. We didn't like each other much, we had less and less to do with each other as the years passed. Sergeant Winters, I don't know why McMillan would go to all that trouble to get rid of me. If she'd asked me for a divorce I would have given it to her."

"She probably told McMillan some sort of story," Smith said. "That you'd fight her in court, spend every penny on lawyers, maybe that you had some sort of hold over her. If McMillan was pressuring her to leave your marriage, and she didn't want to, she would have come up with an excuse as to why it wasn't possible."

Walt took off his hat and rubbed at his head. "The best months of our marriage were after I was arrested. How's that for irony?"

Guilt, Smith thought, but didn't say. Guilt had made Arlene loving.

"It wasn't my intention," Winters said, "to tell you or your lawyers what I surmised, and it is nothing more than guesses and speculation, about what happened after the murder of Sophia. I don't know what you heard, perhaps most of it. It's up to you to decide if you want to share with your lawyer what you overheard."

"What I want to know," Smith said, "is who the heck was the guy found in the woods."

"Sophia's killer. Kibbens and McMillan knew he'd done it, and they tracked him down and killed him themselves. Why Kibbens went along with all this, is something we'll never know. Like I don't know why he saved a few pieces of evidence, the gas station receipt, the photo of the dead guy and the bracelet."

"Maybe Kibbens didn't kill himself after all," Smith said. "Have you thought of that?"

"I have, yes, but the evidence, what's left of it, shows that he was in that car alone, and the autopsy found no drugs or alcohol on the body."

Smith drove into Trafalgar. The rain had stopped and the clouds were rapidly retreating. Tendrils of mist drifted around the nearest mountains, but the distant snows of Koola glacier sparkled in the sun.

"Where to, Mr. Desmond?" Smith asked.

"Where to? That's the question, isn't it?"

"Jack McMillan has friends in Trafalgar," Winters said. "He's got to be worrying about what you'll do now."

"Drop me at the motel. There's an overnight bus to Vancouver. I'll take it. I'm supposed to be meeting with the lawyer this morning to talk about suing the

Trafalgar police for harassment. I'm going to phone him and let him know that's no longer an option."

"Your choice," Winters said.

"It is, isn't it? And with choice come decisions and responsibilities."

"You would be within your rights to sue Jack McMillan, you know."

"I am aware of that. He has nothing I want, except to say he's sorry. And that's not going to happen, is it? No, I don't want to have anything to do with him, not ever again. Let him wallow in his bitterness up there on his mountain."

"Constable Smith, drop me at the station," Winters said. "Then take Mr. Desmond back to his motel. Better you don't walk through the streets of town by yourself tonight, Walt. I'll send a car to take you to the bus."

Smith cleared her throat. "You might want to not send just any officer, sir."

"Point taken," Winters said. "But I think a quiet word or two should fix any misunderstanding that might arise. After you've dropped Walt, come back to the office. The chief might want to talk to you."

"Okay." Smith pulled up to the sidewalk outside the police station. "I…uh…just happened to have the voice recorder on my phone switched on. Do you want to see if it picked up anything?" She handed the phone to him. "The password's 4628."

Winters lifted one eyebrow, as he took the offered object. Then he got out of the truck and opened the back door. "Good luck to you," he said. He put out his hand. Walt took it and the men shook. Winters stepped back and slammed the door.

"Home, James," Walt said.

Smith grinned at him in the rearview mirror. "At your service. Look, I know it's none of my business and you can tell me to butt out, but are you going to see Carolanne again?"

Walt sighed. "No, I don't think so. She's a nice person, and she doesn't need complications in her life."

"Your decision," she said. She let him out in front of the motel room. They shook hands on the pavement, steaming as it dried in the sun. "Thanks," Walt said.

"Any time," she said.

"He was right, you know."

"Who, about what?"

"Your sergeant. About bad cops like McMillan ruining people's trust in the police. I'm glad there are good officers like him. And like you. People who can help restore that trust."

"Thank you, sir."

"Say bye to your mom for me."

"I will."

Chapter Forty-two

"Chief wants you in his office," Denton said when Smith walked into the station.

Barb got up from her desk. "John's with him now. He said I'm to come with you when you get here."

They went into Keller's office. Barb shut the door behind them. Smith's phone lay on the desk.

"Molly, Barb. Take a seat." Keller took a slug of diet Coke. "Barb, I'm calling a press conference for three o'clock this afternoon. Alert the media."

"I've always wanted to say that," Smith said, immediately regretting sounding flip. The confrontation was over, the tension she'd felt up on the mountain was dying. Keller grinned. "Make sure the big boys know that they'll *want* to be at it. Then call the mayor and tell him to drop everything and get over here."

"You're going to tell them what happened?" Smith said.

"What happened?" Barb asked.

Keller nodded to Winters who quickly filled her in on the basics of his conclusions. Her eyes widened steadily as he spoke, and she leaned back in her chair with a muffled, "wow."

"My only aim now," Keller said, "and John agrees with me, is to see Walter Desmond emphatically and publicly cleared of the murder of Sophia D'Angelo. We have no proof of any of this. That the dead man in the woods was Sophia's killer. That Doug Kibbens killed himself out of guilt, and dare I say a healthy dose of cowardice."

Barb gasped.

"I've listened to your recording, Molly, and I'm afraid it's pretty much indecipherable."

"The rain falling on the roof and that creaky porch didn't help," Winters said.

"And, as you know," Keller said, "it was taken without McMillan's knowledge, therefore not usable as evidence. But at one point the interference dies just enough so we can hear McMillian saying he was having an affair with Mrs. Desmond."

"Which isn't proof that he set the man up," Winters said, "but it's clearly a huge conflict of interest and he should have declared it at the time her husband was under investigation."

"I can't believe it," Barb said. "Jack and Doug…"

"Which," Keller said, without a trace of warmth or sympathy in his voice, "is why we must never let personal feelings interfere with an investigation."

"That was the evidence in that box, wasn't it, John?" Barb said. "Proof that Doug helped Jack kill Sophia's killer and bury him in the woods? He left it to be found. And I just shoved it all away. If I'd only…"

"What's done is done," Keller said. "And it was all a long time ago. I hope we've learned a few things since then. All of us." He got to his feet. "I'm going to pay a call on Gino and Rose. They deserve to hear this from me first. While I'm doing that, Barb, I want to speak to everyone in our office who's available. Let's say one hour. Pull in anyone who's not on a call. Is Jeff working today?"

"No."

"Call him, tell him he's to come in. My orders, no excuses. Molly. Stay a minute, will you?"

Winters and Barb filed out. Winters gave Smith a small smile as he passed. Barb looked as though she was in shock.

Keller walk around his desk and thrust out his hand. "Good work, Molly. John told me you kept your head out there."

"That's what I'm paid to do, isn't it, sir?" She tried not to grin as she shook her boss' hand.

"I'll be having a private word with Dave Evans and Jeff Glendenning. Your name will not come up, nor should it, because you didn't say anything about anything that transpired with those two. John's been speculating. He is a detective, after all."

"Yes, sir."

"I understand you were in a difficult situation, and I won't advise you what to do if something similar arises again, except to remember that we are a team here. And a team means everyone."

"Thank you, sir."

"Dismissed," he said. His voice was stern, but he wasn't able to suppress the twinkle in his eye.

Walt pulled back the grimy curtain over the door to check who it was. He wasn't all that surprised to see the young male officer standing there, with an expression that indicated he might be sucking on a lemon. Walt opened the door.

"I'm here to take you to the bus station. Sir."

"Kind of you," Walt said. "Dave, isn't it?"

"Yes, sir. Dave Evans."

"I'll get my pack."

"Let me, sir." Evans pushed past him. Walt's things were packed and ready, his backpack zipped closed and lying on the bed. Dave picked it up and carried it outside. Walt followed, closing the motel room door behind him.

Evans tossed the pack in the trunk and opened the back door of the cruiser. Walt gave him a look. "Why don't I sit in the front?"

More lemon sucking. "I guess that would be okay."

Walt got into the car and fastened his seat belt. He was about to make a joke, as he had with Molly Smith, but decided that might be taking things too far. Good cops. Bad cops. Good people. Bad people. Good people made good cops, and bad people made bad cops. But sometimes you could try to stop good people from becoming bad cops before it was too late.

He'd had a brief call from the chief of police earlier, telling him to turn on the radio; the local station would be carrying a press conference live.

Walt had sat on his bed in the overheated, stuffy, dingy motel room and listened in amazement bordering on disbelief as Chief Constable Keller told the assembled members of the press that new evidence had been uncovered which indicated that the killer of Sophia D'Angelo was not Walter Desmond, but a nameless drifter who had died very shortly after Sophia. He went on to say that members of the Trafalgar City Police had colluded in corrupting the investigation. At that the audience could be heard to let out a collective gasp. Keller, clearly uncomfortable, then told them that of those members, one was now deceased and the other no longer worked for the police service. No names were mentioned. None had to be. Everyone who mattered would know exactly who he was talking about.

Keller concluded by saying the Trafalgar City Police would be working with all interested parties to ensure Walter Desmond was given a fair and just settlement for his wrongful imprisonment.

The radio exploded with reporters' questions, but Keller merely said he had nothing further to add, and thanked them for coming. He then called on Sergeant John Winters to bring them up-to-date on a current investigation.

Winters didn't say anything about Walt; like his boss, he didn't have to. He simply stated that because of DNA evidence and witness statements in the recent attacks on two women in Trafalgar, he wanted to interview one Richard James Anderson, thirty-four, known to the police.

"Startling new developments," said the radio announcer, "in a case that has transfixed the people of Trafalgar for many years…"

Walt switched off the radio. And then he burst into tears. The first tears he'd shed in more than twenty-five years.

The bus left at eight-thirty. Walt had phoned ahead to buy his ticket. He'd also phoned Louise and told her to call off the attack dogs. They'd still try to get what was owned him—five million dollars was meager payment for the loss of a life-time—out of the province of British Columbia, but he didn't want anyone suing the modern-day Trafalgar police department. Louise had objected, but he held his ground, without explaining why, and she had finally relented. He was, after all, the boss.

The long summer twilight lingered and the streets of Trafalgar were busy with pedestrians and cars. The restaurant patios were full and the brightly lit shops still open.

Time to be on his way. Nothing remained in Trafalgar for him.

When they arrived at the bus station, Evans got out of the cruiser and collected Walt's bag. He carried the bag into the small waiting room. Walt followed. He considered jokingly offering Evans a tip, but decided not to. No point in humiliating the guy. "Thanks," he said instead.

"Bus'll be here soon, and I'll…uh…be around if you need anything, sir."

"Do you think I might need assistance?"

"No, sir. You won't."

"Glad to hear it."

A scattering of people were in the waiting room, the type who travelled by bus at night. Young people, mostly, some with high-quality backpacks and hiking boots, others in torn jeans and scuffed running shoes. No children or old folks. They glanced up, curious, when Evans came in, but once he left they quickly returned to their own business, most of which seemed to be poking at their little phones. Walt took a seat next to a young woman with long dreadlocks, multiple piercings, and a single tattoo of a red rose on her neck. He opened a side-pocket of his pack and took out his book. Twenty-five after eight. The bus was due at eight-thirty.

At eight forty-five, the clerk behind the counter called for their attention. Several of the waiting people muttered unhappily. This was not going to be good news. "Sorry, folks, but I just got word there's been an accident on the highway outside of town. The bus can't get through."

Everyone groaned. "Bummer," said the young woman next to Walt. "Did they say how long?" a man asked.

"Police and ambulance are there now. Sounds like it's a mess. Might be a while. Sorry."

"I'm not sitting here all night," the dread-locked woman said. "All right if I go for a walk?"

"Sure," the clerk said. "Check back with me in an hour. Won't be less than that."

Some people got up and stretched and others stayed where they were to continue typing. Walt had no desire to be confined to this small room with the peeling paint and stained carpet if he didn't have to.

There was still one thing he wanted to do before leaving Trafalgar, and now he had the time to do it. He got to his feet and hefted his backpack.

Lucky Smith spent the evening alone in the store. It was Tyler's day off, and Flower had been feeling sick and gone home early. Lucky hadn't been happy about that; she had preparations to do to get ready for Saturday, but after thirty years of running her own store, she'd learned to take things as they came.

Almost closing time. No customers had come in over the last half hour or so.

She glanced at the giant photograph filling the red brick wall behind the sales counter. Andy, Samwise, and Moonlight heading out onto the river in kayaks on a perfect summer morning. Good times, she thought with a smile.

Now, Andy was gone and she was with Paul. More good times coming, she was sure. She lifted first her right leg, and then her left, holding them in her hands behind her, one after the other, to give them a good stretch. She'd been sadly remiss in attending her yoga classes lately, and her muscles were starting to feel it.

She checked her watch. Coming up to nine. Closing time. She was about to flick the lock when the door flew open. She stepped back, letting her professional smile cross her face.

The smile died the moment she saw his expression. This was no customer.

"We're closed." Her voice broke.

"So you are." Greasy black hair spilled from under a ball cap pulled low over his forehead. His eyes were small and dark, his skin sallow, his cheekbones shrunken.

"My husband will be here any minute to pick me up," she said.

"No, Mrs. Smith, he won't." Without taking his eyes off her, he reached behind him and turned the lock, but he didn't check that it had engaged. It hadn't. The lock was old and sticky and you needed to pull the door hard toward you with one hand, while turning the latch with the other at the exact right moment. The man stood between her and the door. He wasn't all that big, but menace radiated out from him and he seemed to fill the room. She glanced toward the window behind him. At that moment, the street outside was empty. She turned and bolted toward the back, hoping to get to her office, slam the door on him, and reach the phone. But he was fast and he was on her before she had taken more than a few steps. He grabbed a handful of her hair and pulled, wrenching her off balance. She crashed into the book rack and grabbed at it, knowing she had to remain on her feet or she was lost. The shelf wobbled, books and magazines scattered. His hand was still in her hair, and a searing pain tore through her left side.

The inside of the store was lit, outside night was falling, the windows were uncovered. Surely someone would look in, see what was happening. As if he'd read her mind, he half dragged, half pushed her behind the counter. Lucky screamed as she fell to the floor face-first, and all she could see were scores and notches in the old wooden floorboards. His weight landed on her; he lifted her head by the hair and pounded her face into the floor. Pain and blood filled her nose and mouth. He grabbed the back of her skirt and pulled it up, jamming his knee between her sprawled legs. She tried to throw him off, but she could barely move.

The door opened, and the air changed as the sounds of the street rushed in. "I'm glad you're still open, Lucky," said a voice. "I'm leaving and I wanted…what the…?"

Lucky spat blood and screamed. At least, she

tried to scream, it came out more like a low moan. But it was enough. She heard running footsteps cross the floor. Her attacker's weight came off her as he jumped to his feet. She heard a grunt, a cry of pain, the sound of a body falling. Hands reached for her and she cried out.

"It's okay, Lucky. I'm here. I'm calling for help. Don't move."

All she wanted was to curl up into a ball and cry. But who was speaking to her? Was it *him*? Trying to confuse her into giving up the fight? She struggled to roll over. Everything she had, everything she was, hurt. The room swayed, the white ceiling tiles overhead danced, the bright shop lights hurt her eyes.

"Mid-Kootenay Adventure Vacations on Front Street. Please. As fast as you can." A face loomed over her. A man held the desk phone to his ear. He looked down at her and smiled. "Help's coming, Lucky."

She knew that face. She struggled to remember. Then she had it.

Walter Desmond.

She passed out.

Chapter Forty-three

Jack McMillan poured himself a healthy slug of Canadian Club. The bottle was almost empty, the last of his stash. He'd have to drive into town for another, but that he couldn't do. He wouldn't put it past Winters to have cops watching for him. Any excuse to pull him over would do, and he wasn't sure how many drinks he'd already had.

He'd called Jeff Glendenning earlier. Left a message. No reply. He doubted he'd ever get one.

The dogs lay at his feet. Horace was asleep, his body twitching, his legs moving as he dreamed of his glory days, but Lenny was awake, watching him. The sun had dipped behind the mountains and it would be dark soon. He didn't get up to turn on the porch light. He didn't mind the dark. He hadn't had the radio or TV on all day. He didn't mind the quiet, either.

A photograph lay on the table beside him. He picked it up, for about the hundredth time that day, and studied it.

Arlene.

This was the only picture he had of her. He'd taken it in her dress store, when she wasn't looking. At first he'd cherished the picture. Brought it out at night to look at, to remember her when he couldn't be with her. Now, he kept it to remember, all right, but to remember betrayal and abandonment. He'd loved her once. Whatever love was.

He thought about the last time they'd been together. He'd been working, and had popped into her shop on his rounds. She'd been alone, and gave him that big grin that meant she was up for anything. He locked the door, turned the sign to closed, and she led the way into the back room. He'd swept all the papers off her desk and they'd made love there. He hadn't even bothered to take off his utility belt or uniform. She said she loved the feel of his gun against her hip as he moved, and it made things even more exciting if she could hear officers talking over his radio. When it was over, he left her straightening her clothes and tidying her hair and went back to the street.

He never much cared if anyone saw him leaving, although she wanted him to be discreet. He'd been after her for some time to leave that miserable prick of a husband of hers, but for some reason she was reluctant.

He hadn't told dispatch he was leaving the car,

and he simply got in and went back on patrol. He was driving down Pine Street a few minutes later, thinking about Arlene and how he might convince her to ask Walt for a divorce, when he saw a man slip out of an alley next to a house with a for sale sign on the snowy front lawn. The man was dressed in a heavy winter coat and thick gloves. It was January, nothing unusual about that, but the man started when he saw Jack's car, pulled his scarf up around his ears and reversed direction, moving at a rapid clip.

Jack turned the car around and pulled up beside him. "Going somewhere, buddy?"

"Just out for a walk."

"Cold day for a walk."

"I like the cold."

"I haven't seen you around before."

"Just passin' through." The guy was in his late thirties, early forties maybe, with a many-times broken nose, pockmarked skin, and an old but nasty scar beneath his right eye. That scar, Jack thought, looked like a knife cut. He wasn't wearing a hat. His bullet-shaped head didn't have a single strand of hair on it. A couple of spots of smeared and dried blood were on the top of his lip on the side of his nose. Idiot had been picking his nose, Jack thought.

He was about to ask for ID, and then decided not to bother. This looked like the sort of guy who'd object, citing his right to walk the streets if he wanted. Lucky for him, Jack didn't feel like the hassle. He was in a good mood. He usually was after a tumble with Arlene.

He drove away without another word.

Ten minutes later he was back, answering a 911 call to the house with the for-sale sign.

Lenny barked, and Horace came instantly awake. Their ears stood up, but they soon relaxed. An elk maybe or a car further down the mountain. Not a man. The dogs wouldn't go off guard if a person was approaching.

He hadn't considered for a moment that Walt Desmond had killed Sophia D'Angelo. But he thought he'd have some fun with Desmond, make the guy sweat a little. Kibbens could be lazy sometimes; he was trying to get through the years until retirement with as little effort as possible. If a suspect was handed to him on a silver platter, he wasn't likely to go to a heck of a lot of trouble looking for someone else.

Jack said nothing to Doug Kibbens or anyone else about the bald guy, but he kept his eye out for him. He didn't intend to let a killer get away. Once he had him in custody, it would be easy enough to make the evidence fit. In the meantime, let Walt sweat a little. Let him know the power Jack had over him. It might even turn Arlene on, and make her realize Jack was the man she needed.

Jack had never been in Arlene's home before, not until he and Doug came to question Walt. Arlene had given him a long seductive wink and run the tip of her tongue over her lips when Walt and Kibbens' backs were turned.

That single gesture had sealed Walt's fate. Jack realized he had a way to get rid of Arlene's husband, permanently. He said nothing about the man with the bullet-head, and when he got the phone call from some guy in Fort Nelson who said he'd helped Walt with his flat tire, he kept mum about that too. He watched as Kibbens' investigation cut corners, missed clues, didn't identify possible witnesses.

Another realtor had shown the house that morning, and when questioned, she insisted she'd locked the door when she left. But her eyes had darted around the room as she spoke and she chewed at her lip. She wasn't sure if she'd remembered to lock up or not, but wouldn't say so, and Doug had simply written down what she said without noticing the hesitation. Jack hadn't pointed that out to him, either.

It was obvious to Jack what had happened. The girl, Sophia, had arrived at the house for her viewing with Walt. Walt was delayed, so she tried the back door, found it unlocked, and went in by herself. The bullet-headed guy had seen her, and realizing the house was empty, followed. Jack had

had a couple of run-ins with Sophia when she'd been in school. Drinking in the street, causing a disturbance, once at a teenage house party that got out of control. He'd been surprised when Kibbens reported that she'd been a polite, well-behaved young lady. You'd expect her parents to say that, but Kibbens hadn't gone to any trouble to interview anyone else. He certainly hadn't asked the hard questions that would get people to open up and spill what they knew.

Regardless of what happened with Walt, Jack had no intention of letting a killer walk free. He kept looking for the bullet-headed man, but there was not a sign of him, and none of his usual contacts had any knowledge of the guy. As the days passed, and then when Walt was arrested, Jack knew he'd played this game for too long, left it too late. He couldn't come forward now and say, "Oh, golly. Guess what I just remembered."

Walter Desmond was charged, tried, convicted. Jack had thought Arlene was putting up a good act as the faithful wife standing by her man. But it hadn't been an act. After Walt's arrest Jack had never spoken to her again. She refused to let him in when he called at their house. She hung up when she heard his voice on the phone. The shop and her house were sold. Arlene moved away, following Walter to Kingston, Ontario, where he'd been sent to the penitentiary. Jack had been watching when she left town for the last time. He'd been shocked at the change in her appearance. She'd aged ten years over the past few months.

He ran his finger down the side of her cheek in the photograph, the same way he'd liked to do in life. Cancer, some said. He had no doubt that was yet another lie: she'd killed herself out of guilt, just as Winters had said.

And then, one day, a couple of months after Walt had gone down, Jack spotted the bullet-headed man. He'd been visiting a buddy who lived up the valley near Winlaw, missed the turn, had to go a long way on the narrow road with crumbling edges before he could turn around. He found himself in a small clearing at the end of the old logging road. A rusting camping trailer sat alone among the trees, a motorbike parked out front. The bullet-headed man had been heading to the trailer. He glanced up at the sound of Jack's car, but the sun was in his eyes, and Jack knew he wouldn't be able to make out the face of the person in the car. He did a tight three-point turn and drove away.

He had no intention of taking the man on his own. He went to work the next morning, walked into Doug Kibbens' office, and laid it all down. If he'd judged Kibbens wrong, he'd have to bluster his way out of it. But he hadn't. Kibbens made all the right noises about reopening the case, telling the chief he'd missed valuable evidence. Jack pointed out that missing evidence wasn't the same as being too lazy to bother looking for it. Kibbens probably wouldn't go to jail, but his career would be over. And that nice pension he was expecting in a couple of years along with it.

Jack didn't mention Walter Desmond. He reminded Doug that nothing they could do would bring Sophia back. Why bring more pain to the parents by reopening the case if they could get rid of the killer on their own? Kibbens had caved, like Jack hoped he would, and agreed to "see what could be done" about the bullet-headed man.

And so they did.

They drove up the valley one pleasant afternoon in early fall when the leaves were beginning to turn and it was elk hunting season. They stopped for gas outside Winlaw. Jack waited in the car while Doug went inside to pay. Then they drove up the rutted and pitted road. When they got near the trailer, Doug stopped a few hundred meters short. Jack jumped out and jogged through the trees the rest of the way. Doug let several minutes pass before he continued to the clearing and stopped outside the trailer. He leaned on the horn and yelled out the window. The trailer door opened, the bullet-headed man stepped outside to see what was going on, and

Jack brought him down with a single shot to the chest. He walked up to the man, and made sure the job was finished with a bullet to the head. He and Doug stuffed the body into a bag and threw it into the trunk of Doug's car. While Doug sat outside, with his head in his hands, Jack went through the trailer. He found Sophia's bracelet in a drawer, along with a few other mismatched pieces of jewelry.

"Looks like she might not have been the first." Jack showed the items to Doug. "Seems like we've done a public service here. If you'd done things by the book, he'd have gone to jail, said he was real sorry, and some bleeding-heart parole board would have let him out in a couple of years. Better this way." He slapped Doug on the back. Doug gave him a weak grin. "Right."

They headed back to the highway. They only drove as far as another old logging road Jack knew led to nowhere. They'd brought shovels and dug a good, deep grave. Only one time had Jack turned his back. He'd faced into the woods to have a whiz. It must have been then Doug took the picture. They finished burying the man and left.

He studied the picture of Arlene.

He slipped the photo carefully back into the case it had been in all these years, finished his drink, called the dogs and went inside. Time for bed.

Chapter Forty-four

"I'm surprised your mom's going ahead with the barbeque," Adam Tocek said.

"She insists she's okay," Smith said. "You know Mom. Doesn't like to make a fuss."

Following the attack on Wednesday evening, Lucky had been rushed to the hospital where the doctor had pronounced her injuries as superficial. Walt Desmond had given her attacker such a punch to the jaw the man had been knocked unconscious, but he revived as the police burst through the door of Mid-Kootenay Adventure Vacations. The man had been identified as Richard James Anderson, wanted for previous assaults on Eliza Winters and Darlene Michaels.

It had been nine o'clock on a pleasant summer's evening when police cars and ambulances poured down Front Street under full lights and sirens. A crowd gathered rapidly and word spread even more rapidly. Meredith Morgenstern had been having dinner in a restaurant when her phone rang with the news, and she'd immediately abandoned her friends and her bowl of half-eaten pasta. She arrived at the store in time to get a photograph of Walter Desmond getting into a police car. Into the *front* seat. The next day's *Gazette* had featured the picture under a banner headline, "Hero of the Day!" A smaller headline read, "Arrest Made In Brutal Assaults." There was no shortage of headlines in that day's paper. Another shouted "Desmond INNOCENT!: Keller."

The next day, Meredith attempted to interview Walt, but the police refused to tell her where she could find him. He'd missed his bus, and had asked to be dropped back at the Mountain View, but Paul Keller insisted on putting him up for the night at the Hudson House Hotel and paying his fare for a flight to Vancouver in the morning.

Tocek turned off the winding forest road onto the long driveway that led to Lucky's house. The driveway was lined with cars. "There seem to be a lot of people around," Smith said. "I thought Mom said just a few friends. Hey." She spotted an SUV with Alberta plates. "I think that's Sam's car. I didn't know they were coming. I hope he brought the kids. That looks like Rosemary's catering truck. Mom must really be feeling the results of Wednesday, if she's got someone else making the food."

"Natural enough," Tocek said. Norman woofed in agreement. Adam squeezed his truck between a gleaming white Lexus and an ancient van that seemed to be held together only by rust and prayer. Sylvester, Lucky's golden retriever, ran around the corner of the house to welcome them. He and Norman exchanged greetings in true dog fashion and then he allowed Smith to give him a pat.

More cars were pulling into the driveway. Smith glanced at the single bottle of wine in her hand. "I'm thinking I should have brought more."

"Sounds like the party's already started," Tocek said. "You go ahead. I'm going to put Norman back in the truck until I see who's here."

She joined the stream of people heading around the house, toward the chatter of conversation in the backyard. Everyone wore shorts and tee-shirts or light summer dresses, and most of them carried bottles of wine or six-packs of beer.

When she rounded the house Smith stopped dead in her tracks. "Oh. My. God." Tocek came up behind her and laughed.

About fifty chairs, covered in white fabric tied with long yellow ribbons blowing in the soft breeze, were laid out on the lawn in neat rows. A small arbor, decorated in masses of yellow and white roses intertwined with fresh greenery, was set up on the banks of the river. Long tables, covered in white cloths, rimmed the lawn. One of the tables was full of sparking crystal flutes and the others had stacks of plates, cutlery, and napkins. Rosemary and Merrill, assisted by several young people in black shirts and trousers under white aprons were placing bottles of champagne into wine coolers.

Paul Keller spotted them and waved. Unlike all the guests here today he was dressed more formally than Molly had ever seen him in a dark gray suit, white shirt, and gray-and-yellow-striped tie. A perfect yellow rose pierced his lapel. His smile was enormous.

"If I didn't know better," Tocek put out his hand, "I'd think we've accidently stumbled on a wedding." If anything, Keller's smile only grew as the two men shook hands.

Smith said nothing. She was too stunned.

Keller handed Tocek a rose. "You're a groomsman. Pin this to your shirt." John and Eliza Winters came over. Eliza's bruises were almost gone, and she was fresh and summery in white capris, a loosely flowing teal blue shirt with turquoise jewelry, and delicate blue sandals. Her husband had a rose pinned to his golf shirt and looked about as confused as Smith and Tocek.

"Your mom's inside," Keller said to Smith. "She told me to send you in."

"What? I mean…"

"She'll explain. Adam, John, I think the bar's ready to open. No shop talk allowed today, except I thought you'd want to know that Jeff Glendenning's put in for early retirement. I approved it last night."

"Just as well," Winters said.

Smith picked her way across the lawn. It took a long time to get to the house as everyone she passed wanted to say how surprised and delighted they were. She saw a number of people from the office, including Barb Kowalski and Dawn Solway. She waved to Keller's son Matt and Matt's girlfriend, Tracey, and recognized Keller's daughter, Cheryl, from the photo on his desk. She climbed onto the deck, where her childhood friend Christa chatted to a frail, elderly woman in a wheelchair. Hugs were exchanged all around. "Jane, you look wonderful."

"I do not," Jane Reynolds, one of Lucky's closest friends, said. "But you do, dear." Jane's eyes flicked to where Adam chatted with Keller and Winters. "Perhaps I'll be invited to another wedding soon?"

Smith just smiled.

"And how is dear Dave Evans?"

"He's good." Years ago, when Evans and Smith had been probationary constables, Dave had saved Jane from a fire-bomb. Perhaps for that reason alone, Smith hadn't reported his harassment of Walt Desmond.

"Did you know about this, Christa?" she asked.

The other woman laughed. "Not a clue. I can't believe your mom was able to arrange all this without anyone getting wind of it."

"Aunt Molly's here. Aunt Molly's here." Roberta just about knocked her down the minute she walked into the mud room. Smith bent down and gave the girl a hug. "Nice to see you too, kiddo. Where's your grandma?"

"Living room," Lucky called.

It was the third day after the attack. Lucky's bruises were at their finest. Her face was a mass of yellow, black, and purple and her left eye was swollen, but her smile was huge and radiant. She held out her arms when her daughter came into the room. Lucky wore a knee-length cream dress trimmed with yellow lace under a matching jacket with three-quarter-length sleeves. Yellow roses and baby's breath were twisted into her hair. She looked absolutely spectacular.

Smith stepped into her mom's arms. They held each other for a long time. When they separated, both women's eyes were wet.

"I'm a flower girl, Aunt Molly," Roberta said. "And you're a bridesmaid. You have flowers, too."

"Why didn't you tell me?"

Lucky grinned. "It all sort of got away from

us. The plan was for a simple ceremony followed by a barbeque for the family and a few friends. But I realized that I don't have a few friends. I have a lot of good, close friends. And then there's the people from Paul's work and his children. We wanted a nice, lovely celebration with all our friends around us, but we didn't want gifts we don't need or people making a fuss with showers and stag nights and all the rest. Are you okay with this, dear?"

"Mom, I am beyond happy for you. Truly, I am. Although," she studied her mother's face, "your wedding pictures are going to look a mite odd."

Lucky laughed. "And that will be something for my great-grandchildren to talk about, won't it?"

Epilogue

Walter Desmond sat on the Stanley Park sea wall and watched people. Walkers, runners, skaters, bikers. Some faces were impassive, revealing nothing of the person within, some were crunched in concentration and effort, maybe even pain, and many were full of the sheer joy of being beside the ocean on a sunny day.

He'd been to the aquarium earlier and then bought an ice cream cone to eat while he walked. What joy the day had been.

In prison every day was the same; the view was the same; the people, whether inmates or guards, were, if not the same, of the same sort. Day after day after day, as the years passed.

A few feet from him a child crashed her bike into the wall. She tumbled to the ground and began to cry. A man, dressed in tight jogging shorts and a yellow spandex shirt, ran up to her. He checked her over, made cooing noises, and then righted the bike. "No harm done, sweetie. Let's go, Mom's waiting." Fear and tears forgotten, the girl hopped onto the bike and pedaled away. The man saw Walt watching and gave him a rueful grin that seemed to say, "Kids. You know how it is?" before jogging after his daughter.

No, Walt didn't know how it was. But that didn't matter. He was happy just sitting here.

The *Trafalgar Gazette*, which had been ready to see him strung up from a lamppost only a few days ago, had called him a hero. He was, of course, no more a hero than he was the monster everyone had earlier believed him to be. He'd wanted to say good-bye to Lucky Smith and thank her for her kindness, and he'd arrived at the right moment to be able to help her.

He'd been taken down to the police station, in the front seat of the cruiser, and put in a pleasant room with nice furniture, a pretty painting on the wall, silk flowers, and even a box of tissues. The detective with red hair and freckles and a Mexican name had been very polite with his questions. He didn't ask about Walt's motives, or question his integrity; he only wanted to know exactly what had happened when Walt arrived at Lucky's store. No more and no less.

The police chief had arrived later, and Walt had been surprised when he'd offered to pay Walt's expenses out of his own pocket. Only later had he learned that the chief was Lucky Smith's partner. A patrol car dropped him at the nicest hotel in Trafalgar, and a taxi was arranged to take him to the Castlegar airport in the morning for a flight to Vancouver.

Chief Keller had called him in the morning, before he went downstairs to meet the taxi. "Thought you'd want to know that the guy who was arrested last night had read about you in the paper. He thought he'd be very clever and throw suspicion onto you with the attack on the woman at the B&B and later on Mrs. Smith because of her known…uh… friendship with some members of the Trafalgar police. He wasn't, so he says, aware that Mrs. Winters was an officer's wife at the time of that attack."

"Thanks, Chief. For everything."

"Good-bye, Walt."

The first thing Walt had done on getting to Vancouver was buy himself a cell phone. It seemed as though everyone had one these days. Now, he took it out of his pocket, along with a scrap of paper. A seagull swooped in from the water, heading for a family group enjoying a picnic on the grass. The father jumped up and chased the bird away with much yelling and waving of hands. Walt studied the phone for a long time. Then he unfolded the paper and punched numbers into the tiny keypad that seemed too small for his fingers.

The phone rang several times. *This was a bad idea.* He was about to hang up when a soft voice said, "Hello?"

"Carolanne. It's Walt."

"Walt," she said with a contented sigh. "Oh, Walt."

To receive a free catalog of Poisoned Pen Press titles, please provide your name, address, and email address in one of the following ways:

Phone: 1-800-421-3976
Facsimile: 1-480-949-1707
Email: info@poisonedpenpress.com
Website: www.poisonedpenpress.com

Poisoned Pen Press
6962 E. First Ave. Ste 103
Scottsdale, AZ 85251

CPSIA information can be obtained at www.ICGtesting.com
Printed in the USA
BVOW08s2330150116

433137BV00004B/5/P